THE NUREMBERG ENDGAME

A novel by

BRIAN D. WALKER

2nd Printing. Revisions.

For my son Liam, my family,

and my family of friends.

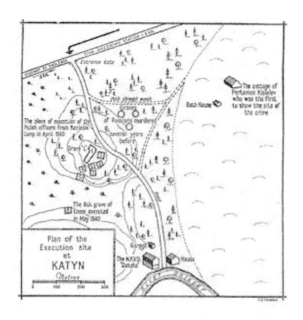

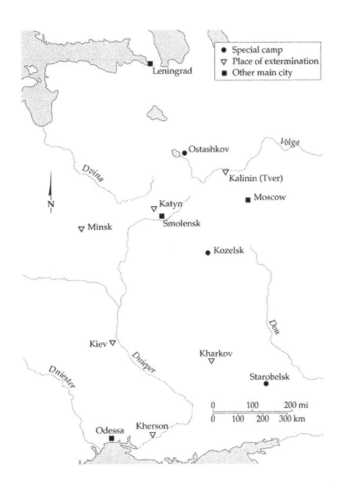

"The privilege of opening the first trial in history for crimes against the peace of the world imposes a grave responsibility. The wrongs which we seek to condemn and punish have been so calculated, so malignant, and so devastating, that civilization cannot tolerate their being ignored, because it cannot survive their being repeated.

That four great nations, flushed with victory and stung with injury stay the hand of vengeance and voluntarily submit their captive enemies to the judgment of the law is one of the most significant tributes that Power has ever paid to Reason."

from Justice Robert Jackson's Opening Statement

before the International Military Tribunal

PROLOGUE

AUGUST 24, 1939

TREATY OF NON-AGGRESSION BETWEEN GERMANY AND THE UNION OF SOVIET SOCIALIST REPUBLICS WAS SIGNED IN MOSCOW. THE TREATY INCLUDED A SECRET PROTOCOL DIVIDING THE INDEPENDENT COUNTRIES OF FINLAND, ESTONIA, LATVIA, LITHUANIA, POLAND, AND ROMANIA BETWEEN NAZI AND SOVIET INFLUENCE.

The Pact remained in effect until Nazi Germany invaded the Soviet Union on June 22, 1941, in Operation Barbarossa.

SEPTEMBER 1, 1939

GERMAN ARMED FORCES INVADE POLAND FROM THE NORTH, WEST, AND SOUTH WITHOUT DECLARING WAR.

SEPTEMBER 3, 1939

POLAND'S WESTERN ALLIES DECLARE WAR ON GERMANY.

SEPTEMBER 17, 1939

THE SOVIET RED ARMY INVADES THE EASTERN REGIONS OF POLAND IN COOPERATION WITH THE NAZIS.

THE PRESIDENT OF THE POLISH REPUBLIC, IGNACY MOŚCICKI, WHO WAS THEN IN THE SMALL TOWN OF KOSÓW NEAR THE SOUTHERN POLISH BORDER, SIGNED AN ACT APPOINTING WŁADYSŁAW RACZKIEWICZ, THE SPEAKER OF THE SENATE, AS HIS SUCCESSOR. RACZKIEWICZ, WHO WAS IN PARIS, BECAME PRESIDENT OF THE REPUBLIC OF POLAND.

The Polish Government in Exile, based in London, was recognized by all the Allied governments.

NOVEMBER 1, 1939

"ONE SWIFT BLOW TO POLAND, FIRST BY THE GERMAN ARMY AND THEN BY THE RED ARMY, AND NOTHING WAS LEFT OF THIS BASTARD OF THE VERSAILLES TREATY."

Soviet Foreign Minister Molotov

CHAPTER ONE

May 1940

Katyn Forest, Russia

HOW HAD IT come to this? How had he gotten here? His mind burned. Thoughts moved in and out of his consciousness, outside of his control.

Every moment invited confusion. Thoughts, ideas, images, pictures, places, sounds, smells, tastes, and memories colliding together. His body felt light, without pain, while his brain – his inner being – twisted under extreme pressure. His hands, tied behind his back, made each step he took awkward. The shrapnel wound in his leg gave him a slight limp.

Over the last few months, he had treated the wounds of his comrades with the sparse medical supplies available. He was formerly a physician and university medical instructor. Naturally, he cared more easily for others than himself, discouraged that his captors would do little, if anything, to comfort the dying. Many of the prisoners faced a slim chance of survival. A couple Soviet doctors had shown some compassion, but what could they do? His hands were tied, figuratively with little resources available to him, and literally from the moment he and his fellow Polish troops had surrendered. They were prisoners of war. Even so, they were supposed to have rights.

He protested their treatment on several occasions. The luckiest of instances, his protest would fall on the deaf ears of his captors. Other times, he might be subjected to a beating, lasting until he fell silent and was unable to struggle or move under his own power. His last protest resulted in bruised ribs and a broken nose. Though relatively still lucky. Speaking up was tantamount to insubordination and led to punishment, even if the complaint was warranted. Others who had spoken out before even "disappeared" (prisoner-ese for killed). Still, he felt it was his duty to speak up, even when those of higher rank suggested he not do so. Good judgment was not going to save them now. None of them. The enlisted men respected him for speaking on their behalf, and beyond that, for keeping most of them alive.

A strong smell of pine and fresh dirt - deciduous oaks, weeds, and rich soil - wafted over him. Freeing him from the restraints of his captivity. He was being led down a path into the woods. His mind raced, a veritable minefield of memories. Smells exploded visions from his consciousness like fireworks. He could barely grasp their significance before they fizzled to nothing, no time to process. So many thoughts, worries, fears, he may never recover but felt the need to replay before they were gone forever.

His body pumped adrenaline, causing a mild euphoria. How unusual. Underneath, a sense of sorrow. Not anger or regret, but sadness. Sadness thinking that he might never learn what happened to his parents or his brothers. If they were alive or dead. Sadness, knowing he couldn't help them either way. Sadness, knowing that he couldn't help more soldiers in his unit who had fought so bravely, and were now succumbing to their wounds. Sadness that his country no longer existed. How did it come to this?

They walked into the forest, down a narrow pathway. All were in uniform, or at least whatever semblance of uniform they had been wearing when captured.

During the past few months, they had been moved several times, from one prisoner camp to another, but never had their hands tied. Today was different. Always prisoners, but today, they were also captive. Every man on the truck had his hands tied. What was different this time? Why the extra precaution?

The men looked at each other, unsure of their fate, but knowing, no matter what lies ahead, the end would not be pleasant. They sought comfort, reason, and salvation as they marched. Finding ease in their routine of marching.

Their minds were all on fire. The looks on their faces, strained, burning with worry. Some men were sweating. Some were ashen with gray skin. Few men held their heads high, with pride, and defiance. The others, low, looking up only occasionally to make desperate eye contact with their comrades, hoping for an escape from their captors, only to look down again in defeat as he realized, this time…there may not be an escape.

He had been called up in August last year when the tensions with Germany had reached their fever pitch. He left the university the day after receiving orders to report to his unit.

Given his relative youth, he hadn't reached the point in his life of constantly worrying about death. In fact, he never really thought about it previously. Now, as if stuck in a loop, his mind pleaded for release. For anything but a violent death. He prayed, no matter what was awaiting them, it did not involve extreme or prolonged pain.

Serving as an Army Reserve Captain brought him his first brush, face to face with death, only a few short months ago.

September 1st. The war had just begun, amid panicked confusion. The German military onslaught had sent the Polish forces, and the government, reeling. Almost overnight, the wounded and dying, both soldiers and civilians, had overwhelmed his medical unit's capabilities. Supplies were exhausted, and, amid the chaos, there was no way to plausibly seek, or expect more assistance. There were too many people to care for in those early days of the fighting. They had hoped eventually to take over the local hospitals, but the best they could do at that point in the war was dispense basic first aid and comfort the dying. He had grown weary of death and conflicted in his role as savior.

Pine needles crunching underfoot as the prisoners, and guards, made their way forward the trees. The men had been walking for hours now, seemingly endlessly deep into the forest. He sensed they were getting closer. They must have been. But closer to what? Closer to their end he remembered.

With heightened senses, he heard everything.

"There!" His mind registered the sound. He heard it again: a muffled "crack." Then another. He knew the sounds well, imprinted on his mind. The costly effect of fighting. These small scars which would stick with him forever. Small arms fire.

Hundreds of prisoners had gone missing. One of his brothers had not been seen in many days.

His brother, an Infantry Sergeant, had fought ferociously from the beginning of hostilities until the surrender. As brave as they were, the Polish Forces were no match against the modern war machinery of the German Wehrmacht. Once the Soviets joined in the attack from the East, it was all over. So swiftly, so violently.

Sunlight broke intermittently through the dense branches. The trees and undergrowth were thick and tangled, but ahead he could sense a clearing.

They were almost there. Then again, he worried what awaited them.

Drawing near the pit, the men prayed aloud, speaking a sort of gibberish, an intimate conversation, between man and his maker. That negotiation one must make, before meeting one's terrible, inevitable end. They were powerless, and rendered their final hopes lost. One man broke down and started begging.

The pressure on his brain was tremendous.

THINK. Think. Think.

So many thoughts flooded his mind. A cascade of thoughts and experiences rushed in like the waters over Wilczki waterfall.

The water thrashed, sloshing around inside of his head. He was full of memories, hope and joy, so full it felt like magic, and it brought him power. A superpower. His senses were heightened. His mind was blazing. He was so close to the answer. To their escape. To their survival.

One of the other men started struggling, shouting obscenities. Two guards restrained him roughly, a third approached. The third guard stuffed what looked like sawdust into his friend's mouth.

The man was robbed of his ability to speak but continued to struggle.

"Crack!"

The struggling stopped.

"Crack!!"

The praying stopped.

"Crack!"

Images raced through his mind. Memories.

"Crack!"

Visions... Prayers...

"Crack!".

People...

Wait, was that him?! The memory leapt from his burning mind. He worked hard to sustain the vision. To make sense of it.

The barrel of a gun was pressed against the base of his skull.

Was that him?

The pressure of the gun. The desire to remember. It was all too much. How had it come to this? He had to remember. His freedom, his legacy, depended on it. He could feel the barrel shift ever so slightly as the finger applied pressure to the pistol's trigger. But...no matter how hard he tried...he couldn't place it, the face, the name...

Was that him? Goddamnit!

Silently he cried out with all his energy. The final tip of the pistol.

"Crack!" A deafening sound.

His eyes closed instinctively. A bright flash blinded him. A searing pain. The bullet ripped through his flesh.

Violently he fell. Into an abyss. He couldn't see anything ahead of him. Or behind. Only that image.

Think.

He understood he was dying.

Think.

But he was no longer terrified.

Think.

He prepared himself for a new journey.

Think.

Face-first he slammed against the bottom of the pit, among other bodies, with brutal force.

He blacked out. All the while his mind kept spinning.

Think. Who was that man?

GREGORZ WAS SICKENED. Never as bad as this. Not since that first day. No, he decided, this was worse.

For the past two days the prisoners had been in the woods, doing dirty deeds for their masters. He had lost his appetite and along with it, his ability to sleep the past few nights.

He couldn't go on much longer, didn't have the physical or mental strength.

He stopped himself. He knew death was his only other alternative, but he wasn't ready to join the thousands of victims in the dark woods. Forcing his comrades, men from his unit, to dispose of him. He couldn't bring himself to it. There was no way out of this grizzly situation.

The first day of the killing was the worst. The men in the "special operations" unit struggled. No one would, or could, say anything about it if they wanted to. The men in this unit never shared their thoughts, emotions, or concerns, if they had any at all.

Gregorz never wanted to be attached to this particular unit. Superficially, they were an army police unit, being used as a tool for more...unorthodox purposes.

One never asked questions in the Soviet Union. These men never shared their thoughts, emotions, or concerns, remember.

His leader had told him he was chosen because he had been a police officer years ago. He wasn't sure how this qualified him for the special unit. As far as he knew, they weren't doing any police work.

He was reluctant anyhow. He had only been able to barely get himself out of the police department with his life intact, merely three years ago. A constant source of surprise to his friends and colleagues, making him a target of suspicion.

Typically, anyone who attempted to leave the police were either killed 'in the line of duty', or simply never heard from again. Which is to say the same.

His unit had been ordered to take Polish enemies into the woods for 'disposal'. 'Enemies of the state' was the term used to classify anyone deemed undesirable. They had learned long ago not to ask questions, just follow orders. Without hesitation. They'd also learned not doing so meant removal, and removal was akin to permanent disappearance.

Long trenches were prepared in a clearing deep inside the woods. His unit had been issued pistols along with ample ammunition, both of German origin. The 'enemies' arrived in trucks; their hands bound behind their backs. Most of the men wore uniforms from various Polish military units, while others were in civilian clothes.

[21]

They were marched to the rim of each trench. Some men were silent, some prayed. Others begged their captors to be set free, to think of their families, to seek prayer, anything not to kill them.

No matter the plea, both the condemned and the executioners knew release was an impossible task. Everyone must die, no exceptions. Those were orders.

Several comrades in his unit were concerningly good at their work, imbuing a grotesque sense of pride in their efficiency. Others enjoyed the warped sense of mercifulness that accompanied extinguishing the lives of the men. The immaculate power of executing the sealed fates of so many.

The Lieutenant instructed them to move quickly once the enemies arrived.

"Less time to react, lest they may resist or escape." Their orders were simple. Two steps. Place the barrel of the pistol to the base of the skull and pull the trigger.

The bodies fell forward into the trenches,

"You may have to give it a shove."

They were instructed to keep moving until the entire group was finished. Carry a spare magazine and pistol in case their weapon jammed.

A simple, methodical, and efficient process.

They 'processed' a few hundred the first day.

His first enemy was slightly older than him and a Captain by rank.

Gregorz will never forget the moment. The image stained his mind. The man stared directly into Gregorz' face, reflecting a combination of defiance, indifference, and scorn.

As little as either man wanted to take part in the act, he knew refusing equated the same fate. Joining the ranks of the other hapless souls. A rifle shot from one of the guards circling the perimeter of the site. The Lieutenant and a couple officers stood a few yards away at the end of one trench, observing the executions.

Gregorz followed orders and took his pistol, placing it against the skull of the Captain, whose eyes closed tightly in prayer. He stood back until he was as far from the man as possible. His extended arm barely graced the man's neck. His face was cold. A chill shot down his neck, his shoulders. His stomach tightened into a knot. His arm weakened as the pistol grew heavier in his hand.

He struggled to focus on his task, but as he gazed past the captain's head to the other side of the trench, he saw one of his rifle-wielding comrades staring across at him. Time stopped. The comrade slowly started to lift his rifle. It was clear what needed to happen, and his comrade was willing to finish the job if Gregorz couldn't. It was both of their deaths otherwise.

Gregorz squeezed the trigger. The strain of his conscience gave way as he pulled.

"Crack!"

The man's head jerked forward. As it had been with hundreds of others, blood exploded outward from where the bullet impacted the head. The body slumped forward, slowly at first, then tumbling downward into the trench. Gregorz took a breath, only then realizing he had been holding it.

It was done.

He had done it.

He had followed orders once again.

As had become customary for survival, repentance became a way of life. Gregorz compartmentalized his thoughts, feelings, and remorse. Entire areas in his mind closed for business. The inhumane acts made him nauseous, but he learned to control his physical self, quieting his emotional instincts, in order to continue the gruesome work throughout the day.

He must have personally disposed of at least a hundred enemies, but he'd tried to lose count.

The sky was dark, permanently it would seem, and the Lieutenant ordered them to head back to camp.

During the truck ride back, Gregorz comrades made sense of their conquests, all while stifling whatever emotions they'd not been properly able to process.

"All enemies of the Soviet Union deserve what they get," said Yuri.

"You're damn right about that. These fuckin weakling Poles surrendered their country, their women, and their children. They aren't real men, they're fuckin cowards." Dmitri added.

The guards sat silently in the truck.

Yorgi chuckled.

"It's like shooting rats... except the begging makes it more fun. Rats don't beg like babies."

A few more men chuckled nervously.

Silence was the only answer. It had become law. Even if you didn't agree with what was said, you didn't share. Those who did, were ratted on.

Later Gregorz skipped dinner to throw up in the latrine. He needed sleep, was desperate for his dreams, to somehow transport him far, far away to a better time and a better place.

Eventually, the guards had all become hardened executioners. Even Gregorz. It was an effect of the work.

Until, that all changed.

Until Gregorz saw him.

Prior to pulling the trigger that day, he had looked many of the men in their faces. Over time, he didn't even see anything looking back. Not anymore. The men had become lifeless faces to him. Seconds from becoming lifeless bodies.

He stopped listening or hearing what they were saying either. Most never spoke at all.

But it all changed that day.

Gregorz had just reloaded his pistol with a new magazine, when, looking up, he saw him.

Was that him?

He couldn't take his eyes off the man as he slowly made his way amongst the group of prisoners toward the trench. The man had not made eye contact with Gregorz, not directly, but as he got closer, Gregorz knew.

He hadn't seen him in years. Not since their families had spent summers together, so many years ago.

He was almost sickened to remember. The fun and laughter, great food and drink their families shared, how different it felt from life now. That summer.

The two had stayed in touch for a number of years since, but, having grown older, everyone had gone their own separate ways. The entire episode had felt like a mirage, disappearing into the distance as life had become darker, more meaningless.

Gregorz hadn't seen, nor heard from the man, in several years. Until now.

Finally, the two men made eye contact. It was pure. He recalled it too. They locked eyes, and the memories flooded them both. That same rush of feeling. The dam burst and the emotions overwhelmed him. It was him. Gregorz' cousin.

His head started spinning, a reaction to the flood of emotion. His body, depleted from the senses for so long, couldn't process the wealth. A quick jolt ran through him, leaving him in a cold sweat.

He had to continue his work, so as not to overwhelm his system, to draw attention to himself. He stepped behind a rather large man, a

Sergeant, and quickly, coldly dispatched him, extinguishing the prayers he was muttering.

Next in line was a Lieutenant, wearing glasses, speaking something incoherent, slowly, over and over, until Gregorz pulled the trigger once more. The body fell forward like all the others.

He stepped behind the next man, and his humanity overpowered him. Those feelings. The memories of his past. He worked to quiet the rising compassion but was desperate to say something. To prevent this. His pistol pointed at the base of his cousin's skull.

And now, his cousin, whom he'd spent many summers pleasantly with, was now an enemy, and he, Gregorz, was by way of grotesque circumstance, the executioner.

He desperately wanted to reach out and touch him, to save him, or at the very least to say something, to say a prayer for him, to apologize. To cleanse his own soul.

He was taking much longer to dispatch than normal. He could feel his hesitation draw the attention of the others. He pretended his gun was jammed. Then, he felt all eyes were on him. He cocked his pistol.

His finger pulled back, and, ever so, he shifted the barrel of the gun away from the base of his cousin's skull toward the side of his neck and lower ear, all in a movement that was smooth and quick, almost imagined.

He pulled the trigger.

"Crack!"

His cousin's head jerked to the side, as the others had before him, and with a quick and forceful shove, Gregorz pushed his cousin forward into the trench. He stepped over to the next man and again pulled the trigger. Continuing with his orders. He was an executioner. A genuine murderer.

Step to the right. Crack!

Step to the right. Crack!

Later that afternoon, after a long day of murdering helpless humans, Gregorz drifted away toward some thick undergrowth. They had just finished their daily duties.

"Where you going? Trucks are this way!" Gregorz' comrade called out.

"We're heading back to get something to eat..."

Gregorz kept walking.

"We're not waiting forever!" called out another.

"I am taking a leak... I'll catch up!" Gregorz yelled back in a weary and sad voice.

He wandered to a small grouping of trees several yards off the trail, opened his trousers, and urinated. The thick scent of pine made him think about how beautiful the trees and forest were. He finished, buttoned up his trousers, buckled his belt, and pulled out his pistol once more, checking the magazine to see if there were any rounds left.

He was overcome with fear. Anger. Hatred. There was no way out of his situation. His future unfolded in front of him. Lines of men. Murdered. At his hand. He was a prisoner until his job was completed. For as many days as it took. As many men as it took.

He wasn't sure how much longer he could go on. But there was no escape. Asking for reassignment was impossible. He could run. But desertion meant starvation, and if caught, death, usually with a good bit of torture at that. This left him no other option. It had come to this.

He pushed the magazine back into the pistol and cocked the hammer. He opened his mouth and placed the barrel upward against his soft palate, then used his last bullet.

APRIL 9, 1943

"POLISH MASS GRAVES HAVE BEEN FOUND NEAR SMOLENSK. THE BOLSHEVIKS SIMPLY SHOT DOWN AND THEN SHOVELED INTO MASS GRAVES SOME 10,000 POLISH PRISONERS".

APRIL 14, 1943

"WE ARE NOW USING THE DISCOVERY OF 12,000 POLISH OFFICERS, MURDERED BY THE GPU, FOR ANTI-BOLSHEVIK PROPAGANDA ON A GRAND STYLE. WE SENT NEUTRAL JOURNALISTS AND POLISH INTELLECTUALS TO THE SPOT WHERE THEY WERE FOUND. THEIR REPORTS NOW REACHING US FROM AHEAD ARE GRUESOME. THE FUEHRER HAS ALSO GIVEN PERMISSION FOR US TO HAND OUT A DRASTIC NEWS ITEM TO THE GERMAN PRESS. I GAVE INSTRUCTIONS TO MAKE THE WIDEST POSSIBLE USE OF THE PROPAGANDA MATERIAL. WE SHALL BE ABLE TO LIVE ON IT FOR A COUPLE WEEKS".

Entries in the personal diary of the German Minister of Propaganda, Joseph Goebbels

CHAPTER TWO

April 20, 1945

Berlin, Germany

"General is on his way!" the SS guard announced as he hung up the telephone receiver. Army Major Werner Ruessel stood up, put out his cigarette, and straightened his well-worn tunic the best he could. He hadn't slept, nor eaten well, for the past couple months, and it showed. He looked haggard and felt exhausted.

Berlin was being annihilated. Anyone venturing above ground these days couldn't possibly keep their clothing - or uniform - clean. Smoke, dust, and soot from burning buildings clung to your clothes and darkened any exposed skin. Even after a wash-up, the smell and sooty film cloaked you in a dark and rancid mood. Everything was collapsing.

He looked out at the destruction and wreckage of what was once the great Reichskanzlei, and wondered, how had it come to this?

The air was thick with airborne particulates from the destruction of Hitler's Berlin. Once the proud city of the German people. The great Teutonic race had been reduced to a scurrying and cowering populace. The symbolism of Berlin was the reason the Americans and British were so intent on bombing it into rubble.

The Soviets had now started an artillery barrage. Pounding what was left as they made the final drive on the Fatherland's capital with all types and sizes of munitions. For the past few days, you could hear the distant rolling thunder, vibrations of war, strong enough to shake hanging pictures off walls. Telephones rung eerily, no caller on the other end.

Lieutenant General Karl Reiniger strode up the last few steps and emerged from the Fürherbunker, catching his breath. It was never easy, nor enjoyable, but deep breaths of dirty air were all that was left.

At 56 years of age, and a head full of salt and pepper hair, he was in excellent physical condition. Athletic as a young man, he still carried himself in a self-confident manner. He wore the best field gray tunic he had available for his meeting in the bunker, but it was a far cry from the sharp and crisp uniforms officers had worn only a few short years ago. How times had changed.

An SS Captain approached the General holding a familiar pistol. "I believe this is yours."

No weapons were permitted to enter the Führerbunker. Not even a highly decorated German Army General was allowed to carry a sidearm. Since the attempt on Hitler's life last year, no one, especially the Army leadership, was trusted around the Führer.

The General grabbed his weapon without acknowledging the SS officer, and as he holstered the pistol, stared into the man's eyes with great disdain. The SS man coolly returned the General's stare with calm indifference. He was dressed in a neat gray uniform. Anyone else would have been shaken to the core with the General's peering sights, but SS officers didn't really care much about army officers, let alone anyone in any branch of service other than theirs. The SS, or Schutzstaffel, was the major Nazi Party paramilitary organization. The particular detachment this officer belonged was the Führer's personal bodyguards. He was untouchable. The SS were a different breed.

"Assholes." The General muttered under his breath as he walked away, without receiving a salute. This was fine with him. He didn't like using the raised arm Nazi salute anyway, preferring to use the traditional military style.

Reiniger had specific feelings about the SS. He knew of the large and small-scale atrocities the SS had orchestrated on innocent victims. He hoped these animals would receive appropriate justice from the eventual victors of this war, followed by a quick descent into the hell he wished fervently to be real.

"Let's go, Major."

"Yes Sir, Herr General," Werner replied loudly with a smart salute. Loud enough so that the SS men guarding the entrance to the bunker noticed.

[33]

The General gave a faint smile, returned the salute, and strode past the Major who followed him closely as they worked their way out of the heavily damaged Reich Chancellery.

"I don't think those people in the bunker realize what is going on out here. They're living in a fantasy down there, Werner," he said in a subdued voice. "Things are far worse than any of us thought."

Few still believed they could win the war, or at least, only a few still acted like they believed it. Even worse.

"Yes Sir." Ruessel paused a few seconds to ask "Where to, Sir?" attempting to change the subject.

"We have an assignment. The city will fall to the Soviets within the week. But we haven't much time. Four or five days at most." The General spoke with indifference and confidence simultaneously.

The Reich Chancellery, once a proud symbol of the German nation and Nazi state, was now a desolate building. The Führer had recently moved underground with staff and various government officials. The place was all but deserted, except for the SS detachment and the handful of military and government officials scurrying in and out of the bunker. The structure had sustained extensive damage, but its sheer size and former grandeur, outlasted, making it an impressive sight to behold.

"What is the assignment, Herr General?" Ruessel asked.

The two men descended the debris-strewn front stairs of the building. The General ignored Ruessel's question.

Both men jumped into the awaiting kübelwagen. The General gave the driver directions.

"The Führer's birthday is today." Said the General blandly, if tinged with sarcasm. "They were sipping champagne and making toasts down there."

Slowly they made their way through the devastated city, avoiding rubble, burnt-out streetcars, abandoned vehicles. And bodies.

Red Nazi flags billowed gently in the dirty air, hung from the tops of building windows in honor of the Führer's birthday. The bright red looked surreal, sharply contrasted with the dull gray surroundings. A sign read "The Fighting City of Berlin Greets the Führer." The sign hung sideways. Several artillery shrapnel holes had ripped through it, leaving it to dangle awkwardly.

A half block away lay the grisly remains of a dead horse, killed recently by the Russian artillery shelling. The carcass hadn't started to bloat or stink yet. A haggard group of civilians surrounded it, carving up the animal with kitchen knives for their next meal. Berliners had become skittish and hungry people. Desperate for meat, really any kind of nourishment. Regular foodstuffs had slowly disappeared over the past several weeks. The city was silent except for that ominous thudding of artillery in the distance.

An occasional woman could be seen, darting here and there, carrying buckets of water, sacks of potatoes, or anything to be used as fuel. Volkssturm units - or the People's Militia - armed with hunting rifles and panzerfausts, stood guard like ghosts and misfits at hastily constructed barricades. The units were comprised of elderly men and teenage boys. Each of them wore a motley selection of uniforms, overcoats, and armbands identifying them as a Volkssturm member. Some were armed with rifles and maybe a couple of rounds of ammunition. Others carried shovels or pitchforks. A few had panzerfausts. Armored vehicles that hadn't yet been destroyed simply sat idle in the streets due to lack of petrol.

Two million civilians remained in Berlin. Mostly women and children. Despite the powerful Soviet armies surrounding the vast city, Hitler repeatedly rejected any suggestions of evacuating the population while there was still time to do so, deciding instead to abandon them to their fate in the doomed city.

Bodies of dead soldiers and civilians could be seen on every street they traveled. Most, killed by artillery or aerial bombs. On one street, a makeshift gallows was erected to hang a hapless soldier. His lifeless body swung slowly back and forth in the breeze. Around his neck, a sign read *traitor. this is what happens to deserters.*

Nearby on the side of another building, graffiti scrawled on the wall read, 'Fight For the Führer – We Will Never Surrender.'

The fate of those remaining in the city was sealed.

The General took in their surroundings, and in a disgusted tone mumbled, "Fanatics." He referenced the graffiti. "They've ruined us."

THEY CAME ACROSS the badly charred remains of the shell of a building. Previously an Army office complex.

The General leapt from the vehicle as they pulled up to a stop.

"Let's go" he said to Ruessel and the driver.

"Begging the General's pardon, but where? Why?"

"Inside Ruessel. Down to the basement." the General replied, impatient with his adjutant.

The men walked over the rubble to the other side of the building. A guard stood wearily near the doorway. As the General approached, a guard stood at attention. He saluted.

"Which way to the file storage rooms?" the General asked.

"Through this door, to your right, and down the stairs, Herr General."

"Thank you, soldier".

The men entered, then found their way to the stairwell leading to the basement. The first level below ground was a central hallway. Rooms on each side. The doors to each were open. Each room contained filing cabinets, shelves, and boxes. Materials from the cabinets and shelves were scattered about on the floor.

A Sergeant looked out from one of the rooms when he heard them walking.

"Can I help you?" Quickly realizing that he was addressing a General and another officer, he stood at attention and saluted. "Sir".

"Of course, you can, Sergeant." The General gave a quick salute and pulled a folded piece of paper out of his tunic pocket. He handed it to the Sergeant, who promptly opened the letter and read.

When finished, he looked up at the General and then at Ruessel.

"Do you understand the orders?" asked Reiniger.

"Of course, Herr General, I shall take you down there."

The Sergeant eased past the General and took them further down the hall to another stairwell.

Berlin had become a city of cave dwellers. Almost all activity in Berlin these days was happening underground. So few people dared to stay above ground as it was.

At the bottom of the stairway, they entered a dimly lit hallway with more rooms, similar to those above them.

Even two floors below ground they could still faintly hear and feel the eerie pounding of distant artillery. Toward the end of the hallway, they reached another room.

"The materials you are looking for should be in here Sir."

"Very good, Sergeant, the Major and I will take it from here," said the General curtly.

"Will the General be needing assistance locating the files?"

"I think we can handle it from here, but please send down some document cases. We'll be needing them".

"Very well Sir." The Sergeant lingered. "May I make a copy of your orders for our records Sir?" He asked.

The General hesitated a moment.

"Thank you, Sergeant. No need to add to the vast accumulation of paperwork and files, especially since you are in the process of destroying them. Silly, don't you think?"

And with that, the General took the letter from the Sergeant's hand and walked into the file room. Ruessel followed. The Sergeant waited briefly, before retreating down the hallway.

"What are we looking for Sir?"

"We're looking for files and materials, Ruessel."

The General spoke quickly, curtly.

"Which files Sir?"

"Ones to take with us."

"Where are we going, Sir?"

There was that faint pounding of artillery.

"We need to get out of Berlin. The sooner the better, it seems."

The General quickly scanned the shelves and file cabinets for specific labeling. Then, he found it.

"Our assignment."

The air in the basement was stale and musty. The file room appeared untouched, compared to those above them, with papers and materials scattered about.

Ruessel glanced around the dimly lit room and surmised the importance of sensitive materials here. More important materials than those in the rooms upstairs. He now understood the Sergeant's need for written orders to retrieve their details.

"Here we are," said the General, pulling a box off a shelf. He placed the box on the floor and opened the lid, just wide enough to glance at the contents. Then quickly he shut it. Satisfied. He started to pull down the accompanying boxes.

"We need all these boxes and anything else associated with them. Look over this general area and pull anything out."

"Yes Sir."

Ruessel looked at the file names on the boxes and proceeded to check the nearby shelves for any related materials. Meanwhile, the General had moved on, searching for other files.

"Here are some more, Ruessel."

The Major walked around the shelving units, watching as the General placed more boxes on the floor. The pile was growing fast.

"Be sure to check all file cabinets thoroughly, we don't want to leave anything behind."

Ruessel bent down to read the label before he opened one. The box was marked, 'International Katyn Commission Findings.' Other boxes nearby read, 'Polish Red Cross Commission' and then, 'German Special Medical Judiciary Commission.'

Ruessel's face went white. His eyes widened.

He knew the files. All too well.

He and the General had been Army liaisons to this investigation back in April of 1943. They were stationed in the area inside the Soviet Union. They were there when the grisly remains were dug up. Forensic scientists from the International Red Cross conducted a thorough investigation to identify, categorize and process the dead. It was a gruesome and sickening task neither Werner nor the General enjoyed.

It was obvious who had killed the men, and only a simple matter of classification for the official record. Propaganda Minister Goebbels had already decided the executioner's identity, as soon as the bodies were discovered, but there was still a need to go through the process to validate his assessment.

That was long ago. The impending collapse of the Reich was a far more important, and timely, issue now.

"What are we going to do? With these files, Sir?"

"Take them with us, Ruessel."

"But, why?"

The General was slightly irritated but responded to Ruessel. "We need to preserve as much evidence as we can, to make sure none of this material falls into the hands of the Soviets."

He continued scanning the shelves for more files as he spoke. "Some of our 'brilliant' leaders actually believe we might convince the Americans and British to join our fight against the Soviets."

"Is that possible?" Werner asked, incredulously.

"Well…" the General hesitated. "Seems more like a fantasy, but folks down in that hole seem to think it's possible." He said with a bit of disgust in his voice. "Seems to me, they need a better handle on reality. And they better get one soon."

An SS Lieutenant appeared suddenly in the doorway to the storeroom along with the SS Sergeant that had fetched the file cases.

"Here are the cases you requested, Herr General. Will you be needing anymore?"

"Very good, Sergeant. Please put them there. I think that should be enough," He ignored the SS officer.

"May I ask, on whose authority are you accessing these files?" the Lieutenant asked. The Sergeant stood back so the officer could enter the doorway. The Lieutenant was wearing a sidearm.

SS men were everywhere these days, watching everyone like hawks, even Army Generals on special assignments.

The General turned and looked at the officer. "No, you may not. But I request men to take these cases up to my car. That will be all, Lieutenant."

The General turned and went back to searching through a file cabinet.

The Lieutenant continued to stand in the doorway, his hands firmly on his hips. "Then, may I *see* your orders?" he asked again, more firmly.

The General ignored the request, continuing to look through the files. The Lieutenant waited several more seconds, then repeated himself. This time in a more demanding tone.

"Sir?"

The General stopped looking and stood up straight, his back to the SS officer. He was struggling to remain calm. He turned and faced the doorway, the Lieutenant. A fire raged in his eyes as he stared across the room at the SS officer. He was furious to hear scum refuse his orders.

"I said that will be all. You and the Sergeant have been dismissed. Please see to it that men are available to help bring these cases to my car. We will be leaving shortly," he said affirmatively, deliberately.

The Sergeant sensed a confrontation and slowly backed away, turning to walk quickly down the hallway.

The SS Lieutenant lingered in the doorway, looking. "Where are you taking the files?" he demanded.

His orders were to supervise the facility. He was assigned to make sure nothing out of the ordinary took place. Army clericals, in and out, secured important documents, and destroyed others. A newly expedient task, now that more and more soldiers and officers were abandoning the Führer to flee the city.

The Lieutenant had grown suspicious over time. He could not allow them to pull one over on him.

"Very well, here are my orders," said the General as he opened his tunic pocket, extracted the paperwork. His hands were shaking.

"Major, please give this to the Lieutenant," he handed the papers to Ruessel.

Ruessel took the papers, turned and walked toward the Lieutenant. As he reached the doorway...

"Crack!"

A shot rang out.

The Lieutenant's head jerked violently. The bullet impacted squarely into the forehead. Blood, skull fragments, and cranial matter spewed from the back of his head onto the wall behind him. His body reeled, stumbling awkwardly backward until he hit the wall across the hallway. The man's legs gave out and he slowly slumped to the floor.

Ruessel stopped in his tracks and watched the SS officer collapse. He swung around, wide-eyed, and saw the General holding his pistol, still smoking. He had it trained on the spot the Lieutenant stood only a second ago.

"I gave him an order. Failure to follow can be costly," The General said in a monotone. "Isn't that right, Major?" he shifted his gaze to Werner, while crisply holstering the smoking pistol.

"Yes, Herr General."

"Make sure my orders are followed. Understand?" He motioned for the Ruessel to give him back the papers. "He displayed no respect...none of them do," referring to SS men.

"Of course, Herr General. My apologies," he said as he stepped away from the twitching body, crossed the room and handed back the papers. "I won't let it happen again, Sir."

Werner had never seen the General fire his pistol, let alone empty someone's skull with it. He seemed calm and composed, as if he had merely stepped on a cockroach, which, to the General's thinking, was only a couple notches up from an SS officer anyway.

The casualty was not going to bode well for them. Should other SS find out that an Army General had just killed one of their own, they'd be eager to return the favor.

"Werner, it had to be done. We don't have time for this crap," said the General, attempting subtlety to minimize or justify his actions.

Werner was a hardworking and dedicated young officer. The General felt sorry for him. Knowing he was witnessing the destruction of their country. That he, and others, will likely struggle to make a new life after the war, presuming they even survived it.

"These orders are from the Chief of OKW - Ober-Kommando der Wehrmacht - and from OKH - Ober-Kommando der Herr. Our job is to get several sets of important files to OKW headquarters in Krampnitz and then onward to a location wherever they can be held safely. Ultimately, we may have to take them to the American or British lines." He paused. "These papers are our ticket out." He began searching the files again.

"Krampnitz?"

"OKW is on the move now. Things are fluid. They're going to stay as close as they can to Berlin, but things are changing quickly now that the Soviets are surrounding the city."

"I understand, Sir."

The Major began working with the General in early 1943. He joined his staff as a Lieutenant after the General had been promoted to his current rank. General Reiniger had made a name for himself after serving admirably in North Africa. He was subsequently recalled back to Germany, and then was tasked with assisting desperate units fighting in Russia.

As operations specialists, he, the lieutenant, and their staff were experts. They were frequently dispatched by OKH, ordered to divisions in distress to get things back under control, typically after a commander had been relieved.

They would hold down each fort, so to speak, until a new commander was assigned, then they would move on to the next troubled division and replace the next commander.

General Reiniger had a reputation as apolitical, not affiliated with party membership. Werner and other staff believed this to be the reason he had not been elevated to a higher command position. Obviously, the Army valued his talents, but not enough to withhold awarding commands to less talented Nazi Generals.

Over the next two years, things deteriorated badly for the Wehrmacht and Germany. Reininger and Werner found themselves in a devastated, and barely functional Berlin with another assignment. They were barely keeping a terminal 'patient' alive.

"I'm sorry if I have been quiet Ruessel, but as you can see, it's all happening quite fast," said the General. "The Soviet are animals. We need to keep these documents in German hands, but if circumstances dictate otherwise, we may need to hand them over to the Americans or British. Anyone but those fucking Russian swine."

"Yes Sir."

"If it looks like the Soviets may get these documents, we destroy them first. Got it?"

"I understand, Sir."

Werner deduced the documents must be incriminating or contain secrets (possibly scientific) if the Soviets must not possess them.

"Who knows we have the files, Sir?"

"Not many, Ruessel. Jodl at OKW knows we are bringing them, and Krebs at OKH wrote out a set of orders on his own. I don't believe their superiors know. I'm pretty sure no one would seriously ask the Führer for permission to remove anything from Berlin for safe keeping so the Soviets don't get their hands on them when they take the city. I suspect that would get a few of us Generals shot. He is probably the only one with a gun down there."

"So, if the SS find us running from the city, they may not like it?" said Ruessel.

"Exactly. So, we avoid them, as well as the Soviets, to get out with our necks," a lame attempt at humor. "I knew you would understand."

Werner always was a smart one.

"But why us, Sir?"

"Because you and I are probably the only ones capable of getting the job done," and after a brief pause, he added, "and because our names are mentioned in some of the documents." Another pause. "Along with others." Then, "If the Soviets get their grubby hands on these files, they will track down anyone mentioned in them –

officers, scientists, witnesses, whomever, and either haul them off for whatever their purposes – or if they know too much, liquidate them."

"Doesn't the Propaganda Ministry or the SS have their own copies? Might they try to get their copies out, as well?"

"They might try. If not, they had better destroy them – for our sake as well as theirs. These are the Army's copies, so we're taking care of them."

"Why not just destroy the documents, or at least the lists of names?" Ruessel asked.

"Because they may be important to our government once the war is over."

The General turned back to a drawer and pulled out a few more files and threw them into a box.

Down the hall came the sound of men approaching. Ruessel glanced at the General and then got up and went into the hallway. There were three soldiers approaching the file room carrying more empty cases with them, slowing down when they saw the body of the SS officer lying on the floor with blood pooling beneath his head.

"This way men – come, come," as Reininger motioned for them to hurry and come into the room. They couldn't help but look down at the dead body. Ruessel offered no explanation.

"Take these cases here up to the street and put them into the General's vehicle. Then come directly back here for the rest," he instructed them.

The men were a bit unnerved, with the dead SS officer, and the situation they were in, but they picked up the cases and left the room, looking down at the dead man as they passed.

"I'll go with them." Suspecting the men might alert others about the dead SS officer, Ruessel decided to go with them.

The General looked at him, understanding, and nodded. "Good idea, Werner. I'll keep working here. Let's get what we need and go," he said, waving him to follow the men.

AT THEIR UNDERGROUND location, beneath a government building, they brought the cases of documents down. The General addressed his remaining staff.

"Our assignment is of great importance to Germany's future."

After a few questions from the men, the General gave instructions "You're to separate into two groups, Colonel Thalberg will lead the second group".

Then he added "Thalberg, I want to congratulate you on your promotion. Your paperwork finally came through," as he took out some more papers from his tunic and handed them to Thalberg.

Thalberg, taken aback for a moment, took the papers and clasped the General's hand for a deeply appreciative handshake.

"Thank you, Herr General, I am honored."

"Actually, I told them it would be easier for you on this assignment if you were a General. I made them fill out the promotion papers at gunpoint," he said with a laugh. Thalberg and the others joined the laughter. "You can use my other tunic. We don't have time to find you a good tailor just now. I think we are about the same size, aren't we?" Reininger held out a tunic and Thalberg stepped forward and donned it. He buttoned the front and turned toward the gathered men. Reininger shook his hand.

The men gave out a cheer, then passed around a bottle of Schnapps. Each shook the new Brigadier General's hand.

They would depart on their missions in the morning.

CHAPTER THREE

April 21, 1945

Berlin, Germany

BY MORNING, THE Generals had secured the vehicles and stocked them with fuel, food and water. The morning was gray, pouring rain, as they prepared to make their way out of the city. Ruessel briefed the men in the small group on their assignment and the importance of getting out of the city.

Ruessel and the General rode in the back of a staff car, closest to the files stored in the trunk. A kübelwagen carried additional files and a couple more men, an armored personnel vehicle and another kübelwagen followed. Thalberg's group would head west and attempt to link up with OKW and onward to Northern Command. Reiniger's group headed southwest to reach the Allies that were rapidly heading eastward toward Berlin.

"Should something happen to me along the way...these papers," the General said to Werner as he patted his top left pocket. "They may save you." He had also given copies of the orders to Thalberg.

THE PATH THROUGH the city was slow and dangerous. The streets were barely passable due to the vast amounts of debris and wreckage. Some were intentionally blocked and barricaded by military units, ordered to defend the city. Meanwhile, Soviet artillery crept ever closer to the city's center.

Relentless bombing by the American and British 'air gangsters' had turned the city into a hellish visage. Violent blasts from the daily and nightly bombing ensured every building sustained some damage. Most met worse fate. Almost all structures were gutted shells. Even fewer had roofs. Everywhere you looked, it was grey or black.

The occasional red flag provided the only color among the ruins.

Torrential rains added to the gloomy feeling of the city. All around them, civilians peered out from shattered windows or doorways, a mix of concern, fear, and resignation in their tired eyes. They watched in silence as the men passed. Two older German's yelled out to the passing group to ask for word. What was happening? Should they leave? Rumors of Soviet takeover in the Berlin suburbs were advancing quickly. What was true?

The soldiers in the group, for the most part, ignored the queries, preferring to avoid conversations to focus on the task of getting quickly through the city.

During one stop, a middle-aged woman approached the group. She was not bad looking, but you could tell the stress and strain of living in these conditions had taken a heavy toll on her.

She politely asked the General what he thought the people of her neighborhood should do. The German people constantly needed guidance, direction, orders. They were looking for someone to tell them what to do. Give them orders, they would do as they were told. Apparently, it had been ingrained in them. They were good followers.

He didn't judge. Being a military man himself, he was used to giving and following orders, as good as any German.

The General replied curtly.

"Prepare for the worst, Madam."

The woman was shocked. The people were used to more positive news. They'd grown used to pandering, to hearing the ridiculous party spin on the inevitable victory that the Führer was orchestrating.

The woman searched the General's eyes. She seemed relieved. The first man with any authority to tell her – tell them – the truth. They had become so conditioned to hearing lies and false promises...lies had become truth...it was all that they knew. How were they meant to have faith in eventual victory when their homes were being bombed? No food. No fuel. Nothing was real or true anymore.

But this man, this General, confirmed the fears they had long suspected. No lies, no party line...just the truth. Strangely, it was uplifting to finally hear, and more so coming from a soldier – a leader. Now their fates were easier to face, knowing the truth – bleak though it was.

Air raid sirens began to wail, and the General warned. "Madam, you should make your way back to your basement or shelter. I wouldn't want anything to happen to you."

A glimmer of a smile on her face as she accepted the General's concern. She turned with the others and walked with new determination back to her destroyed apartment block. The General and the group resumed the journey.

Werner sensed an uneasiness. The General was a compassionate man, but his concern was unusually high for the welfare of a stranger.

The General looked back out of the vehicle, to see the woman retreat. She was about the same age as the General's late wife.

Reininger had lost his wife, Berta, only two months prior, in the firebombing of Dresden. The General had sent her to stay with family members there, with the belief she would be out of harm's way. He couldn't have known that the Americans would attack and destroy an ancient and cultural city like Dresden. Dresden wasn't a manufacturing or industrial center, but it had been targeted as a major communications hub, and thus a worthy target. Conventional and incendiary explosives from American bombers had created a firestorm, roasting its inhabitants in their homes, basements, and streets.

Immediately after receiving the news of the city's devastation, the General feared the worst. Her remains were eventually identified in a basement with several other bodies, older men, women, and children. All of whom were sheltering from the raging firestorm above them. They had suffocated as the oxygen vanished.

The General accepted the news calmly, having become accustomed to death in a way that men at war will. But Werner acknowledged a change inside. He wasn't the same. More reserved and withdrawn from his staff after that.

He considered the link this woman drew to Reininger's wife. Maybe he felt guilty? Maybe he felt that leaving her to her untimely fate was the equivalent of sending his wife into that firestorm.

THEY ENCOUNTERED SEVERAL checkpoints traversing the city. Tough Army checkpoints were not a problem, but the roving bands of SS troops were. They looked for anyone in uniform – or out for that matter – who might be a deserter attempting to flee the city without authorization.

Deserters and defeatists were punished. Examples had to be made. Their group managed to make it through these checkpoints with a few close calls, through which the General skillfully negotiated them.

One of the most massive migrations in history was underway. Millions of refugees were on the move, heading westward from Prussia and the eastern regions of Germany. Reiniger's group fell in with the long column of soldiers and civilians attempting to make it to the American lines and avoid Soviet captivity.

Dejected troops of the rapidly disintegrating armed forces - Luftwaffe, Army, even Waffen SS men - were scattered among civilians streaming in small, fragmented groups, away from the Russian onslaught, carrying their weapons and meager belongings with them. The troops listlessly dragged their feet, some limping from injuries or fatigue. Silently they trudged along, each man for himself. Sunken cheeks, hollow eyes, and stubbled chins. They looked defeated and pathetic. This chapter of the war was a far cry from the Führer's invincible and victorious motorized blitzkrieg armies of 1939.

Civilian refugees carried suitcases, bags, blankets, family heirlooms and treasures. Eventually, as they tired, they would discard items along the roadside. Vast amounts of debris lingered on the roads. Left behind. Trails back to the lives they'd known. Lives they were currently fleeing. Destroyed and disabled military equipment, discarded furniture, pots, pans, clothing marked the paths out of the city. Gruesome human and animal remains lay strewn amongst the hellish flotsam.

The Soviets were attempting to close off all escape routes and take as many prisoners, and loot, as possible. The race was on to see if the Soviet Army could surround Berlin and prevent Germans from crossing the Elbe River to the relative safety of the American or British lines.

Ruessel and the General traveled in silence for most of the day. The General was unusually sullen. The two men watched a disaster unfolding outside the windows of the car as their small caravan crept out of the ruins of the Reich capitol.

"Do you believe we can hold out, Sir?" Werner asked sheepishly.

"No." was all the General had to say.

"Will the Führer break out of Berlin?" Werner asked after a couple more silent minutes.

"I hope not. I was told he plans to stay until the end. The city is indefensible."

"What of the new weapons systems?"

The General grunted, unwilling to chat. "Even if we had them, it would still be too late. We haven't got the men or the resources to go on much longer," he said with grudging resignation.

Ruessel had never seen the General in such a negative mood. They hadn't really spoken of the situation. The frankness shocked him.

"What will happen to the country Sir? I mean the people, the armed forces, our industry…our technology?"

"Well Werner, I think that will be up to the Americans and the Soviets. It's out of our hands now. We only have a few cards left to play, if they're even worth anything at this point."

"Surely the Americans and the British wouldn't let the Soviets have their way with us, would they?"

"They've already carved things up I'm afraid. In fact, some want to take all our industry away and turn us into feudal farmland, back to the dark ages. Make no mistake, the Soviets will have their revenge, of this you can be certain. They'll take everything they can and turn our people into slaves. They'll simply kill off the upper echelons." Then with a hint of sarcasm in his voice, "The Americans will have their hands full trying to hold them back and keep Stalin in line."

"That's why the Americans should help us." Ruessel said with diminishing confidence. He had only heard talk of Americans and British joining the German forces in repelling the Soviet onslaught of Central Europe.

"No, no, Werner. That won't happen," said the General bluntly. He stared despondently out the window. "We are responsible for too much. Too many things have happened during this war. All the cruelty. Make no mistake. We will be crushed, Werner. We must be crushed, you see." Still, he peered out the window. "Look what the Americans did to Dresden, to Berlin. They aren't interested in rescuing us. They'll take what they can, or what we give them, but ultimately, they'll have no mercy. That's for certain. The time has come for reckoning."

"What do you mean, Sir?"

"We're going to be held accountable for the war. The losers always are. Just like the last war. Just like the next." He felt too defeated. "This war was ruthless, you know that. There's been too much death and destruction. We were fools to go along with these Nazis," he said with regret. "The Army was weak in not stopping the madness long ago, but too many of us were under the Führer's spell. His military scheming should have been controlled. We had chances to win this war, but we missed opportunities by being totally devoted to the Führer's military 'genius'."

"All is lost, then?"

"It's been over for quite some time, Werner. We just didn't want to believe it. As long as the Führer is alive there are those that will keep fighting for him."

Werner was a bit worried about what the drivers would think of hearing the General talk like this, especially about the Führer. He motioned for the General, regarding the men in the front seat. The General understood what he was getting at.

"Helmut?"

"Yes, Herr General?"

"Did you and the Corporal hear what the Major and I were discussing?"

"Yes Herr General".

"Everything?"

"Yes, Herr General."

"Do you have anything you'd like to say?"

"No, Herr General. I respect the General's wisdom. We are ready to follow all the General's orders. It's not as if we cannot see for ourselves what is happening."

"Very good, Helmut."

The General and Ruessel sat quietly in the back of the car, staring out the windows at the refugees on the road.

The collapse was almost complete. It was simply a matter of days.

"...evidence of atrocities, massacres and cold-blooded mass executions which are being perpetrated by Hitlerite forces in many of the countries they have overrun and from which they are now being steadily expelled"

From the final section of the Moscow Declaration entitled Statement on Atrocities, signed by the U.S. President Franklin D. Roosevelt, British Prime Minister Winston Churchill and Soviet Premier Joseph Stalin.

CHAPTER FOUR

April 24, 1945

Germany

AFTER THREE DAYS, General Reiniger's group were within a few miles of the Elbe River in the vicinity of the city of Lutherstadt Wittenburg, roughly 50 miles southwest of Berlin. The Soviets were harassing the fleeing troops and civilians with sporadic artillery fire and strafing from Sturmovik fighter planes during the past few days. Hundreds had been killed or injured by the deadly fire, temporarily slowing the panicked rush to escape.

The remains of the fallen, along with their final worldly belongings, were strewn unceremoniously alongside the road. The military vehicles mixed within the column of those fleeing drew the attention of the Soviet fighter planes. All aircraft overhead posed a danger, as the Luftwaffe had faded from the sky weeks ago.

Night was falling as they passed through a small village that was nearly destroyed by bombing. The ragtag column of traffic and refugees gradually came to a stop.

The only remaining structure standing was a battered and scarred church. The surrounding houses and shops were burnt out; roofs, windows and doors all gone. The street was lined with smoldering, broken, and battered walls. Charred brick chimneys remained standing. All reminders that homes, families, once lived there.

The driver brought the car to a stop, and the General opened the door and got out. Ruessel followed.

"Why is everything stopping?" Ruessel asked.

"I'm not sure, Werner. Possibly trouble up ahead," he said with a concerned look on his face.

They looked west up the road toward sounds of artillery, mortar, and small arms fire erupting. The sounds were near, maybe less than half a mile ahead. Ragtag troops in the column moved forward with their weapons drawn. The civilian refugees in the column panicked, running in the opposite direction. Some still clung to their belongings, while others dropped everything as they retreated.

"We're being cut off," said the General, realizing the severity of their situation. "Stay with the car, Werner. You know what to do."

He unbuttoned his greatcoat, pulled the papers from his pocket and pressed them into Ruessel's hands. Werner quickly placed them securely in the pocket of his tunic.

"Where are you going Sir?"

Reininger pulled out his pistol and motioned for the men in his column to follow him.

"We need to get through" he said, surveying the area and taking stock of the men and weapons close by.

Reiniger had made it far enough through this war but knew this could be his last battle. His job now was to get as many of his countrymen across to the American side and take as many damned Soviets with him as he could. Most importantly, Werner and the files needed to get into Allied hands.

He called out and rallied some troops moving forward in the column, ordering them to get their weapons ready. There was no time to waste.

"Men, follow me! We're breaking through the encirclement to the river! Our people will be killed by the damned Soviets otherwise!" He shouted in the loudest voice he could muster. "Let's do our duty! Save our people!"

The formerly sullen soldiers, who had been marching aimlessly for days, transformed. They readied their weapons for action.

He motioned to a Lieutenant and a Sergeant nearby to get the men organized, then started forward. They pushed past the stalled line of vehicles, carts, and the terrified civilians scrambling about. The General, along with the men, disappeared into the smoke and darkness, heading toward their destinies.

Werner stayed with the staff car and the drivers as ordered. He watched the General and soldiers move forward into the darkness and haze. In the distance, the sounds of heated battle became more intense. The sounds drew closer. More troops ran up from behind him in the column, moving forward up the road. He called out the situation, ordering them forward to support the troops already attempting to break through. Then he heard it.

A hissing and spitting sound above him.

Artillery and mortar rounds started dropping on the village, right where he and the column had halted.

Everyone scrambled for cover, hiding in the ruins of the houses, under carts and wagons, or near piles of rubble.

Werner instinctually jumped in the backseat of the car, hoping they might be able to drive away, but there was nowhere for them to go. They were hemmed in by all the vehicles in front and behind them.

Werner could hear it coming.

Whooomph.

A shell exploded a few yards away in a blinding flash. The shockwave and shrapnel lifted the car off its wheels and blew out the front and left side windows of the car. Werner ducked just before the shell landed. Glass, dirt and shrapnel showered him through the window.

Helmut, the driver, had not been as quick.

A haze of smoke and thick dust filled the air in and around what was left of the mangled car. Werner slowly raised himself up from the backseat and brushed off some debris. The concussion of the blast made his ears ring loudly. His eyes felt gritty as he rubbed them furiously. He fought to regain his bearings. His vision slowly came back into focus, and he could see the Helmut 's face had been blown off and was a mass of bloody pulp. His body slumped awkwardly forward on the mangled steering wheel.

Blood was everywhere on him, but it didn't seem to be his blood. The other soldier in the front seat was covered with glass, dirt and blood as well, but alive. He was moving slightly, shaking debris off himself.

"Let's go!" Werner yelled, tugging on the man's shoulder. The soldier, dazed from the blast, was still confused. He grabbed the door handle and tried pulling it open, but it wasn't unlocking. He tried ramming the door with his shoulder, but the thing was jammed and wouldn't budge.

Werner was able to get the back door open, and he quickly rolled out onto the ground. He got to his feet and tried pulling the front door open so he could get the wounded man out next. The door simply would not budge.

Werner yelled at the soldier to climb out of the car through the back seat, and then, turned and ran to the rear of the vehicle. He wrenched the trunk open and pulled the document cases out, looking around and wondering what his next move would be. Time was running out.

Whooomph. Whooomph.

More shells were landing. Flames, dirt and hot shrapnel expanded outward from the impacts. The noise was deafening as larger artillery shells locked on the village. Vehicles and carts, halted on the road, were exploding as they were hit, sending debris and bodies flying.

Staying put meant being killed. Werner weighed his options. The closest cover was the church back down the street. Shells were landing all over between here and there, but he was out of options. He grabbed the cases and took off running as fast as he could.

Whooomph.

The exploding artillery rounds lit up the night with fire, shock, and debris. Those caught in the open realized they needed cover and they ran toward the church as well. He looked back to see if any Bolshevicks were advancing, just in time to see a shell impact directly on the staff car.

Whooomph.

Vehicle pieces and parts flung in all directions, blowing apart the soldier trapped inside. The shock wave lifted Werner off his feet, throwing him headfirst into a pile of rubble. He lay there dazed but conscious for a few seconds trying to catch his breath. His eyes, ears and mouth were full of dirt and dust...again. He spat the material from his mouth and pulled himself up and checked to see if he had been hit. His lower right leg was bleeding. His trouser was torn several inches above his boot top. He reached inside the pants and could feel an opening in his skin, a gash. There wasn't time to analyze the wound. He pulled the scarf from around his neck and quickly tied it around his trouser as tight as he could stand.

With his arms, he pushed himself back onto his feet. He grabbed the cases and resumed running toward the church. He could run on the leg so he knew it wasn't broken, but the pain was slowing him down. His adrenaline was pumping, giving him the strength to make it to the front entrance of the church. He leapt up the stairs past the doors that were blown open.

The church was badly damaged, but it offered cover from the artillery saturating the village. Inside he saw dozens of people seeking refuge. There wasn't much inside the church to use for cover, as most of the furniture and furnishings had been damaged or removed. People were simply huddling together in groups. Some people had covered themselves with blankets or greatcoats. A large, simple wooden cross still hung on the wall at the far end of the room.

Most everyone was quiet, as if staying silent would help to hide them from the explosions. A few people were praying. Light from the exploding artillery outside flashed through the window openings and holes in the roof and danced like a deadly storm. Each detonation shook the structure, stressing the old walls and further weakening the roof.

He scanned the room looking for a place to shelter. On the far side of the church, he noticed some people heading through a doorway. He wove his way across the room with the cases in tow and through the door, which led to a stairwell leading downward, supposedly to a basement. The passageway was dark and narrow.

He was struggling to carry the two heavy cases and put pressure on his wounded leg. He could see two men in front of him, but it seemed that someone ahead of them had fallen and they were now stopped in the cramped quarters of the stairwell.

Whooomph.

Another shell impacted the roof sending a shower of debris raining down into the church. The force of the blast behind made him lose his balance and he tumbled forward down the narrow stairwell along with the cases. As he fell, he pushed the other men downward and they all ended up sprawled together at the base of the passageway. He had let go of the cases as he fell and they flew downward, landing on one of the men's heads, knocking him unconscious. Artillery continued to pound above them.

Whooomph, Whooomph.

Someone a few feet away turned on a torchlight, another lit the flame to a lighter. The basement was thick with smoke and dust. There were about a dozen refugees in the basement – a mix of soldiers and civilians – dazed from the bombardment. This basement might just turn out to be their graves.

Gasping for breath, Werner called out "Who has weapons?" Two soldiers within the group answered, they had.

"Cover the stairwell" he ordered them, fearing enemy troops coming down, or tossing down a grenade. The soldiers moved past him in the cramped space, pulling the unconscious man to the side.

One soldier went to the top of the stairs, while the other took up position at the base.

"Is there any other way in or out of this basement?" he yelled at the group. No one spoke up. There wasn't enough light to see everyone clearly, but he could hear coughs from several people. Finally, a woman spoke up.

"A tunnel. Out to the cemetery."

"Which direction, where?"

The woman pointed toward a far corner in the room.

Werner grabbed the torchlight from the man next to him, pointing the light around the space. The beam cut through the smoke and dust, illuminating the basement. He could see a dozen scared and dirty people huddled in the small room. He aimed the light in the direction the woman had pointed and then walked over to the door. The tunnel had enough room for a man to pass if hunched down. It was pitch black and thick with smoke and dust. He attached the torchlight to his tunic pocket, freeing his hands to pick up both cases. He headed into the tunnel, dragging the cases with him. The tunnel stretched fifty feet before ending at some stairs that led up to a cellar door. He listened for a moment, for any activity on the other side of the door but the sounds of the battle made it impossible to distinguish anything. He slowly pushed open the heavy wooden door. It was dark outside, but the flames from the village were bright enough to see the small cemetery tucked behind the church. The cemetery had a low brick wall around it and several dozen headstones and markers organized neatly in rows. There was an impact crater that had strewn several headstones across the lawn.

He quickly went to work.

Whooomph. Whooomph.

Mortar shells continued to explode throughout the village panicking the refugees. Werner took cover a couple of times, while digging. He stood up when he finished and got his bearings. Hearing small arms fire closing in near his position, he attempted to flank the advancing Russian troops and make a break for the river.

Not sure he could make it on his wounded leg, he fashioned a more secure tourniquet, got to his feet, and headed out in the direction he could only guess would avoid the roaming Soviet troopers. Staying put meant death or capture. He knew there was a river nearby. His only chance.

In the darkness, Werner carefully picked his way through the brush and thickets, finally finding the riverbank. He had been lucky so far, as the Soviets were scattered all over the area. Small arms fire continued in the distance. He spotted a large section of timber floating near the bank and scrambled down the bank to the water's edge. He braced himself and waded into the icy water to get the large piece of wood. The shock of the cold on his injured leg was intense.

The river was wide and dark. It must be the Elbe he thought. Looking to the far side of the river, he could see lights scattered about, flickering here and there, but no artillery shells landing. It was quiet on the other side. No fighting. It must be in American hands. Wading into the water up to his waste, he lay on top of the lumber and started to gently paddle into the water. The frigid temperatures stunned his body as his uniform became soaked. His boots were heavy from the water, and he had difficulty kicking with his injured leg. He tried to be as quiet as he could in the water, so as not to draw attention to himself. His body was very tired, probably in shock from the leg wound, but he continued paddling toward the opposite side of the river. To safety.

Thirty yards into the river, shots rang out above him from the riverbank he had just left. Three Soviet soldiers spotted him, yelling at him to come back.

He ignored them and kept paddling, but with urgency now that he had been spotted. The Soviets continued yelling until one of them raised his rifle and took aim. The shot sailed high and passed over Werner's head. A second soldier took aim, missing high as well. All three were taking shots at him now. They were relishing the target practice.

Werner paddled faster, but the strength was draining from his body. Adrenaline kept his arms moving, pulling him further from the riverbank.

Bullets were impacting to his left and right, whizzing by him into the water. He hoped he could get out of range, but a bullet finally found its mark and ripped through his right shoulder, spinning him off the makeshift raft. Choking on water, he struggled to regain his hold on the lumber. With his left arm and pulled himself halfway back on. All he could do was hold on. He felt so tired. He closed his eyes and relaxed. Everything went dark.

The Soviets continued to take practice at the floating human target for a while longer, until they were bored and lost interest. They turned and headed toward the village. That was where the action was. That was where treasures could be discovered. That was where women and girls could be found.

GENERAL THALBERG'S DETACHMENT attempted to break through the Soviet encirclement of Berlin to link up with OKW headquarters which had now moved to Fuerstenberg. As the Soviets tightened their grip around the city, Thalberg finally decided it was now or never. They needed to make a break for it. The noose was closing.

They headed in the direction of Wenck's XII Army, supposedly on its way to relieve the city and rescue the Fuhrer. It was a fantasy. Wenck's Army, only recently formed out of remnants of battered forces and scattered Volkssturm men, made a sudden turn from facing west to facing east. In the general confusion, the Soviets surrounding the Reich capital were facing an unexpected attack. Wenck's spearhead fought towards Berlin, making some initial progress, but they were halted outside of Potsdam by stronger Soviet forces. This Army of remnants never really stood any real chance of success and were quickly forced back along the entire front.

Thalberg's detachment was surrounded by the Soviets and he and his men fought desperately for their lives as they made a frantic attempt to escape. Their vehicles became disabled from the immense gunfire. They jumped out of the vehicles, fighting until they could fight no more.

Thalberg was hit by several bullets in the arm, leg, and chest. One bullet had damaged his spine. He laid in the street, unable to move his legs. He was not going to succeed in his first assignment as a General. He had failed, and with that he closed his eyes as the Soviet troopers crept closer. The Soviets slaughtered his men, no one survived.

Thalberg's half-track armored personnel carrier was smoldering. A Soviet Sergeant took a quick look inside the vehicle and saw some leather cases. He put down his weapon, reached in, and pulled the cases out. The cases might contain valuables – or gold. He unbuckled the straps on the case and wrenched it open. Files. Papers. He rifled through it to see if there was anything of value. Nothing.

He did the same with the other case and got the same results. He could barely read and write, and certainly couldn't read German. Maybe these papers were important in some other way?

The soldiers surveyed the carnage – man to man - taking whatever they could from the dead. Watches, weapons, badges. Anything of value. One of the men found the General's blood-soaked body. He called his Lieutenant over. The officer confirmed that this man was a General from his tunic insignia.

Thalberg was still alive. He could not move though his hands seemed to twitch on their own. He struggled to breath. His eyes locked onto the man standing above him. The Lieutenant looked at the old man with no remorse or care. The Russian knelt down beside him and opened his tunic, looking for anything of importance or value.

Blood flowed out of Thalberg's abdomen, and from the wounds in his arm and leg. The Russian did not want to go much further in the search, because of all the blood from the wounds. But as an officer, he was bound to have a trinket or two. Sure enough, he found a gold pocket watch and an engraved fountain pen from inside the man's uniform. He also found some papers inside one of the pockets. These may be of importance, so he would give the papers to his captain who would pass them up the chain of command to division if it warranted.

The old man lying on the ground in the mud was taking an occasional gasp now and then, barely breathing, but still staring at him. Blood seeped from the side of his mouth. He was trying to say something, or cry out, but the Russian wasn't sure. This old Nazi was a tough old goat indeed. The Lieutenant offered the soldier standing nearby the honors, but he declined. The Lieutenant pulled out his pistol, locked eyes with the General, and fired into the old man's forehead. The back of Thalberg's head exploded. His body jerked lamely, once, then was still. There was one final retch of blood from his mouth, the newly commissioned General's eyes no longer making contact, but staring upward, into nothingness.

The Lieutenant and his men were glad that they would be getting credit for killing this old Nazi General. Unfortunately, no one had a camera and film to take their picture with their trophy. They may get a medal or commendation for this.

The haul in booty the past two days had been good. The fleeing Germans carried many valuable things with them. It was like a grotesque, macabre shopping trip. Germans continued their attempts to break out of the surrounded city, but most were quickly overwhelmed by the superior forces of the Soviet armies. Many of the fleeing rats were easy to eliminate, but some were fierce warriors and put up a respectable fight. The Soviets had lost a few men in the past week to enemy resistance.

But the bigger prizes lay ahead as they fought their way toward the center of the city. More Nazis to kill. More plunder. More women.

"UNFORTUNATELY WE HAVE HAD TO GIVE UP KATYN. THE BOLSHEVIKS UNDOUBTEDLY WILL SOON 'FIND' THAT WE SHOT 12,000 POLISH OFFICERS.

THAT EPISODE IS ONE THAT IS GOING TO CAUSE US QUITE A LITTLE TROUBLE IN THE FUTURE. THE SOVIETS ARE UNDOUBTEDLY GOING TO MAKE IT THEIR BUSINESS TO DISCOVER AS MANY MASS GRAVES AS POSSIBLE AND THEN BLAME IT ON US."

Entry in the personal diary of the German Minister of Propaganda, Joseph Goebbels
September 29, 1943

CHAPTER FIVE

July 29, 1945

Paris, France

WHAT WAS THAT noise? He could hear it in his sleep. If you could call it sleep. He heard everything even though he desperately wanted to sleep. The sun was up. The room seemed abnormally bright. The sounds of morning were becoming louder.

Then, the pain, slowly but steadily working its way throughout every corner of his skull; a rhythmic pounding mixed with a constant stinging behind his right eyeball. As he rolled over, one of his two pillows fell off the bed.

He was thirsty. He *wanted* to sleep, but first, he really needed water. That would mean getting out of bed though. Through one barely opened eye, he could see a pitcher of water on the dresser only a few feet away, but it was far enough to make getting a sorely needed drink of water too huge an effort.

He slowly swung a leg over the side of the bed and his foot touched the floor. He pulled the blanket off and urged the other leg onto the floor. Then he coaxed his body up into a sitting position. His head was throbbing as he tried to focus on the dresser only a few feet away.

He could now see what looked like a note near the water pitcher. Pushing himself upward into a standing position, he took four slow steps over.

Grabbing the pitcher, he poured the water directly into his mouth. He took several big gulps. His body reacted. The liquid rehydrated him after the previous night of drinking. Water always tastes better when hungover.

He took a break from guzzling and let it settle into his stomach. *Ahhhhh...much better.* He took one last long swallow from the pitcher and put it down. The note next to the pitcher had his name on it. Picking it up, he guessed it to be a woman's handwriting.

He flipped open the note and focused his sore eyes on the message written inside.

> *Doug*
>
> *Thank you for the wonderful night. I hope we can see each other again soon. You can reach me at the embassy. Take care my love. Angela.*

Angela. That was her name. He met her at the reception. She was a translator, or secretary, or assistant or something for the British here in Paris. He couldn't remember all her details, but he did remember she was a knockout; charming and attractive. He also remembered that she could actually carry on a conversation. If only he could remember what they spoke about?

She must have left early to make it to work on time. He wasn't sure after his incredibly intoxicated sleep.

He made his way back into bed, rearranging the pillows so that the pounding in his head might lessen. Searching what was left of his memory of the previous evening, he visualized bits and pieces of their time together.

First, he remembered seeing her with a girlfriend or coworker at the reception hosted by the American military brass in Paris for the diplomats and dignitaries from various countries. They hit it off well. After some initial introductions and small talk. Eventually her girlfriend made an exit, offering them the opportunity to settle into a small corner table of the reception hall at the hotel.

"Is this your first time in Paris?" she asked.

Doug replied, "Yes. Actually, my first time in Europe."

"Oh, really? I would have thought an Army Lt. Colonel and an Army lawyer would have certainly traveled to Europe before."

"Well, I suppose, the one-day layover in England before flying here, but then, that's about it," he offered.

"So, you *have* been to 'Europe' before Paris?"

"Well, technically, yes, if you consider England part of Europe," he said, trying to get what he hoped would be a rise out of her.

She took another sip of champagne, finishing her glass. "Though we're not attached to the continent physically, we are Europeans

[81]

nonetheless, Mr. Walters, you certainly know that...or are you just one more boorish, simple American?"

"So, you've met others? More of my kind?" he said smiling. "Just how many 'boorish and simple' Americans have you met, Miss... I'm sorry, I haven't asked you your last name." He was embarrassed and could tell he had had a few too many glasses of champagne. Though, with a beautiful companion such as this stranger, why not?

"Get me another glass and I'll consider telling you." she said, sitting back in her chair and folding her arms. She paused. Coyly. "Do you remember my *first* name?"

"Of course, I do." He guessed. "Angie'."

She smiled.

"It's Angela."

"Well, your girlfriend called you 'Angie' when she left, so unless you have two first names...?"

As a matter of fact, she had, but obviously as a familiar nickname.

"I suppose she did call me that, but that's my nickname. You are quite observant. I can see you must be good at cross examining witnesses."

Doug waved over one of the servers carrying a tray of champagne, and the server rushed over to their table. He grabbed two from the tray while the server removed their two empty flutes.

"Merci."

"I apologize for being so forward," he said. "What shall I call you the rest of the evening?"

"Well… I guess you can call me Angie." she said. "But you are being quite forward assuming that we will be together the rest of the evening," she said with a grin as she relaxed her posture a bit and gently picked up her new glass of champagne, slowly bringing it to her lips then taking a small sip.

"Again, I was wrong to assume," he conceded, watching her as she ran her fingers down the stem of the flute.

"If I choose to forgive you, will you stop assuming so much, Doug?"

Her charm was working.

"I will stop assuming so much…Miss….?"

"Norcutt."

"The beautiful Ms. Angela Norcutt" he said in an official sounding tone.

"I thought I asked you to stop assuming things?" she said in a playful tone.

He laughed. "It is an unassailable fact that you are beautiful. I was only assuming your status based on the lack of a wedding ring."

She laughed. "From assumptions to flattery… how very American."

He chuckled. "I didn't realize that flattery was an American trait. You must have previously experienced an American who flattered you too much."

"I don't think there is ever such a thing as too much flattery." she said. "It's just a matter of how sincere it is," shifting slightly in her chair.

Doug leaned forward, putting his elbows on the table, and reached over with his right hand and touched hers, gently, staring directly into her eyes before saying,

"Angela, I think you are beautiful."

She sat silently for a moment, not moving her hand from beneath his touch. After a moment, she rolled her eyes and said, "Is that it?"

"Is that it??? What do you mean 'is that it'? What does a guy gotta do to please you?" he said in an exasperated tone.

"Now that is another topic altogether Mr. Walters," she replied in a sultry voice.

After which, he ordered more champagne, and then everything went fuzzy. He couldn't remember much of what happened next. They eventually made their way back to his room, and he could remember that she smelled fragrant. They were equally passionate to each other. Their lovemaking had lasted a couple hours, until they both fell off to sleep.

He hadn't been with a woman in over a year, and only one other time, since his wife died. It wasn't that he wasn't lonely or didn't enjoy the company of a beautiful woman. It was more of having been caught up in his work – especially after Patricia had died in the car accident three years ago. He had focused all his attention on his job as the Assistant State's Attorney in Michigan, or on the war and on his work as a reserve officer and Army lawyer. He thought about the wonderful time he had the previous night. With Angela.

The room phone rang. He reached over to the nightstand and lifted the receiver. "Hello?"

"Good morning, Sir. Sergeant Mills, reminding you about your lunch today with General Gaines at the Savoy."

In a rather raspy voice, he replied, "Yes, of course Sergeant... Thank you for the call."

"You're welcome, Sir. We'll plan on seeing you at noon."

"Very good, and thank you again, Sergeant."

He hung up the receiver and flopped back into bed. His headache pounded so badly his eyes were sore. What time was it, anyway?

With great effort, he forced himself out of bed and walked over to the chair in the corner to grab his trousers. He checked the pockets, but no watch. Where had he put it?

After he and Angie had gotten to the room, things moved rather quickly. He switched on the light to the bathroom, momentarily shielding his eyes from the bright light. There was his watch on the side of the sink. He picked it up and saw that it was already 10:30.

DOUG WAS FROM the small town of Corunna, Michigan, located on the banks of the Shiawassee River near the city of Owosso, right in the heart of the lower peninsula. Corunna was the county seat of Shiawassee County, located between the state capital of Lansing and the industrial city of Flint. The stately four-story county courthouse graced the center of the town, and the two-story clock tower atop the building could be seen for miles. As a kid, Doug had always been enthralled with the great building, and the people that worked inside it: police officers, lawyers, judges, and elected officials. He looked up to and respected what these men stood for, the work they did, the important place they held in the community, and this led him to pursue a career in law.

The town was a typical Midwestern city. Settled in the early 1800s by a variety of immigrants from Europe, many from Germany, England, and the Scandinavian countries. Many were farmers, laborers, small business owners, or they worked for the county. For those that could, they left Corunna to go to college, to find work in Detroit or Chicago, or more recently, gone off to the war.

Doug had been lucky enough to gain entrance to the University of Michigan in Ann Arbor after graduating the top of his high school class. While at college, he joined the ROTC and after graduating, was commissioned as a reserve officer. Law School followed and soon thereafter, he received a job offer at a firm in Lansing. By the end of the following year, he had passed his bar exam.

It seemed so long ago and so far away, now that he was in Paris and far from the small towns of Michigan. Patricia would have loved to come with him to Paris, as they had both talked about traveling together after the war.

Churchill: A prisoner-of-war who has committed crimes against the laws of war can be shot. Otherwise, they would only have to surrender. I gather, however, that the Marshal (Stalin) thought that before they could be put to death they ought to have a trial.

Roosevelt: I do not want it too judicial. I want to keep the newspaper men and the newspaper photographers out until it is finished.

- from James F Byrnes' shorthand record of the Yalta conference. Feb 9, 1945

CHAPTER SIX

April 2, 1945

Lansing, Michigan

DOUGLAS WALTERS HAD been approached by Colonel Billings and Richard McFarland of the U.S. Attorney's district office in Michigan. They were doing some groundwork looking for lawyers who may be interested in working on the upcoming international war crimes commission that the U.S. Government and its war time allies – Great Britain, France and the Soviet Union - were planning on holding at the conclusion of the war.

They all met at a diner near his office in Lansing. After ordering, Colonel Billings opened the conversation

"Doug… Richard and I are glad that you agreed to meet with us."

"No problem, Colonel."

"I think you might already know why we're here, so I'll get right to it."

The waitress came with their coffees. "I've heard some things through the grapevine" Doug said, picking up his cup and taking a sip.

"I figured as much. Well then, here it is. We would like you to consider working on a team we are assembling to work on the upcoming war crimes trials. This is a good opportunity for someone like you to make a name for yourself".

Doug sat down his cup of coffee and added a bit more cream.

"Colonel, I am honored to be considered for such an important assignment, but I hardly think I am qualified to be a part of such a team. I have no experience whatsoever in international law. I have interviewed a handful of German prisoners at Camp Owosso and some of the other camps around the state over the past year, but I am sure that doesn't make me qualified to work with major war criminals."

Doug didn't understand their interest in having him involved, but he was certainly interested in finding out.

"Doug, we need some good lawyers on this, pure and simple. You have the military law background which will be helpful" said the Colonel looking straight into Doug's eyes. "And most importantly, we need some men who aren't from the 'east coast' – if you know what I mean." The Colonel's voice trailed off on the last part. He glanced quickly at McFarland.

The waitress came over with a tray of three sandwich plates. Doug placed his napkin on his lap then took a healthy bite of his sandwich. The other men didn't touch their plates, but sat silently, patiently, while Doug finished half of his sandwich.

"Sorry. I didn't have lunch today, too busy at the office," said Doug as he wiped his mouth with a napkin. "I'm not sure I understand exactly what you mean by 'east coast men' Colonel?"

McFarland looked at Billings and motioned for him to start on his sandwich. Turning back to Doug he said in a careful and thoughtful way.

"Doug, what Colonel Billings means is... a very impressive team is being assembled for these historic trials, and to date, we have plenty of lawyers that hail from the east coast, and plenty of lawyers that are Jewish."

Colonel Billings took a bite of his potato salad, then putting down his fork said, "Now do you understand what we mean Doug?"

"I understand a bit more clearly now Sir, but probably not entirely."

"If we pack the team with Jews the war crimes trials are going to start looking like a Jewish witch hunt. It's not going to look legitimate in the eyes of the world" said McFarland softly enough so that the others in the restaurant could not hear.

Doug nodded as if he understood now. Both McFarland and the Colonel took bites of their sandwiches.

"OK, a couple of questions. One, what would my role be on this 'team' – other than to help 'balance' things out? And two, what do you mean by 'look legitimate'?"

Both men paused for a moment at Doug's questions, and as they finished chewing their bites, they hesitated to see who would respond.

McFarland took them. "Good questions Doug. To your first question, we are not exactly certain what your role will be on this team, but we surmise that it will involve a lot of things. Things like analyzing documents, interviewing defendants and witnesses, preparing indictments, etc. This team is being assembled as we speak, so things will firm up once we have all the right players in place."

He took a sip of coffee, then continued "To your second question. What the Colonel was inferring was that we want these trials to be fair and above board. How we assemble the team, how we conduct these trials, will be important in ensuring that they are viewed as justifiable, reasonable, and valid. That's all. We don't want the rest of the world to think we are conjuring up these trials simply to seek vengeance on the Germans now do we?"

"I should think not, Mr. McFarland," said Doug. He had read in the papers about the controversy and heated debate on what to do with the Nazi leaders – and the German nation - after the war. Last fall the Morgenthau plan – *named after the U.S. Treasury Secretary who had help develop the plan* - had come out as a possible alternative for post-war Germany and of course there were the calls for executing the Nazi leaders once they were captured. It seemed as though no one really knew what was going to happen once the war ended in

Europe. "Because I would not want to be a part of something that turned into a show trial."

"I would agree with you Doug, we don't want that either." said the Colonel. "We haven't fought a long hard war against these Nazis just to turn around and act like they do."

"Colonel Billings is right Doug, and that's why we want – no need – someone of your background, standing, and legal caliber to work on this team. These trials are going to be too important. There is a lot that has yet to be decided. Having a steady hand like yours involved is vital to the success of these trials." said McFarland.

McFarland was really pouring it on Doug now. Why him? Yes, Doug was a solid, well-respected lawyer, and a Reserve Major, but how did this qualify him more than other big firm lawyers with international experience?

"I would imagine, with how important these trials are going to be – as you say – that there would be lots of men with more experience than I, that would be interested in joining the team."

Doug left the question for either of them to tackle.

"Well, yes, you are right Doug" said McFarland after a few seconds. "And we have some of these fine men willing to join the team. But some of those we've approached with this opportunity aren't able to leave their firms for an assignment like this…or…their firms have had prior engagements or dealings with some German companies in the past that might cast a shadow on their participation – if you know what I mean."

"I see. How long do you expect these trials to take? I'm not sure I could be away from my practice for an extended period either."

"To be honest, you see, ahhh, we're not sure how long these trials will take Doug," said the Colonel. "The goal is to have everything wrapped up by the end of this year. There's no advantage in dragging these trials out for a long period of time. It's probably best to get them over and done with so that Germany and Europe can move forward and start rebuilding." McFarland nodded in agreement.

"And your participation may open up some other opportunities for you down the road, Doug, and you could get some good press out of this," said Billings.

"OK. Well, if I were interested in this, when would things start?" Doug asked as he pushed his chair away from the table slightly and reclined.

"As you know, we've got Hitler and his Nazis on the ropes, and things will likely accelerate once the Russians make their next big push towards Berlin. If the Nazis continue to fight as guerillas, or fall back to their redoubts somewhere, the war may drag on longer. Once the war ends in Europe, we'll get the team assembled and working as fast as we can." said McFarland. He could tell now that Doug has some level of interest in working with them.

"Okay. Where would I – or we - be working? And would I be there as an officer or as a civilian?"

"More good questions Doug. We anticipate having a team in Europe, as that is where the trials will be held. We're not sure where they will be exactly, but I would guess that they will be held somewhere in Germany. It would be difficult and wouldn't look good to hold them in London, Paris, or Moscow. We'll know more as things progress" offered McFarland. "As to whether you'll be there as a civilian or as an officer, I think that your participation as a military lawyer would be best – for both the team – and for you. Having a military rank in a post-war environment could be helpful. In fact, the Colonel I believe, is prepared to recommend that you be promoted to Lt. Colonel should you decide to join the team."

"Okay" said Doug "And that leads to the question of who will be involved in these trials? I mean what countries? Will this be a U.S. run operation? Military? Civilian?"

"The Brits, the French and most probably the Russians are going to be involved with this, as we want this to be a trial of international proportions and amongst the united nations in order for it to hold any weight" said Colonel Billings with great authority. "We cannot say that it will be a 'U.S. operation' as you put it, but I think that we'll clearly be in the lead on much of it" he offered with less authority.

"As to whether it will be a military or civilian operation... the answer is yes. Both. Or at least that looks like how things are shaping up at this point" added McFarland.

"Sounds complicated... and intriguing all the same" said Doug as he took another sip of his coffee. "Should we order some dessert? The apple pie is very good here" he asked.

"I'm sure it is, but I'll take a pass this time...thank you" said McFarland and the Colonel waved his hand to indicate that he did not care for any pie either. "So, you would be interested?"

Doug took a few seconds to respond. He fiddled a bit with his napkin, then put it on the table. McFarland and Billings both pushed back from the table a bit and awaited Doug's answer.

Doug turned his gaze to McFarland "I am interested, Mr. McFarland. But...I would like to have some time to think things over before I give you a definite answer. I need to talk with my partners first."

"Very good Doug...we're glad to hear it" said McFarland as he smiled and glanced at Billings and then back to Doug. "Take your time...and let either myself or Colonel Douglas know if you have any other questions that we can answer. Of course, as soon as you make your decision, please let either of us know, as we want to be able to add you to the team. If you decide against it, please let us know too, as we need to then find an alternative for you."

Doug waved to the waitress to bring the check.

"I appreciate your interest in me for this assignment, and for your confidence in my abilities." Doug stood. The other men followed. They shook hands. The waitress approached with the check. Colonel Billings reached and took it from her.

"My treat, gentlemen."

DOUG STILL COULDN'T understand why they were interested in him. He had heard their arguments. But, something inside him told him to be cautious, something just didn't seem right. Another part of him though, told him that this might be a great opportunity landing at his doorstep, and he shouldn't miss this chance.

He had talked to his partners at the firm, and they too cautioned Doug, but also agreed that this might be an offer too good to refuse.

"Think of the publicity and the new business" they encouraged. "Doug, you'll be part of the world's greatest international trials."

DOUG WALTERS WAS perfect. Billings and McFarland agreed. He was just the right amount of young, aggressive, and successful. An Army man too – albeit reserves – and best of all, he was a team player.

He was widowed, not involved in any questionable organizations, non-political, and was viewed by almost everyone they talked to as being a real straight shooter. And he was not Jewish.

They had done their research.

IN MID-APRIL, President Roosevelt died, and the new President, Truman, vowed to carry on in FDRs footsteps and finish the fight against the Axis powers. By the end of the month, Hitler was dead from suicide in Berlin. By the first part of May, the German Armies still in action had surrendered and the war in Europe was over. The war in the Pacific raged on with increased ferocity.

Doug contacted Colonel Billings and agreed to become a part of the team. Billings told him that he would be heading to Europe sometime soon.

"WITH THIS SIGNATURE THE GERMAN PEOPLE AND THE GERMAN ARMED FORCES
ARE FOR BETTER OR WORSE DELIVERED INTO THE VICTORS' HANDS.
IN THIS WAR, WHICH HAS LASTED MORE THAN FIVE YEARS, BOTH HAVE ACHIEVED
AND SUFFERED MORE THAN PERHAPS ANY OTHER PEOPLE IN THE WORLD. IN THIS
HOUR I CAN ONLY EXPRESS THE HOPE THAT THE VICTOR WILL TREAT THEM WITH
GENEROSITY."

Colonel General Alfred Jodl statement to
General Walter Bedell-Smith after the surrender of German Armed Forces.
May 8, 1945

CHAPTER SEVEN

August 5, 1945

Nuremberg, Germany

DOUG HAD NEVER flown before in his life. He had traveled on plenty of trains and buses, but never on an airplane. He was now on his third plane ride in the past month. So far, he found air travel agreeable, though this flight tested his resolve, it was far bumpier than the previous two. He had never traveled outside of the Midwest, except for one trip to Denver for a friend's wedding. Now, he'd been to Detroit, Philadelphia, New York, London, Paris.

The past couple of weeks he's spent reading and reviewing materials pertaining to the upcoming trials. He found time to see some of the city's cultural sites, the Louvre, Notre Dame, Arc de Triomphe and even a day at Versailles. Paris seemed so crowded, so noisy, so full of life.

The rugged twin-engine C-47 aircraft of the U.S. Army Air Corps was loaded with mail bags, parcels, and three large crates. Four other passengers were on board - two Sergeants, a Lieutenant, and a Major, all accompanied with their duffle bags and luggage. They sat in the troop seats toward the front of the aircraft. They exchanged

[101]

introductions and then settled back in their seats and tried to get comfortable for the long flight. The aircraft's engines roared as it climbed off the runway and up into the billowy clouds sitting above Paris. The pilots pointed the nose of the aircraft toward Germany.

Everyone, except one of the sergeants, who looked as though he wasn't enjoying the flight, watched the thin clouds and German landscape slip below from the plane windows.

The pilot powered back the engines and nosed the plane downward as they started their descent. The rugged transport plane glided earthward, banking gently a few times to line up with the runway at the Furth airfield, situated northwest of the city center. Until 1945, the airfield was used as a factory airfield for the Luftwaffe, but now it was occupied by US troops. The main gear touched down smoothly, then finally the tail wheel. The pilots taxied the plane for a few minutes, then braked to a stop.

The rear doors on the olive drab C-47 swung open and the men climbed down the steps and were officially on German soil.

Doug had arrived in Nuremberg.

FROM THE AIR, Doug noticed the war damage - bridges destroyed, ruined towns, remains of buildings. The sight from above had not prepared him for what he saw entering the city of Nuremberg. Allied bombing had devasted the medieval heart of the city and the industrial peripheries.

Corporal Franklin was sent to collect Doug at the airfield. Franklin helped load his luggage in the back of the jeep before they hopped in and headed for the Grand Hotel, where Doug was to be housed.

Doug had a sense Corporal Franklin shared in his shock. Whatever war damage he had seen in London and Paris was nothing compared to this. This city was utterly devastated.

Piles of rubble everywhere. Twisted metal and broken glass. The charred and shattered remains of commercial buildings, four flats, homes – a man-made nightmarish landscape of a horrific destruction. How could anyone have survived?

"It's a bit of a shocker isn't it, Colonel?"

To say the least. Doug was aghast. The smell was sickening.

"I…wasn't aware the damage was as extensive" was all he could say.

"I felt the same way when I first got here a couple months ago. It's actually getting better here now. Our boys in the 7th sure gave them Nazis a beating when they took the city back in April. I heard that some Russians were fighting alongside the Nazis too. Go figure that" Franklin said.

Doug couldn't imagine that this was 'better'…and that it could have been *worse*. "You mean to say it was worse? That seems hard to believe."

"I know Sir. But when we first got here, the bodies were everywhere out in the open…some piled up. They've gotten most of that taken care of already. And you can get around the city a little better now that some of the streets are passable."

"I see."

"The place still smells a little, but not as bad. You'll get used to it after a bit." said Franks.

Franklin was right. The smell was distracting. It was the smell of death and destruction.

"Where I come from, the worst cow manure smells better than this."

"Haha... me too. I'm from Wisconsin... Where are you from Sir?"

"I'm from Michigan, right across the lake from you."

They drove past wreckage, destroyed military vehicles, and what seemed like hundreds of refugees – each carrying bags holding their meager possessions - walking nowhere and anywhere, towards infinity. Most of them appeared lost. None had any idea where they were going. You could see it in their eyes, their tired and withdrawn faces.

In contrast, here were two Americans, dressed in clean and neat uniforms, glowing, healthy and well fed, driving past them effortlessly in a nearly new U.S. Government issue jeep.

"There are a lot of people moving about," Doug said.

"Yes Sir. The DPs. It's been this way since I got here."

"DPs?"

"Displaced Persons."

"All of these people are DPs?"

"Pretty much. Most of them don't have places to live, so they go from camp to camp. You know, they say this city had about 300,000 living here...and after we bombed her to pieces, killed about half of them, and the rest ain't got a decent place to live now" offered Franklin, matter of factly. "Most of them live underground now... as you can see there isn't much left above ground.

"It certainly does seem that we laid this city to waste."

"They're still digging bodies out of the rubble... that ain't helping the smell at all."

Having just left the excitement and luxuries of Paris, he now found himself in a hellish wasteland. In a matter of minutes, Doug had lost any excitement he had about coming to Nuremberg.

"I'm not sure what to expect for my accommodations here.'

"Oh, don't worry Sir...you're at the Grand. All the officers are staying there. Relatively speaking, it's in pretty good shape."

"I hope you are right."

They drove through the devastation... the rubble that was once the city of Nuremberg.

The City of Nuremberg, located in the German State of Bavaria, was famous for its medieval walls and ancient Kaiserburg castle, but these were heavily damaged now too from Allied aerial bombing. The Allies had selected Nuremberg for the International Military Tribunal. It was determined an appropriate location given that it was in the American zone of occupation, and the Americans were taking the lead in pressing for the trials.

Beyond convenience it was fitting symbolically, given that this historic old Germanic and imperial city was closely connected with the Nazi Party. The extravagant Party rallies were held there, all the Nazi leadership attending the party congresses, and the famous anti-Semitic laws were announced here. For some, it seemed proper to bring the Germans to justice in the now destroyed 'heart of Nazism'.

Though the city was heavily bombed by the Americans, several buildings were still in standing, including the Palace of Justice, and a prison capable of holding the defendants. Both the Palace and the prison were damaged, but they would receive repairs and renovations compliments of Uncle Sam. All in time for the historic trials.

CORPORAL FRANKLIN DROPPED Doug at the Grand Hotel. At first, he wasn't sure if it was habitable. The main building was heavily scarred, without water, missing walls, windows, and ceilings. Apparently, there was one section of the once 'grand' hotel that was habitable and that's where they would stay.

Built in 1897, the hotel had been considered one of the world's greatest. Five stories in height and taking up almost a full city block, it was still a formidable structure. The first-floor windows had all been bricked over, giving the building a fortified look. Interestingly, in the late 1920s, the owners had refused to rent a room to Hitler, as they disagreed with his politics. Hitler never stayed there again.

The lobby had seen better days, all the former opulence had been stripped away, replaced by utilitarian military furnishings. A large message board covered with posters and a few notes dominated one wall. Most of those in the lobby were military types, with a few in civilian clothes. A Lieutenant was stationed at a desk inside in the lobby. The lieutenant helped him get checked in, and offered to help him with his bags up to his room. His room was on the fourth floor. After climbing the stairs, they entered a long, and dark, hallway. As they walked to his room, they had to pass over some rough lumber planking that covered a hole in the flooring. Above the damaged flooring was more planks nailed to the ceiling, covering some damage. They reached his room, and the Lieutenant had to give the door a bit of a shove to get it to open. It was relatively dark and warm, about fifteen feet by twelve feet in size. They placed his bags on the wood floor. The furnishings included a bed frame with a single mattress, one basic wooden chair in the corner, and three drawer dressers opposite the foot of the bed. On top of the dresser was a wash basin and pitcher, and a couple of white towels folded neatly. There was a reading lamp next to the dresser with a rather dated Victorian style lamp shade topping it. Part of an interior wall was missing and there were holes on the outer wall, probably from bomb shrapnel delivered compliments of the US Army Air Forces. Crude patches had been attempted.

The Lieutenant sensed Doug's discomfort with the room. "This is about the same as the others, Colonel...plus you have a window..."

he cut himself off when he noticed the window had a couple of panes of glass missing that were replaced by cardboard. He walked over to the lamp. "The electricity is still spotty." He reached under the lamp shade to tighten the light bulb, pulling the chain a couple of times but the lamp did not turn on. He looked at Doug and gave a shrug. "If you're hungry, we've got a canteen downstairs. Laundry service as well, usually takes a day, just ask at the front desk."

He walked back to the doorway. "There is a lavatory at the end of the hall. Water is spotty as well." He pointed further down the hall. He paused before departing.

"The staff here is German. A few speak English. Some. They haven't seemed to cause much trouble, but I tell all the guests to be watchful. If you have any belongings that need securing, we have a safe in the lobby."

"Good to know. I'll do that," was all Doug could say.

The Lieutenant took off toward the stairwell they had just climbed and with that, Doug was a temporary resident of Nuremberg. For how long he still wasn't sure.

He noticed the floor in the room was soft in several areas. He decided he should count his blessings, realizing he was better off than all those DPs who knew nothing about their future, and had nothing, except what they carried or dragged along with them. Doug had food, clothing, shelter, a job - and a home to go back to when he was finished here. He didn't have a wife or family, but he felt certain few of them had no families to return to either.

After grabbing a quick lunch, a BLT and a cup of coffee, he decided to visit the Palace of Justice. His workplace for the foreseeable future. The drivers in the motor pool offered to give him a ride, but because the sun was out, he decided that if it was within walking distance, he would walk.

He needed the exercise after the past few days of travel. He asked for directions to the Palace and the soldiers gathered outside the hotel entrance obliged with quizzical looks of judgment on their faces. Doug thanked them, saluted, put on his cap, and started walking.

A Sergeant called out to him "Sir. Sir. I can't let you go off like that."

Doug stopped and turned around.

"Why is that, Sergeant?"

"We are not allowed to let Officers or staff venture out without an escort or without...a sidearm in your case" the sergeant said matter-of-factly.

"A sidearm? What for?"

"Sir. Venturing out alone is dangerous. You see, there are vagrants, ex-military, uhhh...undesirables here and there. It's best if we take you to the Palace. Otherwise, I must insist you wear your sidearm. I assume you have your sidearm in your belongings?"

Doug took in what the Sergeant said.

"Yes, I have it in my room." He started walking back toward the hotel entrance.

"Sir, I can send someone up to get it if you want." said the Sergeant. "It's not a problem at all." He turned and waved for a private standing nearby to come over.

"That won't be necessary, Sergeant. I'll take you up on your offer to give me a lift" as he thought twice about venturing about on his own.

"Best choice Sir."

The Sergeant turned and led Doug over to a waiting jeep. Doug hopped in and asked the private driver to be taken to the Palace.

"Yes Sir" said the driver and he put the jeep into first gear and pulled away from the hotel into the gray and dirty air of the war-scarred wasteland.

CHAPTER EIGHT

August 5, 1945
Nuremberg, Germany

A FEW MILES southeast of Nuremberg was a prisoner of war camp formerly known as Stalag XIII-D. This former Allied POW camp now housed German prisoners. The prisoners were known to possess extensive Nazi backgrounds. The camp was built in 1939 as an internment camp for enemy civilians on the famous Nazi party rally grounds.

During the war, all types of prisoners had been held in the camp including Polish, Russian, British and American. Now the camp housed 15,000 Disarmed Enemy Forces, or DEFs, including former SS military personnel, and other German civilian leaders. Guarding the camp were over a thousand American GIs. They were encamped there in large tents alongside the prisoner enclosure. It was an expansive prisoner camp and well-guarded, with two dozen tanks positioned around the perimeter.

Beside the battle-hardened American GIs, there were more than a thousand other troops encamped there. Former Polish troops. They were now considered DPs. These Polish soldiers had fought bravely over the course of the war alongside the Allies against the Nazis. Their country had been invaded by both Hitler and Stalin in 1939 in a swift and deadly campaign. The spoils of Poland were divided up by the two dictators. Many Polish soldiers died defending their country, as did many civilians trying to flee the onslaught. Some of the soldiers were able to flee the country before capture. They were now living in the camp waiting to be repatriated back to Poland, not knowing what their fates would be.

Under the warm August sun, a group of Polish soldiers were challenging a team of Americans in a game of soccer. A soccer field had been laid out with goals on an open stretch of field next to the camp. The sidelines were lined with both Polish and American troops cheering their teams on. The Polish team was up by three goals and the Americans were struggling to learn the game, as they weren't as familiar with soccer, and the Poles were easily beating them.

Major Chet Walters was on the sidelines yelling and coaching the Americans. He was one of the senior officers at the camp, and a proponent for playing sports and games as a good way to keep the men occupied.

The American team had a few good athletes too, but the Poles were just too skilled in the sport. Walters planned on having the Poles teach the men soccer in order to help keep them in shape. He hadn't ever played soccer himself but had been a varsity athlete in high school playing football, baseball, and basketball.

The final score was 5 to 1 in favor of the Poles.

Chet went over to congratulate them on their victory. More invested than usual, he'd also placed a gentleman's wager on the match. He made the deal earlier in the day, with the Polish Army Captain who was coaching the Poles.

"It seems I owe you a case of Budweiser," Chet said to the Captain.

"Indeed. Today was a good day, Major. But I believe your boys are making progress. We'll give them a few more lessons" Captain Mazur said, with a bit of pride, and a big smirk.

"Agreed. I think your boys are getting better at baseball" Chet finished, not to be outdone.

Both men stared for a moment, before their grin appeared, and then a couple of hearty chuckles.

"I'll drop your winnings off in an hour or so Mazur" said Chet as he slapped Mazur on the back.

"Looking forward to it, Walters. My boys and I are thirsty."

CHET HAD SERGEANT Nichols acquire six cases of Budweiser beer to bring with them to the Polish camp. Four cases for his men and two for him. Nichols had been with Major Walters, then only a captain, since their arrival in England. They had fought through some desperate situations with the men after arriving on the continent in July of the previous year.

Chet's men saw plenty of action. Beginning in France. Ending here in Germany. Now with the war over in Europe, he and his men had been waiting patiently for their next assignments, whether that included deploying to the Pacific theatre or going home. For now, they were stuck here doing boring prison guard duty to these SS bastards. A couple of cases of beer would help dull their boredom.

Captain Mazur welcomed them both into his tent. Inside, they were joined by two of his Lieutenants who offered Major Walters and Sgt. Nichols seats. Nichols set the cases of beer on the low table in the middle of the tent. Chet handed beers to Mazur and his Lieutenants.

"This is Lt. Wojcik and Lt. Zielinski. Two of my faithful comrades" Mazur said.

"Good to meet you gentlemen." Chet handed them an opener for the beers.

"Likewise Major" both men said, almost simultaneously.

"Your generosity is much appreciated," Wojcik said.

"Generosity had nothing to do with it really," Chet explained. "I lost the bet." He raised his beer as did the others. "Cheers."

Chet recognized them from the soccer pitch.

"And this is my Sergeant, Nichols. He's been with me a long time." Nichols nodded to the Polish officers and they nodded back.

Mazur motioned for everyone to sit.

"Major Walters, is it alright if we share the rest of these beers with the men?" asked Mazur.

"Absolutely." Chet nodded to Nichols. Nichols grabbed the beer and exited the tent. The Polish soldiers awaited their American beer.

Both Mazur and Walters took long sips. The taste was a relief, but Chet preferred his beer ice cold, and this beer was definitely not. Wojcik and Zielenski then took sips of their own. He pulled out a pack of Pall Malls, took one and tossed the pack to Mazur. Mazur took a cigarette and tossed the pack to his lieutenants sitting next to each other on a cot. They each repeated the cycle.

Chet flicked his lighter and lit his stick, then offered it to the others. Mazur waved it off,

"We'll have ours later, but thank you."

"Keep the pack" said Chet, knowing cigarettes were as good as currency. The men thanked him.

The tent was very spartan. Three cots, four chairs, a small table, a small black stove and their personal gear. The air inside was stale and had the smell of canvas. All of the Polish troops had been disarmed after hostilities had ended in Europe.

After a few moments, Chet asked Mazur "Any news?"

A few days back Chet had been chatting with Mazur and said they were awaiting news about how long they might be staying in the camp.

"Regarding our fate?" Mazur replied.

He took another long sip of the beer.

"Nothing more really. Just more rumors and confusion."

"Understood." was all Chet could say. He was aware that there were complications about what was going to happen with the Polish troops that had fought in the West with the Allies, but he didn't know all of the complexities or the politics of it.

Formations of Polish troops, loyal to the Polish government-in-exile, were first formed in France and its Middle East territories following the defeat and occupation of Poland by Germany and the Soviet Union in September of 1939. After the fall of France in June of 1940, the Polish formations were reestablished in England. The Polish Armed Forces in the West had made enormous contributions to the allied war effort, helping to ensure the defeat of the Third Reich. Now the men of these forces had become displaced persons and were relegated to camps in the allied zones. Their military contributions to the Allies had been forgotten within a few short months. They were now a political liability to the British, French, and Americans. In fact, there was growing anti-Polish sentiment in Britain, mainly because they were fearful of Polish immigrants taking post-war jobs.

"We have received word that the Americans are forming some Polish guard companies here in the American occupation zone. Some of our men will undoubtedly join up. The men need jobs. They need purpose. It also seems that even with your large occupation forces still here, you still need our help. Occupation requires lots of guards, police, trained soldiers to guard your newly acquired bases and prisoner camps. Especially if the US Army will eventually leave" Mazur said.

"Yeah, interesting. I guess I may have heard something about this coming down the line."

"Of course, Wojcik, Zielenski, and myself wish to return to our country, our homes...our families, whatever might be left of them. It seems the path is not clear as to how that might happen." said Mazur.

Chet looked at the other thoughtfully, nodding his head slightly in acknowledgement.

Lt. Wojcik spoke up. "What region are you from in the United States Major?"

"I'm from Michigan. You may have heard of it." Chet responded.

"Yes indeed. The Great Lakes region."

"Yup, exactly. You're good with geography."

"I've heard many good things about that area. Very beautiful I understand. I actually have distant relatives in that area, last I knew."

"Yes, it's certainly a beautiful place. Good industry and plenty of natural beauty." Chet added as he took another tug at his beer.

"Now imagine, that after everything you have done in this war, the sacrifices you made, the men you lost, that you were told you could not go back to Michigan." said Mazur. "That is what we are being told."

Chet leaned his head back while he contemplated the question. He hadn't thought about this at all really. What it would be like not to be able to return home. And he hadn't thought about what he would tell him men if they couldn't return to their homes.

"I hadn't thought about it much to be honest, but it sounds like a raw deal if you ask me" he finally offered.

"Raw deal?" asked Zienlenski, not sure what that saying meant. He looked at both Wojcik and Mazur, who in turn looked back at Chet.

"Screwed" offered Chet.

"Yes, screwed" said Mazur, who then drained the remainder of his beer. Both Wojcik and Zielenski both understood that term. "Do you have family Major? Are you married?".

"Yes, I have family. No, I am not married." Chet said with a smile of a single man. My parents live in Michigan, and I have an older brother, who is also in the Army. I actually just received word a couple of week ago from him saying he was going to be heading to Nuremburg, believe it or not. He's supposedly going to be working on the Nazi trials. He's a lawyer. What a kick. Haven't seen him in over two years and now he's heading over here." Chet paused for a moment. "It'll really be great to see him again."

"Certainly, great news for you indeed. Reunited with family." said Mazur. "You must be proud of your brother, given he will be involved with bringing the Nazis to justice."

"Yeah, well, he's getting over here a little late for the war." said Chet with a chuckle. "But now he'll be involved trying to get this 'peace' sorted out I guess."

"We Poles are likewise interested in how this 'peace' will be sorted out." said Mazur. "That reminds me, Wojcik here received word a few days ago, via a letter delivered here at the camp, that he may have a brother to reunite with. Tell him Wojcik."

"Yes. My older brother is a doctor and served in the Polish Army. When the war began, he was called up, and was later captured by the Soviets. We had received some information that he had been in a prison camp for some time, but then no more word of him or his whereabouts. Of course, we feared the worst." said Wojcik. "Given the treatment of Polish soldiers and civilians by the Soviets."

"The first enemies we faced in this war was the Soviet Union, and Germany. Now the Soviets occupy all of Poland." Mazur said with barely disguised contempt.

Chet was the only one smoking, but the smoke hung in the stale air of the tent. Clearly these men had grievances. And they weren't shy in sharing them.

Wojcik continued "My brother sent word to me here in the camp that he had traveled here to the Nuremburg area and that he wants to see me." Wojcik was smiling, then he added "He also said he is here because he has information that he wants to provide at the war trials."

"Interesting" said Chet. "Where's he staying?".

"Well, he wasn't specific. He said he would reach out again soon, once he felt it was safe." replied Wojcik.

"If you ask me, the Soviets should be on trial as well." said Mazur.

'Why do you say that?" asked Chet.

"Because they invaded my country. They killed our people. They stole our property and plundered our wealth. They are as bad or worse than the Nazis. I know, they didn't win, and the Nazis lost. The victors will decide who's guilty. But Americans will regret getting into bed with the bastards." Mazur got out of his chair and knelt below his cot. He pulled out a bottle of Whiskey. It was the same bottle Chet had 'paid' him after a lost soccer match a couple weeks prior. He stood, uncorked the bottle, and handed it to Chet. "To the future" he said int toast. Chet looked up at him and took the bottle, put it to his lips, and tilted it back, taking a healthy slug. He gave the bottle back to Mazur who did the same. Mazur then passed it to Zielenski, and both he and Wojcik took slugs of the whiskey.

CHAPTER NINE

August 6, 1945

CHET SENT WORD to the Grand Hotel to see if Doug had arrived as planned. Doug received his message and had sent word back that he had, and that he wanted to see him. Doug suggested that Chet make his way into the city and they meet at the hotel.

Chet and Sergeant Nichols set off for the old city center of Nuremberg, where Doug's hotel was. Chet had brought along a bottle of whiskey as a reunion gift to his older brother. On the drive, they passed a couple of check points, which they were quickly waived through. There was still an endless procession of refugees on the roads. Some heading into the city in search of essentials like food, shelter, and work. Others were leaving the city because there were none of those essentials available. Those traveling were mostly on foot. There were a couple of horse drawn carts now and then, typically overloaded with furniture or riders. A few travelers pedaled by on bikes.

Water and electricity were still relatively non-existent. Where there was a working spicket of water, long queues of inhabitants stood for hours to get a bucket or two filled to use for cooking and hygiene. Women were cooking over campfires. Men and boys scavenged for firewood and anything of value that could be traded to the Americans. Children played among the ruins. Elderly women and men sat quietly in the summer heat. Others shuffled about aimlessly, still trying to comprehend how their birthplace, their businesses, their homes, their families had been destroyed. Nuremberg had once been a city of great architecture, art, religion and education. Gone were the museums, parks, quaint shops, and world class restaurants. It was now a city in shame from its celebrated Nazi past. Consumed by human desperation.

The city streets were full of debris caused by damage inflicted from the Allied aerial bombing campaigns and the battle for the city back in April, passable for jeeps, army trucks. Or a Sherman tank. Motorized vehicles were operated by the occupiers, as petrol was not available to civilians. The few civilian vehicles remaining in the area had been located and liberated from local Nazi dignitaries and pressed into service by the Army. These cars were used to shuttle around the growing number of staff members moving into the city in preparation of the coming war crimes trials.

Visible across the expanse of ruins were a handful of heavily damaged church steeples and spires. Most notably were the solid single steeple of the Frauenkirche and the twin spires of St. Lorenz church, both towering above the surroundings of gutted and demolished buildings. American soldiers were stationed throughout the city, including at those churches. Chet and Nichols made their way to the Grand Hotel, realizing how good they had it compared to Germans living in the city.

They pulled up to the hotel and an MP waived them toward a parking area across the street. Nichols pulled the jeep into and open space. They jumped out and Chet grabbed the bottle of whiskey from the back seat. They crossed the street and noticed the hotel had seen better days. Walking in the entrance, they were stopped the guards at the door. They provided the appropriate identifications and walked into what was the hotel lobby. A dozen people were milling about, many in uniforms. They spotted a reception desk. Before reaching the desk, someone tapped Chet on the shoulder. He turned around and before him stood his big brother Doug, broad shouldered and with a big smile on his face.

"I'll be damned." said Chet. A big smile took over his face. "It's really you." They embraced each other. Doug was two years older than Chet, but they had been inseparable throughout childhood. In high school they had played on varsity teams together. When Doug went off to college their parting had been hard on them both. They had never really been apart before. Doug made it home as much as he could during college breaks to watch his brother play football, or basketball, or baseball. That helped them both deal with the separation. The brothers held their embrace for several moments until Doug noticed Nichols standing behind Chet watching them.

"Are you the one responsible for taking care of my kid brother?" asked Doug to Nichols.

"I did the best that I could Sir" responded Nichols. Doug clasped his hand gave it a healthy shake. "But the Major can certainly take care of himself, and the rest of our boys."

"I'm sure he can. And did. Never doubted it, considering who taught him everything" said Doug with a wink and a smile.

"Alright. Enough of that. It's been a minute and you're already taking credit for stuff." interjected Chet. "This is Sergeant Nichols. None better."

"Sergeant, Great to meet you. And thanks".

"Likewise, Colonel."

"What you got there?" asked Doug, staring at the bottle Chet clutched in his hand.

"Oh, just something for us to sip on while we catch up." as he held up the bottle.

"Always planning ahead. Well so did I." Doug grabbed a package on a nearby table. "I got us some sandwiches for lunch. Thought we could get out of here for a bit. This hotel isn't as 'grand' as I was told it would be. Plus, it's pretty crowded. And depressing."

"Sounds good." said Chet. "Anywhere you want to go in particular?"

"Is there anywhere we can get out of the city center and into some fresh air?" asked Doug.

Chet looked at Nichols "We could head up to the airfield, or we could stay closer in and go to the rally grounds." said Nichols.

"Let's do the rally grounds." said Doug. He put his arm around Chet's shoulder and they strolled out the front door.

NICHOLS DROVE THE jeep into the rally grounds complex and parked in an open area. Several jeeps, and a couple of cars, parked in the vicinity. GIs had put together a makeshift baseball diamond in the large expanse of grass and were now playing a lively game. Players had their shirts off and were taking in the sun, the fresh air, and the exercise playing America's pastime. They had enough ball mitts to field a team, but after each at bat the team in the field dropped their mitts so that opposing side could use them. Local German boys watched from the sidelines as the ball went around the field. The Americans noisy, hollering and cheering as the game progressed. The German boys hoped to pick up some snacks or candies from the GIs that were willing to share.

The Nazi Party rally grounds covered about 4 square miles in the southeast of Nuremberg. Six prominent Nazi Party rallies were held there between 1933 and 1938. Hitler had declared Nuremberg the "City of Nazi Party Rallies" in 1933, and so construction began on monumental buildings for the party's mass meetings. In 1934, Nazi architect Albert Speer constructed the Zeppelinfeld stadium.

Located east of the Great Road, it was built to resemble the Pergamon Altar in Ancient Greece. At the front of the great stadium was the famous Zeppelintribüne grandstand, atop which sat a massive swastika.

This location and these architectural structures were known the world over, having been seen numerous black and white newsreels over the past ten years that showed the Germans in various uniforms marching, goosestepping, and saluting. No other German city was more deeply under the spell of National Socialism, and the city provided a welcome setting for the Nazi rulers' propaganda events.

The damaged stone remains of huge structures bore witness to the megalomania of the National Socialist regime. The massive swastika had been demolished in a spectacular explosion back in late April by U.S. troops after taking the city in a hard-fought battle. Hitler had been alive at that point, cowering in his bunker in Berlin, but only a few days longer as it turned out.

Scattered clouds slowly floated across the sky, but it was a wonderful sunny day. It was good to get out of the city center where the sights and smells were dismal and desolate. Seeing his brother again already lifted his spirits. The men jumped out of the jeep to stretch their legs. Doug pulled out the package with their lunch. "You guys hungry?" he asked.

"We never say no to chow' cracked Chet. "What you serving?"

"Looks like we have a couple of sandwiches, and half of a roast chicken." Doug looked at Nichols. "What'll you have Sergeant?"

Nichols waived his hand at Doug. "Go ahead Sir, you guys pick what you want, I'm good with anything". Doug tossed him one of the sandwiches. "Much obliged Colonel" he said with a nod.

Doug turned to Chet. "You get the other sandwich" as he tossed it to him. "I'll have the chicken". They all leaned against the hood of the jeep and started eating their food while they watched the GIs battle it out on the makeshift ballfield. It wasn't like watching the Tigers play the Red Sox at Briggs Stadium, but it was certainly fun to watch.

After finishing his ham and cheese sandwich, Chet fetched the bottle of whiskey and some cups from the jeep. He pulled the cork out of the bottle, poured a healthy amount in, and offered it to Doug. At first Doug waived it off, but Chet wasn't having it. "Hey, it's been a couple years since we've had a drink together, come on." With that, Doug relented and took the cup. Chet poured two more cups, one for him and another for Nichols. Chet held up his cup in toast "Here's to the end of the war." Doug and Nichols raised their cups and said cheers. They each took decent sips and settled back into watching the game.

After a while Chet asked "How in the hell did they get you to come over here?".

Doug knew this question was coming. He gave out a small laugh. "I'm starting to wonder that myself."

"Let me guess. They got you on the patriotism stuff...it's your duty stuff, huh?"

"Well...." Doug scratched his head and gave a quizzical look. "They did mention that stuff."

"I knew it. You always were a sucker for that kinda thing."

"Yeah, well, kinda thinkin twice about it now. Especially after seeing my room for the next few months." Doug said jokingly. They all gave out a good laugh. Even though he was joking, he wasn't expecting the level of devastation in the city and the conditions he would be living and working under. Still, he was better off than most everyone in Nuremberg. Especially the Germans and displaced persons traveling throughout region. And far better than the bodies of people still being discovered and unearthed from the rubble.

"Maybe you should stay with us, we're just a few more miles from here" offered Chet. "I've got some space in my tent."

"Yeah, yeah... as enticing as that sounds, I'll stay put for now" said Doug. He leaned over and bumped his brother shoulder to shoulder. "I'm close to the Palace, and the grub ain't bad. Well, at least it's plentiful."

"You settled in with your new job yet?" asked Chet.

"I just arrived yesterday, so not really. Just met a few people and getting set up in a space. And they've got troops everywhere. At the hotel, at the Palace. Security is pretty tight. They won't even let me walk around without an armed guard. Not sure if that makes me feel more - or less - secure."

"More secure for sure." said Chet. "We've heard reports about some of our people getting jumped and roughed up. There's plenty of desperate people around. You've got everything they don't have. You have a sidearm, don't you?"

"That's what they told me at the hotel too. Lots of us staffers are staying there. Plus, some Brits and Russians as well. Yeah, I have my sidearm, just not used to wearing it around."

"Take my advice, get used to it." said Chet.

The GI at bat took a big swing and hit the ball a country mile over the heads of the outfielders.

"Whoa... now that's a hit. Let's see if he can run it out." said Doug. "You know Nichols, my brother here was a pretty darn good pitcher. And a decent hitter. I taught him everything."

Chet sat there silently. Then he rolled his eyes and took a long sip from his cup.

"Well Sir, it doesn't surprise me. I haven't seen him throw a baseball yet, but I certainly saw him toss a few grenades that sure were on target." said Nichols. He made a throwing motion with his arm. "He sure made those Krauts pay. The Major here...he's a pretty tough fighter."

The men sat silent for a bit while they watched the batter round third base and head for home. The shortstop received the relay throw and turned and dealt the ball to the catcher. Both the ball and the base runner arrived at the same time. He was called safe, and the opposing team gave out cries of disbelief.

Doug hadn't heard about Chet's experiences upon arriving in Europe. The letters they had exchanged weren't vivid in detail, mostly general information about his health, asking about mom and dad, and other relatives. Doug figured his brother would share what he wanted, when he wanted.

"That I don't doubt. He was never one to back down from a good fight."

"Now it's Doug's turn to make the Krauts pay." said Chet. "Exactly what are going to be working on here?"

"Well, I'm part of an investigative team that is helping gather information, evidence, and witnesses that we will use in various phases of the trials against the Nazi leadership, government officials, generals, etc. Part of the team is based in Berlin. The rest of us here, but I'll have to go to Berlin off and on as needed."

"I hear you're putting Göring and Hess on trial?"

"Yup, they're part of the large group of prominent Nazis. But there will be plenty of other trials after them where we pursue others that are guilty of war crimes, atrocities."

"Like the ones running these death camps?" asked Nichols.

"Yes. We'll be pursuing them for certain."

"We've got thousands of them SS bastards penned up. That's what we've been spending our time the past few months doing. We're basically camp guards and security details now." said Chet. I'm sure we've got a few war criminals in there." After months of fighting these men to the death, and losing several of his men in the process, Chet was not inclined to be lenient on these SS soldiers.

"You know, we also passed through a couple of their death camps. Some really sick bastards, the whole German lot if you ask me."

Doug shook his head in acknowledgement. He had only seen what had been shown publicly about the atrocities in the Nazi death camps. Newsreels. Newspaper reporting. Photographs. It was disgusting and beyond comprehension. But he was surely going to see and hear more about it as he sifted through and analyzed evidence that would be used to prosecute the Germans. "Our goal is to find those responsible and bring them to justice."

"Justice? You mean line them up and shoot 'em? Put them in prison? Maybe you guys can give them a piece of their own medicine. Lock them up in some camps and starve them to death." The whiskey was kicking in and Chet was not shy on expressing his thoughts. He took the half empty bottle of whiskey and added more of the brown liquid into everyone's cup. "If you haven't been in one of those camps and seen what they did, well, it's hard to explain. It does something to you when you've seen something like that."

"I'm sure some of them will be facing a death penalty for their actions. Who and how many, that I don't know yet. And it will certainly take a while to build cases and prosecute them all. It's a complicated process. We've haven't had trials like this before. War crimes of this scale. Hell, we don't have laws to point to that says it was a crime, we're still writing them."

"Save time. Do it my way. What's good for the goose is good for the gander. What laws do you need? Murder is murder. And they are guilty as hell. Period."

Growing up with Chet, Doug knew he was very intelligent. Exceptional with math. He'd graduated from college and was a math teacher. Until the war started. When Chet had a drink or two, he could become passionate. And he always loved to talk to Doug about topics like the law, philosophy, and history. Doug's passions. "Well, you have a point. There are many at home, and over here, that feel the same. But I know it's the whiskey talking. You don't really mean that."

"The hell I don't." Chet shot back, enjoying the brotherly debate.

"Okay, well, we aren't going to be doing it that way. Besides, if we did, we wouldn't be any better than them, now, would we?" countered Doug.

"I knew you'd say that" as he turned to Doug. "We aren't *anything* like them."

"Agreed. So, let's make sure we don't act like it." They all sat watching more of the game. Two young German boys, probably around ten years old, made their rounds around the ball field, talking to the GIs, came up to them. The boys were skinny, and their clothes, once of high quality, had since been heavily worn and soiled. None the less, they looked clean had smiles on their faces. One of the boys spoke up "Baseball is good" he said pointing toward the ballgame. The men looked at them and smiled. The boys stepped a few yards apart, one taking up a batter's stance, and the other acting like the pitcher. The pitcher hurled a pretend pitch, and the batter hit a pretend home run. Both boys laughed and gave a thumbs up, and repeated "baseball is good." They stood there looking at the men, their eyes trying to convey friendship. Nichols hopped off the hood of the jeep and fetched a bag from inside. He pulled out a Hershey chocolate bar in a brown wrapper. He walked over to the boys and tossed them the candy bar. Their eyes lit up as the treasure flew toward them. One of the boys caught the candy. "Danke, Danke. Thank you" and they both bowed toward the men. They stood up straight and saluted. Doug, Chet, and Nichols all raised their arms and gave them salutes in return. They watched the boys take off running, happy to have the chocolate.

"Wars...and the aftermath are complicated." said Doug. "So many things have changed. Some of it doesn't make much sense. Trying to put together war crimes trials here in Germany, and we're still fighting the Japanese."

"Complicated for sure." said Chet. "We have some Polish soldiers encamped near us. These guys fought with us against the Nazis, and now they're in camps. Disarmed. They don't know for sure if - and when - they'll be able to go home. That's crazy. These guys deserve better than this."

"I've not heard much about it."

"These Poles are getting the twice over by the Russians. First in '39 with the Krauts they invade Poland. Now they're back and have the whole country. Not sure Uncle Joe's going to welcome these Poles back." Chet was of course referring to Joseph Stalin, leader of the Soviet Union. Stalin had surprised the world by securing a pact with Adolf Hitler. The German-Soviet Nonaggression Pact was an agreement in which the two countries agreed to take no military action against each other for the next ten years. Europe at the time was on the brink of another major war, and Soviet leader viewed the pact as a way to keep his nation on peaceful terms with Heer Hitler. It also gave him time to build up his military. Meanwhile, the German chancellor and **Führer** used the pact to make sure Germany was able to invade neighboring Poland unopposed. The pact also contained a secret agreement in which the Soviets and Germans agreed how they would later divide up Eastern Europe. Of course, the deal fell apart in June 1941, when Hitler and his Nazi forces attacked the Soviets, pushing them out of Poland and deep into the heartland of the Soviet Union itself.

"As I said, things are very complicated now. We've got to work with the Brits, the French, and Uncle Joe, to pick up the pieces here and get this country up and running again. We've got to work with them in these trials as well. The Soviet concept of justice is much different than ours."

"Yeah. Sounds like the Poles are going to get a dose of Soviet justice." said sarcastically. "I'm sure they're wondering what we Americans are going to do for them."

"Good question. I haven't met any of my Soviet counterparts yet, but I'm sure I will soon enough."

"Once you get settled in, one of the Poles we know says he has a brother that wants to provide evidence in the trials. Not sure if it's legit or not."

"Interesting. Yeah, I've got to get a handle on things, get things organized. We've got a ton of work ahead of us. I'm sure we're going to have plenty of people willing to testify against the Nazis."

"Well, I got the impression this guy's brother was looking to testify against – the Russians."

Doug turned to Chet to see if he was joking. Chet shook his head that he wasn't. "Now that *is* interesting."

CHAPTER TEN

August 7, 1945

ERNST HAD A hard night. One really didn't sleep these days. You sort of dozed off for a bit. It didn't help that you were constantly hungry. You were nervous and anxious. Your body ached. Your feet were sore.

Ernst had been walking for the past six weeks. He began his journey carrying two large suitcases. They contained clothing, a small photo album of family pictures, some medications, and a file containing birth certificates, deeds, and education credentials. It was all he could squeeze into the cases before he left. But he was now down to only the one case. One had been stolen from him while he dozed off one evening. It was just as well, carrying both cases was physically taking a toll and wearing him down.

He had survived the six long years of war. He had been living in what was left of his damaged home in Leipzig, primarily in the basement for the few months of the hostilities. The American forces advanced and took the city in late April, but in July, the Americans withdrew from Leipzig, retiring westward to the line that marked the designated postwar zones of occupation. Then the Red Army moved

[137]

in. That's when Ernst, and thousands of other Germans, packed up what they could carry and fled as the Americans withdrew.

His goal was to make it to Stuttgart, in the American zone, where he had some family. He had no idea if they were still there, still alive. Ernst had lost his wife to illness just as the war started. His daughter had married and last he knew she was in the north of the county. His son was in the Luftwaffe as part of a flak battery, but he hadn't heard from him since February. His son was on the Eastern front facing the Red Army. He had no idea if his son was dead or alive, but the odds weren't good. Ernst was all alone.

Ernst made his way to Nuremberg and was lucky enough to receive some food from a Red Cross aid station. It wasn't much, but it was something. He considered staying in Nuremberg, as it was in American hands, but as with everywhere in Germany, there were no jobs, housing was scarce or non-existent, and the availability of food was never assured. He slept in the open air in a park along with hundreds of other travelers.

He rose in the morning just as the sun started to rise. He drank a few swallows of water from a canteen he had and ate his last bit of bread. He grabbed his belongings and started walking.

Others like him were wondering the roads in the early morning hours before the sun and heat would begin to take a toll. After an hour, a man started walking alongside him. A fellow wanderer. He was one of a thousand similar men he had seen since leaving Leipzig.

The man eventually spoke. "Sir, would you be willing to help me out?".

Ernst heard this request many times before. Fellow travelers asking for help. He learned to ignore it and focus on his walk, his journey. He didn't respond to the man. Again, the man spoke. "Sir, would you be willing to help me out with a small favor? I can offer you a bit of food."

Ernst listened, now but kept up his pace walking. He wanted to cover several miles today. "What kind of favor? What kind of food?" responded Ernst without looking at the man. Maybe this man was for real, or maybe he was trying to trick him, or worse yet, rob him.

"The favor is to simply deliver this letter to the sentries at the camp about a mile ahead." said the man. "I can offer you a couple of potatoes and a carrot in return."

Ernst kept walking but turned his head slightly to look at the man who had started walking beside him. The man spoke with a slight accent and had a jacket on with the collar pulled up. Even with his cap on, Ernst could see he had sustained an injury of some sort and had most, or all, of his ear missing, on that side. He didn't want to stare, so he faced forward and kept walking. "Why don't you just deliver it yourself?"

"I don't want to be seen too many times by the camp, that's all." said the man.

Everyone had reasons, stories, for everything these days. Some stories were true. Others were half-truths. Most were lies. Germans, including himself, had been living with, and telling lies, for the past twelve years. Deceptions, lies, and misinformation is what brought the Fatherland to its current state of total destruction. Millions of lives lost. His country prone and occupied. His family destroyed. All the lies. They became used to them, accepting of them, willing tellers of them. What harm would it do to listen to one more lie, especially if it got him some food for his belly. Without looking at him or breaking his stride, Ernst replied "Put the letter – and the food – in my pocket."

The man pulled the letter from his inner jacket pocket and slipped it into the side pocket of the overcoat Ernst was wearing. He pulled two potatoes and a carrot from his front jacket pocket and reached over and slid them into his coat. "Thank you, Sir, I truly appreciate your kindness and understanding." He walked alongside Ernst for a bit longer then stopped. Ernst didn't look back. He knew the man was gone.

Ernst kept walking. Dropping a letter at the camp really wasn't asking too much, so why not? Especially since he received some food for his trouble. One less meal to have to worry about today. A mile ahead was the camp. He crossed the road and walked toward the gate where an American GI and a couple of other soldiers were standing and talking. He approached the men. The men noticed him and stopped chatting. Most walkers simply trudged by with their heads down and ever approached the camp. In general, most Germans avoided interacting with any foreign troops unless it was necessary. Ernst stopped a few feet from the GIs and put his case down. "I would like to deliver a letter."

The men looked at him for several seconds. The American looked at the other two men. One of the soldiers understood some German. He said something to his counterparts, translating. Ernst stood there with his hands by his side. The American said "What letter?", to which the other man translated to German and repeated to Ernst. Ernst made a movement to reach into his pocket. All three men in front of him took a step back. The American put his hand to his sidearm.

The soldier who spoke German said in a slow and calm, but anxious voice, "Nice and slow there mister." as he held out his arm in front of him with his palm facing Ernst, signaling him to stop.

Ernst realized that these men thought he might have a weapon. Ernst withdrew his hand from his pocket quickly and raised both arms in the air and froze, scared that he had put himself in danger. "I just have the letter in my pocket. Really, is this necessary?"

The soldier translating walked slowly towards Ernst. He put his hand on the outside of Ernst's jacket pocket. He felt something solid, round. He quickly took a few steps back. "There's something in his pocket alright!" he yelled.

The American pulled out his .45 and aimed it at Ernst. The war was over and he was biding his time until he got shipped back home.

He wasn't about to get killed now, after all he had been through during the war, by some crazy old bitter Kraut. "Tell him if he moves again, I'll kill him." He pulled back the hammer of the gun with his thumb.

The soldier translated to Ernst, who was now concerned and annoyed. "No, no, I don't mean any harm. I don't have a weapon. Don't be ridiculous." Ernst was tired and impatient. These foreign soldiers were bossy and arrogant, they never listened.

The soldier didn't understand the language completely. He misunderstood what Ernst meant about 'not' having a weapon and doing harm. He looked at Ernst. 'What weapon?" in a concerned tone. He took a few more steps backward away from Ernst.

That was all the American solider needed. He squeezed the trigger. The bullet impacted the side of Ernst's forehead. His head jerked back, then his body followed as he fell backwards onto the gravel of the driveway. Ernst was dead. The threat eliminated.

Afterward, the men found the letter in his pocket, along with some potatoes and a carrot. They found other papers in a file from his suitcase that identified him. He was a professor or teacher. They found a photo album containing pictures of the man and what looked like his family.

The letter he had supposedly been attempting to deliver was in his jacket pocket. It was addressed to Cilas Wojcik. The soldier translating knew he was a Polish soldier in the camp, a fellow brother in arms. He served with Lt. Wojcik and delivered the letter to him. He explained how it was delivered.

UNDER HEAVY PRESSURE FROM THOSE WITHIN AND OUTSIDE OF POLAND, THE POLISH GOVERNMENT-IN-EXILE SOUGHT AN INVESTIGATION AND IMPARTIAL INQUIRY INTO THE MASS GRAVES. THEY CALLED ON THE INTERNATIONAL RED CROSS TO EXAMINE THE KATYN SITE.

THE RED CROSS AGREED, BUT WITH A STRICT CONDITION THAT SUCH AN INVESTIGATION WOULD BE ACCEPTABLE TO ALL GOVERNMENTS.

THE SOVIET GOVERNMENT IMMEDIATELY VETOED THE PROPOSAL AND BROKE OFF DIPLOMATIC RELATIONS WITH THE LONDON POLES ON 25 APRIL 1943. THE SOVIETS ACCUSED THEM OF "A HOSTILE ATTITUDE TOWARDS THE SOVIET UNION."

CHAPTER ELEVEN

August 8, 1945

DOUG ROSE AT 6 a.m. He used the bathroom, brushed up, threw on his uniform, and headed to lobby to grab some coffee and some eggs. People milled about lobby, chatting in small groups. It wasn't the normal early morning crowd. At the front desk he dropped off some laundry. He had laundry to pick up but told the man behind the counter he would pick it up in the evening when he returned. The man was German, and he spoke English with a thick accent. Doug noticed that the man, and all other Germans working at the hotel, never really looked you in the eye, whether speaking to you or passing you in a hallway or on the street. He assumed they acted this way because they were a conquered people. That they have some trepidation about those around them, some fear of their own pasts. With a hotel, and a city, full of investigators looking to put Germans on trial, and possibly to their deaths, one had to be cautious.

On the way to the canteen, he stopped and asked the Lieutenant manning the desk what was going on. "What gives? What is everyone excited about?"

"We received news about the bomb Sir, an atomic bomb dropped on Japan. President Truman made an announcement about it."

"Atomic bomb?"

"Yes Sir. New weapon I guess. Sounds like it knocked out a whole Jap city. Maybe it'll get them to quit."

"Maybe Lieutenant, maybe. Let's hope it does." said Doug. He let the information sink in and questions filled his thoughts.

"Anything I can help you Sir?" asked the Lieutenant.

"No, no, I'm just going to grab a quick breakfast then head to the Palace." said Doug. The news of this new weapon, and atomic bomb took the edge off his appetite.

"We should have drivers out there waiting to take you over when you're ready Sir."

"Yes. Yes. Very good Lieutenant." Seeing first-hand the devastation the aerial bombing and artillery had wrought upon Nuremberg, Doug tried picturing a single bomb powerful enough to do similar, or worse, damage. Whatever this atomic bomb was, it certainly captured everyone's attention this morning. He assumed that if a single bomb had destroyed an entire city, thousands of civilians must have been killed in the blast. Presumably women, children, and elderly. That was starting to sound like mass murder.

DURING THE SUMMER of 1945, SHAEF, or the Supreme Headquarters Allied Expeditionary Force, and the organization that replaced it, USFET, or U.S. Forces, European Theater, conducted a survey of possible locations across Germany to conduct the International Military Tribunal, often referred as the IMT. Nuremberg was selected despite the fact that more than three quarters of the city lay in ruin. As it were, Nuremberg contained the only suitable, and relatively undamaged, facilities — the Palace of Justice — extensive enough to accommodate the trial of this magnitude. The Palace contained 20 courtrooms and a prison capable of holding up to 1,200 prisoners. The American, British, French, and Soviet delegations all recommended to their governments that Nuremberg be the site, though the Soviets only agreed to this with the provision that Berlin was designated as the seat of the tribunal. Of course, Berlin was in the Soviet zone.

The Americans were spending enormous sums of money and resources getting the facilities ready for the upcoming trials. Parts of the facilities sustained damaged during the war, so reconstruction was underway. Plenty of attention was being paid to Courtroom 600, where the main trials would take place. It was being refurbished to allow space for the defendants, their defense teams, the prosecution teams, translators, and of course, the press. These trials would not be held in secret, but in the open for all the world to see.

Doug pulled up at one of the side entrances to the facility. He hopped out, grabbed his case, and thanked the driver. The driver parked the jeep around the block in a parking area set up for military and designated civilian vehicles. A stone wall and metal fencing surrounded the grounds. Scattered around the perimeter of the huge complex were tanks and armored personnel carriers. Each entrance to the facility had a guard shack and two to three guards posted at all times. Many of these guards wore brown drab uniforms and distinctive white helmets, belts, and gloves. The U.S. Army was taking security seriously, and without the proper credentials, you weren't getting in. Period. Colonel, General, Judge. No credentials, no entry.

Doug presented his credentials and made it through the checkpoint at the outer wall without any trouble. He made his way to the entry door leading inside the office section and up ahead of him he saw her. The woman had stopped to check something in her bag. As he drew closer, she turned her head slightly and he knew it was her. Angela.

He walked up beside her and he said "Something wrong Miss?".

Angela was wearing a dark grey dress and matching jacket, almost uniform in cut. She wore a hat that was black and fairly basic, nothing haute couture. Even in the drab utilitarian looking outfit, she was still striking. She closed her bag and turned toward him. "Well hello Doug. I mean Lt. Colonel Walters." She smiled, turning to face him.

A big smile grew on Doug's face. After their parting in Paris, he hadn't expected to ever see her again. But yet, here she was, within arm's reach. He wanted to reach out and hug her, but this wasn't the place. "I thought I might eventually run into you" she said as way of breaking the momentary silence.

"Well, I hadn't planned on seeing you here, but it's certainly a pleasant surprise." he said. "What brings you here, I mean, how did you get here?"

"Work brings me here. And I suppose I *got* here the same way you did, by aeroplane." she said with a smirk.

Doug was till caught off guard, but he registered what she had said "Ahh, yeah, funny, aeroplane." She still had that attractive sense of humor. "You're working here as well?"

"Yes indeed. I was 'dragooned' into coming here to work in records, translation, interpreting, those kinds of things. I guess my skills were needed desperately."

"A woman of many talents" Doug added.

"In the pursuit of justice, of course"

"Looks like the British delegation made and excellent choice."

"I'm one of many talented professionals on our team. Maybe you've already met some of the others?"

"No, no, can't say that I have." Doug couldn't wipe the smile off his face. "Where are you staying by the way?"

"Oh really, we've only been talking a minute or two and you want my address. You're being very forward Colonel."

"Uh huh. Not what I meant. Just wondering where in this pile of rubble of a city you were able to find a place. I'm at the Grand Hotel. It's not much, but seems, secure."

"Ah yes, the Grand Hotel. We didn't end up there. We were assigned to home of some former Nazi official. They patched up the roof, fixed some of the windows. I was told they had to remove the bodies of this Nazi fellow, and his unfortunate wife and children. Seems he wasn't willing to face the consequences, I suppose. There are 8 of us on the team sharing the housing. There is a local couple, husband and wife, caretaking for us. Not sure I trust them." she said with a wink.

With that, Doug put out his arm and motioned toward the doorway. They walked toward the building, and as they reached the door, Doug opened it for her.

"Thank you, Colonel."

"You're welcome, Miss, Northcutt." he said as he passed through the doorway after her. "And I'm glad to hear you have an adequate housing situation. And hopefully secure."

"Oh yes, we have an armed guard at the house at all times. A house full of female...professionals, could become a target I suppose."

"Or an attraction." he said with a smirk and a wink. He removed his visor hat and was standing there looking at her. Angela started for a staircase and took the first few steps and then looked back at Doug. He was still watching her. He gave a nod and as he turned to walk away, he said "And I have a room all to myself. Oh, lonesome me." He didn't wait for her reaction as he headed down a hallway.

ANGELA CLIMBED THE stairs to the second floor. She walked down a long hallway, then took a hallway to the right. She reached her destination and opened the office door. The room was rather long and narrow, with a window at the far end. The window let the early morning sun fill the room with warm light. Several desks were set up with a typewriter and stacks of files. Female colleagues were sitting behind their desks leafing through files. Angela walked over to her desk, put her bag down, took off her hat, and placed it on a nearby rack. She straightened her jacket and walked over to a doorway at the far end of the office. She gave the door a light knock with the back of her hand. A few seconds later she heard 'Yes' from behind the door. She opened it a jar, just enough to speak through.

"Any progress Miss Northcutt?" said a man behind the door.

"I've made contact just now Sir." she replied to the query.

"Excellent news. Keep me posted." was all the man said.

Angela closed the door as the conversation was over. She walked back to her desk and sat down. She took a clean sheet of paper from her desk drawer and rolled it into the typewriter. She sat there for a few seconds, then started to type.

DOUG WAS THINKING about Angela all day while he worked. Could their brief encounter in Paris lead to further encounters? Unfortunately, this wasn't Paris. This was a dreary, creepy, city that smelled of dust and death. Not a place you could take someone out to dinner. No proper places to eat, or drink, or dance. Maybe that was by design. Everyone in Nuremberg was working was under enormous pressure, with tight deadlines, and mountains of files and evidence detailing the deeds, crimes, and sins of a corrupt regime. The teams in Berlin, and throughout the country, had were securing vast amounts of incriminating evidence from the extensive and far-reaching Nazi bureaucracy. The Germans unknowingly provided the Allies with a gold mine of archives to guide the prosecution teams to their guilt. Even the most damning crimes of the Gestapo and SS were thoroughly documented and cataloged.

Given the high stakes of this historical undertaking, it was probably best there weren't many, or any, distractions. Doug assumed that they both worked in the same complex, he would have opportunities to see her. Maybe grab a coffee. Take a walk. He could find ways for them to spend more quality time together. Somehow.

Doug retuned to the hotel after a long day. He passed through the lobby and someone from behind the main desk called out to him "Colonel Walters?". Doug stopped and walked over to where a Sergeant sat behind the desk.

"Yes Sergeant, I'm Colonel Walters."

"Yes, Sir Colonel. You received a couple of messages today. Here they are." and he handed Doug two envelopes. Doug took the letters and headed up the stairs to his room. The hallway was very dark. One solitary light shown farther down. This meant he'd be lucky tonight and have some electricity in his room. He opened the door and set his case in the chair. He took off his tie, then his shirt, and kicked off his shoes. He sat on the bed then leaned back and put his head on the pillow. He reached over and grabbed the envelopes. He ripped the first one open. It was a note from Angela. Doug smiled. Another note from Angela. In the note she said she was so happy they had crossed paths, and that she hoped they could do so again soon. It seemed that she had been thinking as much about him as he had been thinking about her. How best to proceed he thought?

Doug opened the other envelope. This one was from Chet. He was following up on the Pole who supposedly had information about some war crimes he wanted to come forward with. The witness was very secretive and not very trusting. Did Doug want anything to do with this or should he just let it go. He said the Poles in the camp were asking him to see if he could help. Doug lay there for a bit. The August sun was setting. A bright orange glow was coming through his window. He got off the bed and poured himself a glass of whiskey. He tried his luck with his lamp, and sure enough, he had electricity tonight. At least for a while. He took off his pants and laid them nicely over the chair. Damn. He had forgotten to pick up his laundry before he came up. Oh well, he'd wear the clothes he had worn today again, or go down in the morning to pick up his clean clothes. He opened his case and pulled out a file and a pencil. Between the light from the window and the lamp, he could read for a while. Before he could sit back on the bed, there was a knock on his door.

"Who is it?" Doug called out. He was in his t-shirt and underwear, not prepared for visitors.

"Sir. It is Alfred from the laundry service." said the man in thickly accented English.

"Who? Alfred?" it wasn't registering with Doug who the man was.

"Yes Sir. Alfred from the laundry service downstairs."

Then it clicked and Doug remembered it must be the guy from this morning. "Oh Alfred. What can I do for you?"

"I have your laundry here with me Sir."

"My laundry?" Doug walked over to the door and opened it a crack. Some light from the room shown through the door opening into the dark hallway. Doug peered through the opening and barely recognizing the man standing there. The man shifted so that Doug could see his face in the light. The man didn't make eye contact, holding out a bag toward the door.

"I noticed you come through the lobby a bit earlier, and remembered you had some laundry with us. I just figured I would bring it up to your room in case you needed it." said Alfred. "My apologies for disturbing you Sir."

"Ah, no worries...Alfred. I was actually just thinking about my laundry. It seems you've saved me a trip downstairs." Doug opened the door a bit wider and grabbed the laundry bag. "Thank you for bringing it up."

"You're welcome, Sir." Alfred bowed then walked away.

Doug closed the door and opened the bag of laundry. Sure enough, it was his clothes, folded and pressed. He put the clothes in the dresser.

What it a coincidence? He had just been thinking about his laundry, and there it was. Alfred was providing excellent service. The Germans employed at the hotel wanted to stay on the good side of the guests. This was his second coincidence today. He had been at the right place and right time to run into Angela this morning. He finished off his whiskey and laid back on the bed, opening a file. A couple of pages into the document, something in the back of his mind said 'there are no coincidences' over and over. He was tired and stressed, but the investigator in him wouldn't let it go. He needed to focus his attention on the document he was reading, get through it, and make notes for tomorrow.

ALFRED RETURNED TO the lobby front desk. He glanced over to a man in a brown suit sitting in the lobby. The man was reading a newspaper. He lowered it just enough so he could see Alfred. Alfred looked at the man for only a second, then averted his eyes.

Alfred slowly nodded his head, then walked from behind the counter into the back room.

Alfred had been a member of the Nazi party, serving as an economic development executive for the city of Nuremberg and the surrounding region. His job had been to bring industry and tourism to the area. He didn't consider himself a fervent party member, but everyone who wanted to find opportunities or move up had to join the Party. It was the way things were. Now he was concerned that his 'party membership' could cost him this job, or more. He found that even now, after the war, he had to cooperate, again, if he was going to survive.

CHAPTER TWELVE

August 16, 1945

BY MID-AUGUST, many of the high-profile Nazi military and political leaders who were slated to stand trial arrived at Nuremberg from various prisoner holding camps. They were kept in the prison facility connected to the Palace of Justice. These men had surrendered shortly before the official cessation of hostilities in May, or soon thereafter. Before arriving in Nuremberg, they had been housed in several locations that were decidedly not prisons. Some were housed in former spas or hotels, albeit, under guard. When word spread through the press that war criminals were living in relative comfort, the perception was not well received by the Allied political and military leadership, nor the general public. Once the prison facilities in Nuremberg were ready, prisoners were transferred. This prison was what one would expect, and the prisoners realized the situation had significantly changed in their status, and not in a good way.

A steady stream of documents arrived from Berlin, various German cities, and from areas previously occupied by the Nazis.

Doug's team worked hard to sort, organize, cross reference, and catalog the daily intake of files. The prosecution and investigative teams had ready access to the prisoners to conduct interviews, gather information, and verify documents. Doug was an investigator, and now that prisoners were finally here, he wanted to have access to them to follow up on information they had provided in previous testimony in interviews about in-depth military strategy, political and governmental organization, technology and armaments, and regime leadership. Before their arrival in Nuremberg, the prisoners had cooperated in the interrogation process and were willing to share their knowledge, expertise, and opinions about the Third Reich and the war. Now they found themselves sitting in a small spartan cell inside a formidable prison, thinking twice about what to share.

One of the prisoners on Doug's list was Alfred Jodl, the former Chief of the Operations Staff of the *Oberkommando der Wehrmacht*, the German Armed Forces High Command. He held the rank of Colonel General in the Army. He had worked Hitler and all of the top Nazi officials, and had signed the German Instrument of Surrender on May 7th in Reims as the representative of Admiral Karl Dönitz, Hitler's successor. Jodl had an abundance of information to provide on the Nazi regime, but he also had a lot to answer for as well.

There was an interrogation of Jodl on the schedule for that day, so Doug arranged his schedule so he could sit in the testimony, but not as the lead interrogator. That interrogator was an Army Major by the name of James McDaniels. Everyone on the staff called him

Mack. He had a good reputation for being exceptionally prepared. The appointed time for the meeting was at 1 p.m. Doug arrived a few minutes early so he could introduce himself to Mack and two other officers, a psychiatrist and a historian, that planned to observe and take notes. At 1 o'clock the four men entered the interview room. The room was 20 x 20 feet in size, with a wooden table in the middle, six wooden chairs on one side, and two chairs on the other side. A small table off to one side had a tray that contained a pitcher of water and four glasses. Another wall was a chalk board. There were no windows. On the other side of the room was another door. Two bright overhead lights hung from the ceiling and provided ample light to read and take notes. Doug and the other two observers grabbed chairs and sat away from the table. Mack had a chair at the table, where he proceeded to spread out various folders from his case, and a legal pad to take notes.

At 1:01 p.m., the door on the other side of the room opened. A guard held the door open and looked at Mack. Mack looked up and waived for them to come in. Jodl stepped into the doorway and then into the room. Behind him stepped in an Army Sergeant who was there to interpret. Mack did not rise from his chair but waived for them to come in and sit in the two chairs. The guard closed the door behind them as they took their seats.

Jodl was 55 years old. He was nearly bald, with a bit of hair on the sides of his head. His face was pale, his cheeks sunken. His eyes were big and round, his nose pointed and thin, and his ears sticking out more than normal from his head. He wore his grey military uniform and riding pants, and his black boots. His insignia and decorations had been removed from the tunic. All that remained were the shiny buttons down the front. Some of the military prisoners continued to wear their uniforms, while others chose civilian suits.

Jodl sat upright in his chair and placed his hands on the table. Mack looked through his notes. Doug sat off to the side behind Mack, with a legal pad resting on his lap. Jodl did not acknowledge Doug or the other men in the room. He looked straight ahead at Mack, indifferent to him and the others.

Mack checked the identity of the interpreter and swore him in. He then looked up at Jodl "State your name."

"Jodl'"

"Have you heretofore been interrogated?"

"Yes."

"At that time were you sworn?"

"Yes."

"You understand you are still under oath and you have promised to tell the truth, the whole truth, and nothing but the truth, so help me God?"

"Yes."

"I have before me five sheets of legal-sized paper, with writing on both sides, which purports to be in your handwriting. I ask you if these sheets of paper are material that you have presented to us for evaluation and inclusion in your record?"

"They contain the answers to questions that were put before me."

'You identify these sheets as being in your handwriting?"

"I have written them myself."

And so, the interview began. Jodl was calm and matter of fact in his answers. A man like him had risen to the heights of the military and had dealt with the likes of Hitler and other Nazi cronies. He was not one to be ruffled. In his previous interrogations he was known for his eye for detail and providing very precise answers. Up until this point, all the questions he had been asked regarding the planning and waging war were not feared as possible war crimes trial information. He was a military man. He had provided information on various aspects of the German military structure and the views of the General Staff towards technology and the use of tactics and weapons during the war. Now the questions were taking a different tack. Jodl knew that the trials would be forthcoming and that he would be accused of things were no laws existed.

During Mack's interview, he was asking specific questions regarding Jodl's signature on the 'Commando' and 'Commissar Orders'. The Commissar Order was issued by OKW in 1941 and instructed the Wehrmacht that any Soviet political commissar identified among captured troops be summarily executed. The Commando Order was issued by the OKW in 1942 and stated that all Allied commandos engaged in Europe or Africa should be killed immediately without trial, even if in proper uniforms or if they attempted to surrender. The High Command lawyers, officers and staff had prepared the order, and Jodl distributed a handful of copies in secret with instructions that the order was 'intended for commanders only and must not under any circumstances fall into enemy hands. Jodl's handwriting was literally all over these orders.

Mack moved through his list of questions. Who had been involved with drafting these orders? He needed names. Who, if anyone, had been opposed to them? Why were the orders kept 'secret'? Did he know of anyone who disobeyed those orders? Who had obeyed them fully? After almost two hours of questions, Mack suggested they take a five-minute break. He needed to rest his hand from taking copious notes. The sergeant interpreting the interview needed a break. Jodl rose from his chair and was escorted out by the guard. The psychiatrist and historian put down their notepads and left the room, heading toward the restroom. Doug figured he should relieve himself as well, as from the looks of Mack's files, he had plenty of more questions to go through with Jodl. Mack stepped out of the room and lit up a cigarette. He offered one to Doug, but he declined and headed toward the restroom. Mack walked over to an open window in the hall and looked out. The building was warm from the August heat, but a bit of air was flowing in, providing some air movement at least.

Doug walked into the restroom at the end of the hall. Both the psychiatrist and historian were standing at the urinals. Doug walked to the only other available urinal and unzipped his trouser. The men were discussing the interview. Jodl's ability to recall minute details, places, people. And his calm and composed manner of offering up the information. The men finished their business at the urinals and walked over to wash their hands at the sinks.

"He seems so flat, one dimensional. Not much of a personality." said the historian.

"Yes, well it would seem so. I'm trying to understand that side of him as well. What makes a man like him tick? He has a highly logical side to him, a heavy reliance on obeying orders, and an appreciation for laws and societal norms." said the psychiatrist as he wiped his hands on a towel.

The historian turned to Doug who by now had finished and was tucking in his shirt and zipping up his trousers. "Your thoughts on Jodl, Colonel?"

Doug walked toward them and stood in front of the sink. He turned on the water and soaped his hands. "Oh, that guy has a personality for sure. And he has a lot more he wants to tell us. Right now, he's just answering the questions we give him."

The two men opened the bathroom door and exited. Doug finished washing up and straightened his shirt and tie in the mirror. He headed back to the interrogation room. Outside stood the psychiatrist, the historian, and Mack, talking. Mack opened the door to the room and the men entered and took their seats and settled in for more questioning.

JODL COULD SENSE by the line of questioning that the interrogators were interested in having him provide information that would incriminate him. He had been providing details and information willingly about military tactics, war economy, technology, and the incessant interference by Hitler and senior officials into military matters and strategy. As expected, it would only be a matter of time.

Jodl, along with other like-minded General Staff officers posted in various theatre commands, knew that the war was lost in the winter of 1941-42. He, and several others, took steps to correct the situation as it progressed, but to no avail. Hitler and his Nazi Party hacks had mucked it all up. Should he have resigned, like other generals had done? Should he have stood up to the Führer more? Would have it made a difference, or would he have ended up sidelined, replaced, or worse? He was a cog in the machine. Subordinated to Field Marshall Keitel, and to Hitler himself as commander in chief. He implemented the wishes and orders of those above him. Those damn Commando and Commissar orders were problematic for him.

He needed to redirect. Go on the offensive. Buy time. Sow doubt. He was due to receive a defense counsel team, but in the meantime, he needed to work on his own. His break time was over and the guard led him back to the interview room. He walked in and sat down. The Major interviewing him picked up with his questioning.

"How many copies of the secret Commando Order were distributed?" asked Mack.

Jodl thought for a brief moment before answering. "Twenty-two."

"Why keep it a secret?"

"The order was given in retaliation for Allied commandos employing in their conduct of the war, methods which contravened the International Convention of Geneva. We had evidence that your commandos had instructions not to take prisoners during their actions."

"Yes General. You expressed this in an earlier interview. I would still like to know why it was kept secret? If you were following the Geneva Convention, what was your worry or concern by having this be more widely known?"

Jodl sat silently looking at the Major. He moved his hands from the desk and crossed them in his lap. He leaned back in his chair, crossed his legs and assumed a more relaxed posture. His hesitation in responding had caused a pause, and the American officers in the room took their eyes from their legal pads and looked up at him. He took his eyes from the Major and in turn looked each American officer in the eyes for the first time. He held the gaze of the Lt. Colonel for an uncomfortable time. Doug was used to staring down suspects and witnesses, so he was game.

Jodl then fixed his attention back on the man sitting before him. "Major, who ordered the fire-bombing of Dresden?"

Mack leaned back in his chair and looked at the General, but he did not answer.

"The Commando and Commissar orders maybe accounted for a few thousand deaths of enemy *combatants,* at most."

Mack continued to sit in silence. Doug flipped to a new page of his legal pad. The interpreter was growing uncomfortable. He looked at Mack and the others, not sure what was happening.

"Again, I ask who gave the order for the attack on Dresden? It is my understanding that the firestorm killed upwards of 25,000 *civlians.*"

Mack stared back at the General. "I'll be asking the questions prisoner Jodl. Now, where were we? Oh yes, why were these specific orders shrouded in secrecy? Obviously, you had something to hide, to be guilty off perhaps. Surely at some point you must have known that these orders would be revealed and that you were the man behind issuing them." Mack had not changed his tone or voice from his earlier questions. He was slow, factual, and deliberate in his delivery.

Jodl decided to keep up his line of questioning. "I understand the American armies and government are in possession of a new and very powerful weapon. An 'atomic bomb'. It seems you have used it on the Japanese. Better them than us. How many *civilians* were killed in these bombings? Who gave the order?" He again looked at all of the men in the room.

The historian shifted in his chair. Mack was silent as he leaned forward and scribbled a note for his files. He was content to let Jodl carry on.

"Who knows, it might be that you have to use your new 'atomic bombs' on your Soviet *friends*. It seems rich that you question me about orders to eliminate combatants, especially when your Soviet allies did as much or more. To both Polish and German combatants and civilians."

Mack, no longer looking at Jodl, continued to scribble notes, ignoring Jodl's questions.

"Now you sit hand in hand with the Soviets and attempt to seek justice as victors. If you want seek justice for war crimes, look at them first."

The interpreter was nervous and was struggling with accurately translating what Jodl was saying. He had to stop and restate a few sentences.

Jodl looked at him for the first time, giving him an annoyed look. He wanted his questions accurately translated.

"Katyn Forest."

Now Mack stopped scribbling and looked up at Jodl. "Excuse me? Katyn?"

"Of course, you must be aware of it Major. Please, it is public knowledge. I thought we were being honest with each other." Jodl was happy to have struck a sore note.

Mack was aware of it, as were the others. It was interesting that Jodl was bringing it up, given that he had never made mention of it before in earlier interviews. Mack hadn't seen any notes in the files to that effect. He was intrigued to know where the General was going with this.

Jodl looked at each of the men. He could tell by their faces and postures that they had indeed heard about Katyn before. "Your Soviet friends massacred thousands of Polish prisoners in the Katyn Forest. Shot them all in the back of the head and then neatly buried them." He paused for a moment. "Of course, they couldn't have known we would find and expose their war crimes after we pushed them out of Poland and deep into Russia."

Doug was intrigued, given his conversation with his brother about the Polish soldiers, and this mysterious Pole with information to share. Doug was vaguely aware of the Katyn massacre, as it had been in the news a couple of years back, but of course very few people put much credence into the story of Soviets being responsible. Especially given that the news was coming from the Nazi propaganda machine. At the time, it was presented as a ploy of the Nazis to try to cause a fracture in the alliance of the Americans and Brits with the Soviets. He hadn't seen any specific evidence except that which was filtered through American press for public consumption. Doug wasn't naïve enough to put it past the Soviets to have committed such acts. Stalin was brutal. He had purged his officer corps prior to the war, filled gulags with dissidents and those thought to be a threat to him. He perpetrated acts of violence against his own citizens throughout the Union of Soviet Socialist Republics.

Jodl relished the dramatic pause in the conversation. "We have the proof from the international investigation."

"Proof of what?" asked Mack.

"That the Soviets committed war crimes." More silence. "Once the Americans gave up and we realized that the Soviets would take Berlin, I made the decision to have various classified documents and files moved out of the city. The Soviets would no doubt destroy any evidence we had on Katyn, and other war crimes they committed, as they attempt to rewrite history." In his earlier interrogations, he had not mentioned sending the documents out of Berlin. He hadn't felt the time was right, until now. It was becoming increasingly clear that the war crimes trials were going to be conducted, and that he and the others were now in jeopardy.

"These 'documents'... where did you send them?" Mack had decided he would pursue this tangent of Jodl's a bit further. He had not seen this topic mentioned in the notes on Jodl.

"I had them sent to the American and British zones." stated Jodl. He was referring to the Allied occupation of Germany. To the west of the Oder-Neisse line, the rivers that had previously separated Germany from Poland prior to the war, Germany was divided into four occupation zones by the Allies. This preemptive establishment of administrative zones had been agreed to in London in September 1944. The division was officially ratified at the recently concluded

Potsdam Conference in July and August. Each zone was to be occupied by the allied powers who defeated Nazi Germany, the Soviet Union, the United Kingdom, and the United States. France was also given a zone. American forces had pushed beyond the previously agreed upon occupation zone boundaries during the final weeks of the fighting, sometimes by as much as 200 miles. The American forces withdrew during July 1945 from the areas they were holding but were in the Soviet zone.

"You knew of the zones?" the historian blurted out. Mack had been asking all the questions, but he nodded to the historian and then looked back at Jodl.

"Of course, we knew. Your government had made prodigious public announcements to the effect. We knew which cities would be in which zones."

"How was this 'evidence', these documents moved?'

"I entrusted the Katyn documents to a trusted officer, General Reiniger. He took that documentary evidence out of the city a few days before it fell. I assume you have him in custody."

"What did the 'evidence' consist of exactly?" asked Mack.

"All of the documents from the investigation at Katyn. Photographs, forensic analysis, testimony from locals. Even Reiniger. He was an Army liaison to the investigation. He saw the bodies dug up. He said it was gruesome. You could use him as a witness in fact."

Again, the historian spoke up "If I may, what about all of the Jews and slave laborers that were 'liquidated'?"

"Jews and slave laborers... at Katyn do you mean?" Jodl was confused by the question. He looked at the interpreter again to double check if he understood the question correctly.

Mack jumped in "What he is asking is why is it you seem to know so much about the Soviets killing everyone, but you don't seem to know anything about all the mass murders and killings of millions of Jews and laborers in your concentration camps? We don't seem to be having any problem gathering proof and evidence on this fact, yet you and your crack investigators didn't see anything in your own back yard."

Jodl decided against responding further on this subject. It had served its purpose for now. He looked at the historian and back at the Major. He had planted some seeds. Hopefully they would grow and bear fruit. By discrediting the Soviets as war criminals, guilty as anything the Nazis did, he could possibly discredit the coming trials overall, or at least the case against him. He would regroup and plan his next moves.

Mack had enough for the day. Jodl's discussion had given him a few more things to consider. Best to wrap things up. "Let the record reflect that prisoner Jodl refused to answer the question posed to him regarding the secrecy of the orders he issued."

AFTER JODL LEFT the room, Mack gathered his files and notes. The other participants did as well. Mack leaned back on the table. "Thank you all for joining today. We got a few things."

Doug and the others nodded in agreement.

"My report, the official report, will not be reflecting the accusations by Jodl that the Soviets are war criminals. As you can imagine, that is a touchy subject. Keep your personal notes to yourself, at least for now, I've made some of my own as well."

Doug opened the door and the psychiatrist and historian exited into the hallway. Doug started out behind them. "Doug, everything good?" asked Mack. Mack had noticed he seemed a bit distracted after the conversation with Jodl.

Doug stopped and turned back "Yes. Good info. Stuff to track down."

"Agreed. But these bastards are crafty. Take Jodl for instance. He's figuring it out. He knows he's in deep. Deep enough to be swinging. Once he gets his defense counsel, things will change. Better to get what we can out of him now."

Doug nodded.

"You're staying at the Grand right?"

"Yeah, but I prefer to call it 'Not So Grand'." Doug joked.

Mack laughed. "You are right about that. A few of us from the various delegations were going to meet up there tomorrow evening for cocktails. Join us."

"Great. Count me in." Doug turned and walked out of the room. He headed back to his office to check on the progress his team had made today while he was in the interview. At his desk, he pulled the page from his legal pad out and gave it to one of the secretaries to type up. He made a couple of corrections first, then she started typing. It was a simple list:

Katyn Investigation – Germans 1943?
Gen. Reiniger: rank, background, record, location
Poles – Missing? Explanation

CHAPTER THIRTEEN

August 16, 1945

DOUG RETURNED TO the hotel. He made his way in the entrance and noticed his brother standing at the American desk talking to a Lieutenant.

"Chet, what's going on? How are you?"

"Oh hey, here he is." Chet said as he turned and shook hands with Doug. "I was just leaving you a note."

"What was in the note?"

"Well, the note was to let you know I was checking in on you, I haven't seen or heard from you in a few days."

"Yeah, I know. Sorry about that. I guess I've jumped in full force into this work. And last week I had to go up to Berlin for a couple days to work with the team up there."

"Really? How was Berlin?"

"You hungry? You want to grab some food?"

"Nah, I'm good, but if you want something."

"Yeah, I'm kinda hungry. Let me go over and grab a sandwich. Grab us a seat over there somewhere." Doug pointed to the lobby area which had a few stuffed chairs, mall tables, and some wooden office type chairs lined up around the walls of the room. The large showcase windows that had once looked out to the street had been bricked and painted over. The tables and chairs were scattered around the room, and a there was an open table with three chairs open. Chet walked over and took a seat.

Doug returned a few minutes later with a plate in one hand, and a couple of Coke bottles in the other. He saw Chet and walked over and joined him. "Got you a Coke." and he handed one of the small soda bottles to his brother.

"Thanks. There wasn't anything stronger?"

"I've got that up in my room."

"This'll do I guess."

Doug's plate had a couple of ham and cheese sandwiches. "Sure, you don't want some?" as he held the plate up toward Chet. Chet waived the plate off. "Berlin is as big a mess as here. Some sections are just uninhabitable. The Soviets sure flattened it. Still digging up bodies like here". Then he took a big bite from his sandwich. He'd skipped lunch so he could make the Jodl interview, and he was starved. He sat back in the chair with half of the sandwich in his hand. "Was a pain getting there and back. Berlin is in the Soviet zone and there are a lot of formalities." Doug rolled his eyes.

Chet took a sip form the soda bottle. "So besides being a tourist, what else have you been doing?"

"Funny guy" said Doug as he took another large bite of his food. "All work and no play." He finished half of sandwich and washed it down with some Coke. "Oh, I did run into an acquaintance here."

"What kind of acquaintance?"

"The good-looking kind."

"Got it. Where and when did you become acquainted?"

"Paris. A few weeks back when I was transiting through."

"I see. How long were you in Paris?"

"Only a couple of days."

Chet gave out a whistle. "Fast operator. That's really not your style."

"True." Then he reached over and grabbed the other half of sandwich. "Saw an opportunity and took it."

"You've never put move on a girl that fast in your life." Chet had adored his sister-in-law. She had been the light of Doug's eye. They had met her in their first year at college. It took until his sophomore year until he made his 'move' on her and asked her out. They married after they graduation. When she died it had devastated Doug. He had sunk himself into his work. This was the first time he heard Doug mention a woman in years. "I think you found yourself a Parisian girl that was looking for a ticket to America."

"Hey, that's not what happened smart ass. And she's not French, she's British. And she's here now, working in the same complex as me. What are the chances?"

"As crazy as the world is now, who knows? Have you been seeing her?"

"Actually no." Doug said with a sign and a frown. "Been too busy, and if you haven't noticed, there aren't many places around town to take a girl on a date."

"Yeah, I guess that's true. Any plans to try something though?"

Doug had finished the sandwich and wiped his mouth with a napkin. He polished off the rest of the Coke. "I'm thinking about it. Need to figure a way to get here to the hotel. She's bunking with several her colleagues, under guard no less."

"Oh really? Where is this? Maybe we can arrange an assault?" The brothers laughed loud enough get the attention of the others sitting in the lobby.

"I may take you up on that. What have you been up to?"

"Still holding our position. A few of the guys are starting to rotate back home. Everyone is ready to get back. Now that the Japs have surrendered, it's a load off our minds. Those atom bombs sure did it. Could've used a couple over here."

"Looks like we achieved the same results with those bombs"

"These fucking Nazis fought longer than they needed to. Drop a bomb on Berlin and boom... Hitler is gone. Would have ended things sooner and saved my guys."

"Yeah, it would have changed things, I mean, it changes things."

"Damn right it does. These Russians are going to think twice now about messing with us."

"That's what we would assume" Doug said thoughtfully. They both took a moment to think to themselves about this new bomb and the power it gave the United States.

Chet's thoughts were interrupted when he remembered something "Oh yeah, those Poles keep asking me about whether you can help them or not with the brother that has some evidence to present for the trials. If you are too busy, they asked me to meet with him. Not sure I should be getting involved with this, but they are persistent."

Doug thought about it for a moment. "Maybe you can meet with the guy and get a feel for what he has to say. If you think there's something there, I can step in. It'll make you look good for helping them, and if it's nothing, I don't have to waste time on it. I mean, if you want to do it."

"Sure, I can do that. No problem. I'm currently *not* as busy as you." Chet finished his Coke. "Best if I start heading back to camp."

"You come alone?"

"No, Nichols and a couple others are waiting across the street. We'll try to make contact tomorrow and get this over with."

"Let me know how things go."

"Sure thing. And remember to keep me posted on this acquaintance." Chet said with a smile. Both men rose from their table and walked through the crowd toward the entrance. Doug put his arm around his brother as they walked.

"I'm going to try to get reacquainted soon."

THE MAN SITTING near Doug and Chet's table folded his newspaper and watched the men part at the entrance. He rose quickly, tucked the newspaper under his arm, and made his way out the front of the building. He stopped on the sidewalk amongst GIs guarding the entrance to the hotel. He scanned the area, spotting the man who had been talking to Walters, walk across the street toward the parking area full of jeeps and American GIs. His civilian car was just down the block. He raised his arm and waived toward it. The car engine started and it sprang to life, slowly rolling toward the entrance. One of the American guards at the hotel approached him.

"Can I help you Sir?"

"No thank you Sergeant. I'm with the Soviet delegation and my car and driver are just here." He bowed slightly to the guard then stepped over to the car that had rolled up. He opened the door and jumped in. He said something to the driver who put the car in gear and pulled away from the curb. The car headed in the same direction as the jeep with the American officer was going.

CHAPTER FOURTEEN

August 17, 1945

CHET RETURNED TO the camp, and he and Nichols took a walk over to the Polish camp to see Mazur and Wojcik. The Poles were glad to see them, welcoming them into their tent. They took seats and Mazur grabbed his bottle of whiskey, but Chet begged off, thanking him for the offer. Mazur asked if Chet had been able to speak with his brother. Chet said he had, just an hour or so earlier, and that his brother may possibly be interested in learning more about Wojcik's brother and the information he had. He explained that his brother was naturally very busy, suggesting that Chet go with them to meet the brother first. Mazur and Wojcik seemed less than excited about that plan, but Mazur agreed to it, explaining that at least it was a step in the right direction.

Wojcik received detailed instructions to locate his brother. Roadmaps were useless these days, given the extreme damage to the city and surrounding area, and the lack of street and directional signs. The directions Wojcik had relied on landmarks. They agreed to go in the morning. Chet and Nichols would have a jeep ready for them.

AT 9 A.M. CHET and Nichols rolled up to the gate at the Polish camp. Mazur and Wojcik were waiting. They hopped in the back and Wojcik pulled the letter from his brother with the directions out of his pocket.

"Okay, where to?" said Chet. Over the past two months, he had built a camaraderie with Mazur and the Polish men. He didn't mind doing this, but it all seemed a bit much. This brother of Wojcik's seemed overly mysterious. Why just send notes? Why not just come to the camp himself? Hell, if he has such important information to share, why not just go to the Palace and knock on the door? Somebody there should be interested. This was becoming a bit 'cloak and dagger' for Chet. For whatever reason, Mazur and Wojcik believed it was important and real. They didn't seem like crackpots, so maybe there is something to this. Hopefully after today, it would be all over with, and he would have fulfilled his promise to help them out.

Wojcik gave the first part of the directions to Nichols, who put the jeep in gear and pulled onto the road toward Nuremberg.

A HALF MILE down from the camp sat a black Volkswagen, parked just off the road. Two men sat in the front with the windows rolled down. The procession of refugees on the roadway had started at sunrise and was steadily increasing. The men in the car had taken turns napping through the night while they watched the road. Four U.S. Army trucks had passed thirty minutes prior, heading toward the camps. No other vehicles had passed. The man sitting in the passenger seat was awake and heard the distant sound of an approaching vehicle from the direction of the camp. He turned his head and could see a jeep heading toward them. He nudged the man beside him who jolted awake. The jeep sped by them. It contained four men. He recognized the two men in the front, but not the two in the back. The driver started the car and slowly pulled forward toward the road. They waited for a break in the foot traffic of refugees and pulled out. They could see the jeep ahead of them.

AFTER AN INORDINATE number of turns at various landmarks, they were lost. They followed the directions given them in the letter. They took the second right at the plaza, the left at the park, another left, two rights. On and on. Chet and Nichols tried remaining patient. It had been over and hour already. Mazur and Wojcik became frustrated themselves, hoping this wasn't a farce that would embarrass them in front of the Americans. The endless rows of damaged buildings all looked the same. They slowly drove through the ruins, passing GIs on foot patrol. Germans milled about, sifting through the rubble. Women and children queued in lines for water.

Nichols pulled the jeep to a stop. They reached the end of the street where it dead ended into a cross street. They had to either turn left or right. The sat for a moment while Wojcik reread the directions. All it said was follow the cross. Wojcik jumped out of the back and walked into the intersection to get a better look. He looked both ways but didn't see any 'crosses' on the street or on the buildings. What did his brother mean?

Mazur saw that Wojcik was confused so he jumped out and walked over to him. "What was the direction again?"

"Follow the cross" said Wojcik, looking at the letter again.

Mazur looked down one length of street. He scanned the street and buildings for a cross of some sort. But he saw nothing. He turned and did he same in the other direction, but again saw nothing. Then he saw it. He grabbed Wojcik by the arm and turned in in the direction he was looking. Wojcik looked again down the street. Mazur raised his arm and pointed. Then he saw it. Far down the street in the distance was a church steeple barely visible above the buildings.

THE CHURCH WAS a simple medieval design. Rough stone exterior two stories in height, but with a steeply angled roof that rose higher into the air. A single steeple rose even higher and was topped by a cross. Like all structures in the city, it had sustained damage during the war. Parts of the ornate decoration on the exterior had been torn away. The stained-glass windows on the sides were pockmarked with holes. The church as not big nor imposing like some of the others in the city. It looked like a basic neighborhood house of worship. A brick wall surrounded the church grounds. A single tree stood in the courtyard of the church, lifeless and blackened. Nichols parked next to the wall where he could find space between the piles of rubble. The men got out and stretched.

Chet scanned the area. A handful of the buildings surrounding the church seemed to be more or less intact, while others received direct hits, rendering them burned-out hulks. Ragged looking pedestrians passed by. Chet noticed a woman in a third story window looking down on them. Chet and his men had not enjoyed seeing faces in windows a few short months ago. Back then, you directed fire into those windows. When the woman realized Chet was looking up at her, she quickly withdrew out of view.

"This is the place?" asked Chet.

"I believe so Major" replied Wojcik.

"Alright then, let's find this brother of yours." Chet said with a clap. "Mazur, why don't you walk the perimeter. Take this". Nichols pulled his .45 from his holster and handed it to Mazur. Mazur smiled and nodded, and tucked the pistol into his belt, then started walking around the wall surrounding the church.

"You hang here and Wojcik and I will go inside" Chet said to Nichols who had his Thompson on the front seat. Nichols nodded and pulled out a cigarette and lit up.

Chet and Wojcik walked around to the front entrance of the wall surrounding the Church. The gate doors were no longer there, though the hinges that once held them were. They walked up to the tall carved wooden doors of the church. Chet grabbed one of the large iron handles and gave it a pull. It swung open easily. Wojcik stepped through the doorway followed by Chet. The interior was dark, especially because they had just been outside in the late morning sun. It took a few seconds for their eyes to adjust. Light was filtering in through the stained-glass windows. You could see dust swirling lightly about the space. Long wooden pews spread out from the aisle that led to an altar. A tall wooden cross was mounted on the wall behind the altar.

Chet and Wojcik stood there for a minute looking around the space. No one was inside. They both started to slowly walk down the aisle toward the altar. Halfway down the aisle they heard a door open. They stopped and waited. A figure appeared through a doorway behind the altar and walked a few steps into the room just within view. The dim lighting didn't give them a good look at the person who stood before them. The man wore a grey jacket, brown trousers, and a grey military style cap with the brim pulled down low. Wojcik strained his eyes to see who the person was.

"Brother, is that you?" he called out in Polish,

"Yes, it's me" replied the man standing in the shadow.

Wojcik recognized his brother's voice and a smile appeared on his face. "You're alive, thank God. I really thought you were dead.

Are you alright?" He took a couple of steps toward his brother.

His brother raised his arm and with his hand motioned for Wojcik to halt. Wojcik stopped.

"Is this the American?"

Wojcik turned and looked back at Chet standing there. "This is the American Major, Major Walters, we have been talking with. He wants to help us, I mean you. His brother is a lawyer working to put the war crimes trials together." Wojcik realized he was speaking in Polish. He switched to English "Major, this is my brother."

Chet looked at the man and nodded.

"Were you followed?"

Wojcik was surprised by the question. "Followed? What do you mean? Who would follow us? I mean we barely found this place ourselves."

"I instructed you to make certain you weren't followed brother." the man said sharply. "Who else is with you?"

"My Captain, Mazur, is outside, and the Major's Sergeant."

"Do you trust them?"

"Of course, I do brother."

Chet was sure exactly what was going on in the conversation, but it seemed very tense and awkward. Wojcik's brother seemed suspicious of them, which in turn made him suspicious of the brother.

"Why didn't his brother come instead. I thought that was the plan? He is the one I need to speak to."

"I know, forgive me. His brother is a Lt. Colonel and is very busy doing investigations. He asked that we find you can contact you to learn more."

"I see. Too busy to meet with a crazy Pole."

"No brother, that is why we are here, they want to help." replied Wojcik.

The brothers fell silent. "Is everything Okay?" asked Chet, wondering what the men were saying.

Wojcik's brother understood English but wanted to converse in Polish. "Tell him the information I have is about war crimes. And I'm not sure who I can trust with it."

Wojcik translated for Chet. Chet shrugged his shoulders. "I'm not sure who he can trust either, but, given I don't what these war crimes are he is talking about, I'm not sure how I can help."

"The information is about war crimes by.... the Soviets" said the brother in English.

"I see. That certainly complicates things now, doesn't it?" Chet looked at Wojcik, then back at his brother. Given that the Americans and Soviets were wartime allies, it was obvious that information of this sort would be, uncomfortable. "So, I assume you don't want this information getting into the hands of the Soviets."

"No. It must go to the Americans, but, only Americans that can be trusted with it. Ones that will *do* something with it."

"Well, I don't know much about all of this stuff. It's not my area of expertise. But I'd trust my brother with anything."

"As you should, you are brothers. Would you trust him with your life?"

"Always have. Always will." said confidently.

"And you think I should entrust him with my life?"

"From the sounds of things, I'm not sure if you have a whole heck of a lot of choices my friend."

"You're probably right Major. Tell him my information is about Katyn."

"Katyn? What is that? What about it?"

"I was there. I survived."

The door of the church opened, and Mazur stepped through the doorway. "Everything all right in here? Did you find him?" he called out

"Yes, he's here Captain" said Wojcik "My brother is alive."

"Glad to hear it, but it seems we have some men nosing about out here."

"You were followed." said the brother. He had seen the jeep with the Americans and his brother approach and park outside the church. He had watched them get out. He had also scanned the street that they drove down to get there. He only looked for a few seconds but hadn't seen anyone following them. He should have watched longer but he was anxious to see and talk to his brother. After all he had been through, losing his patience and being sloppy could put him in danger.

Chet turned and started walking toward the Mazur "Are you sure?"

"Pretty sure Major."

Wojcik turned back to his brother, but he was gone. He walked over to where he had been standing, then to the door where is brother had emerged. He swung the door opened and it led to stairs leading down. It was dark. He called out "Brother! I'm so glad you are alive! Please trust us!" He messaged echoed downward into the darkness.

Mazur yelled for Wojcik "Come on, bring your brother now!"

Wojcik ran to the doorway where Mazur stood.

"Where's your brother?"

"He's gone for now."

"What? Why doesn't he come with us?"

"He will. When he's ready." Wojcik presumed.

Doug walked out the front of the church "What men are you talking about?" he asked Mazur.

The Sergeant and I saw a car with two men inside drive by kind of slow a few minutes ago. Then we saw them drive by again. Same guys."

"I see, what kind of vehicle?"

"A black Volkswagen."

"Were they in uniforms?"

"No, suits."

"Well then, let's wait a bit and see if they drive by again." They walked to the front gate and he motioned for Mazur to go to the right. "Wojcik, why don't you hang here, and Nichols and I will go around the other way." They proceeded to walk the perimeter of the church yard. A few more people peeked out from windows from buildings around the square, but more sign of the men in the car. After thirty minutes, Chet rounded up everyone and they headed out, satisfied that the mystery men weren't returning.

CHAPTER FIFTEEN

August 17, 1945

AS MACK MENTIONED, there was a reception being held at the Grand Hotel that evening. Doug arrived at the hotel and went up to his room to freshen up, put on a clean shirt, his tie, and his jacket. He needed to look decent in front of his colleagues, and, more importantly, he wanted to look smart for Angela. He had run into her at the Palace and asked if she was planning to attend the reception that evening. She said she had heard about it, but wasn't planning to attend. But, if he was 'inviting' her, she would reconsider. Doug formally invited her, and she agreed to attend.

Doug ran a comb through his hair one more time and then headed down to the lobby. People were starting to arrive, and he saw some familiar faces. Before joining the group, he checked at the American desk for messages. The Lieutenant checked and sure enough, he had one. Doug opened it. It was from Chet. He read through it.

Just then, Mack appeared in front of him "Doug, glad you decided to join us."

"Absolutely. Hard not to, as I live upstairs." said Doug pointing upward with his index finger. Both men laughed.

"And not far to go when the party's over right?"

"Correct again." Doug took the message he had been reading, folded it, and tucked it in a pocket inside his jacket. "Shall we join?"

Mack and Doug walked over to the area set aside in the lobby, basically the whole lobby, for the reception. "How many people will be here?" asked Doug.

"You never know who will show up to these things. But we invited the Brits, the French, and even the Russians. Always good to have some contact with them, in less formal settings. You never know what you might learn."

There was a bar set up over in the corner of the room. A couple of attendees had queued up for drinks. "Grab a drink?" asked Doug.

"I thought you'd never ask." replied Mack.

The bartender was serving British Gin, American Whiskey, French red wine, and Russian Vodka. An appropriate offering given the evenings guest list. Doug got a whiskey, Mack opted for the red wine. They grabbed seats at an empty table. Doug sipped his whiskey. "How's your wine?" he asked Mack.

"It's nice. Not my usual poison."

"I'm not much of a wine drinker myself. Never developed a taste for it."

Mack nodded. "It takes some getting used to." then he took another sip. "Hey, I heard somewhere that you have a brother over here, close by. Is that right?"

"Yeah, my brother has been over there longer than me. He saw some real action."

"I imagine. Is he doing okay?"

"He is. He and his men are camped just outside of town, somewhat close to the Nazi rally grounds. As you can imagine he and his men are less than engaged. They all want to get back to the States. They're pulling guard duty at the prison camp holding the SS men. And they're watching over the camp with the Polish troops."

"Right. But pulling guard duty sounds a lot safer to me than slugging it out with the Krauts."

"Agreed. Those Polish troops seem to be in a kind of limbo."

"Kind of a raw deal for them I know. Not much we can do though. They are the Soviets to deal with now. We have enough problems putting these trials together for god's sake. I'm sure the American government has plenty of people working on this with the Soviets. It's really not our problem."

Guests were filing the room. Some men were in uniform, others in suits. A few women had joined the crowd. Doug as watching to see if he could spot Angela anywhere, but she hadn't arrived yet. Mach went over and grabbed them each another round. As he arrived back at the table, Colonel Timmerman saw him and came over.

"Gentleman."

"Colonel"

"Do you mind if I join you?"

"Please do." as they motioned to an open chair.

Colonel Timmerman was a level or two above Doug and Mack in the growing bureaucracy of the investigative and prosecution teams. Doug had prepared some reports for him but hadn't interacted with him at a personal level much. The men then proceeded to talk a little shop and get to know each other more. Doug kept watch on the hotel entrance during the conversation. A server wearing a white jacket approached their table and offered them some hors d'oeuvres. Doug recognized him. It was Alfred from the laundry. He must be pulling extra duty.

Most of the tables and chairs filled with guests and the conversations in the room grew louder. Everyone seemed to be enjoying themselves.

A man approached in uniform, a British officer. Timmerman recognized him "Colonel Burton, please join us." The Colonel waived to the empty chair and Burton took a seat. "Gentlemen, this is Colonel Charles Burton, a member of the British prosecution team." Introductions were made around the table.

"It seems our Soviet counterparts are at it again...they certainly have a way at these functions." said Burton. One of the members of the Soviet prosecution team had a table across the room and was laughing rather loudly, toasting to this and that, filling and raising their glasses.

Everyone at the table turned at looked at the commotion. "You've got that right Charles... they always seem to make these affairs interesting, to say the least. But if we don't invite them, they make a fuss and we have a mess on our hands. Some allies with aren't worth the trouble it seems... of course you Brits are alright, but the French and Ruskies are another story altogether." said Timmerman.

The loud Russian starts to shush and quiet the crowd around him. He fills his glass and encourages the others at his table to do so as well. He raised his glass and began his toast. He spoke in Russian, talking slowly so that his interpreter could translate into English. "May these trials proceed quickly, a wise court to render the guilty judgment, so we can get down to the business of hanging these Nazi criminals." The crowd around him listened intently to the last part of the translation in silence. The Russian tipped back his glass and downed the vodka. Those who had raised their drinks in toast slowly follow suit. The American's and British in the crowd were uncomfortable with the Russian's toast, so they slowly lowered their glasses. The Soviet team noticed this, and they were confused. And slighted.

"Ahh, how appropriate. Never ones to mince words these Soviets. Well, we certainly needed them a few months ago to finish off these bloody Nazi diehards. And now they certainly are doing their best to get revenge on the Hun. It seems they want to finish the rest of them off… especially our war criminals. No surprises there. Stalin had proposed shooting several thousand German officers straight away." said Burton.

"There's some victor's justice for you. How are we possibly going to keep these trials legitimate and fair in the eyes of the world when we're supposed to work with these… these…"

"Allies." Timmerman finished his sentence.

"Yes, I dare say it's a bit too late to ask them if they plan to be fair as we attempt to figure out a way judge these Nazi bastards. These Soviets have paid dearly during this war. The carnage they endured. Hundreds of thousands, probably millions killed. Their country laid waste. No, I'd say they have a grudge against these Huns they can't wait to avenge. Did I mention that Stalin wanted to line them all up and shoot the lot of them straight away." offered Burton rhetorically, with a smile on his face.

"Doesn't that make them as bad as the Nazis? They have done as bad or worse. Now we have them sit in judgment beside us. It would seem to make all of this, all our work, all we're hoping these trials will represent, seem a waste and meaningless?" said Mack. The alcohol seemed to loosen his tongue.

"Now wait Major. We're going to make sure these trials don't turn into some Soviet kangaroo court. No show trials here. We'll have not have this court made into a circus." interjected Timmerman.

"Let us hope we can reign them in. They are a rather single minded and stubborn lot. These endless meetings over procedures and such are growing tiresome, aren't they?" Burton shifted in his seat.

"To say the least. We're spending more time placating these Soviets than preparing to prosecute these Nazis." replied Timmerman. He took the last sip of whiskey from his glass.

"Maybe we should prosecute some of the Soviets for some of their war crimes." said Doug sarcastically.

Burton nodded his head no. "Good god man, keep it down. You want to rile up these Soviets more than they are already? Plus, we have no proof that the Soviets committed any war crimes."

"No proof?" said Mack. "Ole Doug here and I interviewed Jodl yesterday. Smug bastard. He says the Germans had proof, evidence, of some sort on a massacre of Polish troops. Of course, he may be lying. Couldn't tell for sure."

Doug watched the reaction of Timmerman and Burton. They both looked at each other, wondering who might talk first. Doug then glanced back the entrance. Still no Angela.

Timmerman took the lead "Yes, we have come across this situation already, and are aware of it. We have sent a couple of officers to do some initial investigation on these claims. Of course, we agree that the Soviets ought best to drop these charges against the Nazis – given what is already known. But it sounds like you might have come across a new lead with Jodl. Let's not necessarily make it a priority though, shall we?"

"Will do Colonel." said Mack.

Doug nodded in agreement. He took what Timmerman and Burton said as something they, or others, were working on. Something sunder the surface, not to be brought out into the open. At least not yet. Doug was brought in to help investigate, find evidence, sort, catalog, and make available the information for others on the prosecution team to utilize as they saw fit. He wasn't prosecuting cases directly. Neither was Mack. That wasn't their role in all of this. He decided he wouldn't mention his brother and the meeting with the Pole yet, not until he spoke with Chet.

Alfred, the waiter, returned to the table. He held out his tray and offered them a new item. Something on a cracker. Everyone at the table grabbed one and popped it into their mouths. Doug noticed her walk in the front entrance. She took off her hat and ran her fingers through her hair, fluffing it. She looked around the lobby and spotted the gathering taking place. She walked in that direction, scanning the crowd. Doug set his glass down and stood up. "If you'll excuse, me I'm meeting someone, who just arrived." Timmerman, Burton, and Mack all nodded. "It was nice to meet you Colonel Burton, I'm sure we'll see each other more."

"So nice to finally meet you as well Colonel Walters."

"I'll see you tomorrow, Doug." said Mack.

He straightened his jacket and made his way through the crowed over to Angela. He waived, catching her eye. She waived back with a big smile. She wore another of those popular 'utilitarian' style dress suits with broad shoulders, rounded collars, nipped-in waist, and a simple pleated skirt that hung just below her knees. She looked exceptionally good in it, despite its austere design. Other men in the crowd took notice of her as well.

Doug walked up to her and stopped. He wasn't certain what the proper welcome should be. A kiss on the cheek, a handshake? He stood there awkwardly for a moment while Angela smiled back at him. "Miss Northcutt, so glad you could make it."

"Lt. Colonel Walters, so nice to see you. I apologize for my tardiness, what did I miss?" she said with a grin. She held out her hand and Doug gave her a polite shake.

"You basically missed a few cocktails, lots of shop talk, and a couple of hors d'oeuvres. I wasn't sure you were going to make it."

"I wasn't either. I was stuck at the 'office' late, and then was having trouble getting a ride over here. I had to pull a couple of strings."

"I hope it wasn't too much trouble for you."

"No trouble at all." They were both standing there smiling at each other. A few people passed by them leaving the gathering, other arriving.

"Oh, would you like a drink?" He turned as if to head toward the bar.

"As much as that sounds delightful, I should be honest and tell you that I only have two hours." she said coyishly. "My driver will return then to fetch me."

Doug turned back to her "So no drink?"

"Not unless you have anything to drink in your room."

Doug thought for the briefest of moments. "I do happen to have a bottle in my room. Whiskey."

"That'll do." was all she said. It had been several weeks since they had first met in Paris, and then, spending the night together. She felt 'imprisoned' with her colleagues at the house they were living in here in Nuremberg. She and the other women were getting along well together overall, but they were in their 20-30s and had individual needs and desires. Bringing a gentleman back to her lodging was against the rules, and impractical even if she wanted to break said rules. The women had to find ways to satisfy their needs outside somewhere. Doing so in a city like Nuremberg was next to impossible. Being invited to a party, at a hotel no less, was not to be missed.

"Whiskey it is then." Doug motioned toward the staircase leading up to the guest rooms. He had been hoping this would be the eventual outcome of the evening, but things have progressed quickly. They walked toward the stairs and he wondered what it might look like to others at the gathering, or if anyone noticed or not. Even if someone noticed, he really didn't care what they thought. He was with a beautiful woman, they were not. Good for him.

DOUG GOT OFF the bed and walked to his dresser. He picked up his watch.

"What time is it?" asked Angela. She was lying across the bed, her long legs and bottom showing, but her breasts covered with the sheet.

"You have about 15 minutes." Doug set his watch back down and turned to look at her lying there. In his mind he was trying to figure out how she could stay longer, maybe even the whole night. He knew logistics were problematic. On the bright side, they had spent the last hour reliving the time they had together in Paris. This time was more intense, more passionate. At least to him. Probably because he had had time to think about her, fantasize, for the past few weeks, and he was eagerly awaiting the time he could get her clothes off. Kiss her soft lips. Taste her breasts. Okay, get ahold of yourself Doug. They didn't have time to extend this evening. Should he ask if she wants to stay longer? He could arrange a ride back for her. No, this was enough, for now. "I need to use the restroom. Be back in a bit." He pulled his trousers on, then his shirt. He slipped his feet into his shoes without bothering with socks. His jacket was slung over the chair, right where he had tossed it after they had gotten to the room. He looked back at her and she sat up on the bed.

"I'll just get dressed then."

"Okay, back in a few." He grabbed his towel and walked into the dark hallway toward the restroom. He relieved himself, then washed his hands, splashing some water onto his face. His hair was ruffled so he worked it back into something presentable. Heading back to the room, someone was walking toward him. The lighting in the hallway was not good, and he couldn't see clearly who it was. As they drew closer to each other, he saw it was a man, in a suit. Doug avoided making eye contact with the man, and they passed each other in silence. Doug stopped at his room door, but before he went back into his room, he glanced down the hall to see if the man had gone into a guest room. The man was gone.

Angela was buttoning up her suit jacket. She gave him a warm smile. A satisfied smile. He now felt that awkwardness that one had after having extremely good sex, then having to part on a professional basis. "I'll walk you downstairs."

She looked in small mirror hanging above his dresser and tried to put her hair back into shape. "That won't be necessary Doug. I can manage." Her hair was not cooperating like she wanted it to. She looked to Doug "My hat?"

He picked up her hat from the table and handed it to her. She affixed it on her head, using it to cover the messiness. Finally, she was satisfied. "How do I look?"

"You looked better before I left the room."

"Is that so?" she walked over to him and leaned up on her toes and kissed him. Before Doug could bring his arms up to hold her, she pulled back and smiled at him. "When is the next party?"

CHAPTER SIXTEEN

August 18, 1945

DOUG WOKE UP early. He felt refreshed. He had the best night's
sleep since arriving in Nuremberg. He thought about his wife
Patricia while he was getting freshened up and dressed. He missed
her dearly. He thought about her every day since she passed. It had
been eight long years now. Today was no different, except that he
was also thinking about Angela as well. He didn't feel bad about it,
but made a mental note to himself. Maybe he did have a chance at
pursuing a romantic life after all. He grabbed a plate of eggs and
ham in the canteen then headed to the Palace. There was one
colleague working in the office that early. Maybe he'd had a good
night's sleep like Doug. If he were only that lucky.

At his desk he started to reacquaint himself with the work he
had been doing when he left the office yesterday. He found his was
struggling to focus on his work. Angela kept popping into his
thoughts. He was reviewing some of notes on his legal pad, when a
young women opened the door to the office. She saw Doug's
colleague standing at a file cabinet. "Is Colonel Walters in yet?"

Doug overheard heard her. "Yes, I'm here."

"Oh, there you are Sir. Colonel Timmerman asked that you see him in his office once you arrived."

"Okay. Thank you, I'll be right there."

"Very well Sir."

Doug figured he'd need to take notes, so he went to the supply cabinet to get a new legal pad and couple new pencils. The cabinet nearly bare. There wasn't much left on the shelves. They were constantly short of office supplies. Paper clips, staples, legal pads. They were forced to ration everything. There were two legal pads on the shelf and Doug grabbed one. He felt guilty about it, but it's not like he wasn't using them.

At Colonel Timmerman's office he was waived in by the sergeant at the front desk. The sergeant tapped lightly on the Colonel's door "Colonel Walters is here Sir."

"Send him in."

Doug walked in the office where Timmerman was standing behind a desk, stacked with files. Two other men were in the room.

"Doug, this is General Tucker. And you know Colonel Burton." Doug saluted the General who returned the salute and held out his hand for a handshake, and he nodded to Burton. "Grab a chair, will you?" Doug sat down. Brigadier General Henry Tucker was with the Army Judge Advocate General's department. He was in his early sixties, over six feet in height, and barrel chested. His face possessed a commanding jawline and piercing eyes, set below bushy eyebrows.

He wore his green Ike jacket, his pinks, service ribbons on his chest, and a star on each shoulder. The General was a lawyer, but looking at him, you wouldn't think twice if you saw him leading a cavalry charge on horseback, or, parachuting out of airplane into occupied France.

The scale and scope of atrocities and war crimes committed during the war was overwhelming. The allies had made declarations and plans in prior years promising that these atrocities and war crimes, or crimes against humanity as it was now being referred to, would be identified, and the appropriate parties would stand trial. The Allies were knee deep in turning these 'declarations' into reality. There were many moving parts and Tucker was here to help keep them moving.

Timmerman and Tucker sat down. "Thanks for coming over Doug. The General and Colonel and I were just catching up on a topic we briefly discussed last night at the party. It's in regards to our Soviet friends and the, well juvenile, attempt to introduce charges of war crimes against the Nazis for the massacre of those Poles back in '40, back when Stalin was bosom buddies with Hitler. At one point they held half of Poland, and the damn mass graves were in Russia for Christ's sake."

Tucker jumped in. "You see Colonel, we're not very convinced that it was the Nazis. The Soviets occupied much of Poland after they invaded and had rounded up thousands of prisoners. Given intelligence we have, it may be, more likely is, that it was the Soviets

[207]

that carried out the killings." Tucker had a cigar lit in an ashtray on Timmerman's desk. He picked it up and took a long puff. "As I'm sure you can imagine, that puts us in a difficult spot."

"Indeed" added Burton. "If we let Ivan try to blame the Germans for something *they* did, an atrocity, a war crime, well then we find ourselves in a bit of a tight spot in trying a myriad of cases of war crimes committed by the Nazis." Burton shifted in his chair. "You see, we have enough evidence to try every single Nazi to hang them each thrice over, no need to attempt to hang them for something they *didn't* do."

"Then of course we have the other little problems." said Timmerman. "Even if we convince to give this farce up, it really doesn't, well, look good to the world if the Soviets are sitting in judgement of the Nazis for similar things they have done. But we're stuck with them on pursuing these trials. They'll have judges helping sentence Nazis for legitimate crimes. If we want these trials to have any value, any meaning, they can't be smeared with judges, juries, and executioners with similar blood on their hands."

Doug sat there listening intently. Timmerman poured himself a glass of water from the pitcher on the table behind his desk. Tucker continued to puff on his cigar as he looked at Doug.

"So, I assume you thinking 'what if Ivan did do it'? What do 'we' do about it?" said Burton. "That's where this whole mention by Jodl of some evidence is worrisome."

"What was your impression of Jodl and what he had to say?" asked Tucker.

"He's a cool customer. Knowledgeable. Good attention to detail. Not one to make mistakes. Believable." replied Doug.

"Would you put him on the stand?"

"To prosecute, or defend him?"

Tucker laughed under his breath. "Sorry, what I meant was, do you believe what he says about having some sort of evidence on this Polish thing."

"I believe 'he' thinks there is some evidence, somewhere."

"Got it. We think that he, and some others, cooling off in their cells over there, are trying to muck up the works, drive a wedge between us and the Soviets. Delegitimize the trials. That sort of thing."

"This would do it General." said Doug. "I would think" he added.

"Right." Tucker reached over and tapped some ashes from his cigar.

"Have you come across anything related to this?" asked Timmerman. Tucker and Burton were looking at him.

Doug was on the spot. Should he mention anything about his brother and the Poles? And this mysterious witness? He really had no evidence. He had just heard from his brother last night in a note that he had made contact with the Pole, and that from what he could tell, they guy might be legit. Should he share this, or was it just some sort of a goose chase that he shouldn't be involved in. But what was the point in lying? They were all on the same side.

"Well Colonel, I hadn't thought to mention it, as I'm not sure it's material, or haven't looked into it, but I was made aware by my brother, who is stationed just outside the city, that some of his Polish counterparts may have a witness that has information about 'Katyn'." Doug felt that what he just said came out sounding amateurish.

"I see. Your brother, is?" Timmerman was intrigued.

"Major Chet Walters, he's helping guard the SS prisoners in the camp out there, and I guess, watch over the Poles as well."

"I see. How did your brother become involved?"

"It's my understanding that some Polish officers approached him and found out I was working here on the tribunal. One of them has a brother that is a potential witness. They asked my brother to pass this information along to me."

"What have you done with this so far?"

"I honestly haven't thought about it, nor done anything. I asked my brother to do a bit of legwork for me to see if any of this was legit."

"He's qualified to do this sort of thing?" asked Burton. "Do you trust him?"

"He's my brother. I'd trust him with anything Sir." Doug was a bit stung by Burton's question. Of course, he didn't know his brother like he did, but his brother was a decorated infantry officer who had put his life in the line of fire. More than Burton ever did. "He's certainly not a trained investigator, but he's got common sense and a good feel for people. As I said, I wasn't prepared to put any of my time or resources toward this. At this point."

"I'm sure the Poles are pushing for this." said Tucker. "They're pushing us on a lot of fronts."

"Indeed. We're having a devil of a time trying to sort this Polish question out." said Burton. "Stalin has all of Poland and they're looking for anything and everything to bugger us into helping them get it back."

"Well Burton, didn't you guys go to war in the first place because Stalin, and Germany, invaded Poland?" asked Timmerman. Tucker found it amusing. Burton did not.

"You are correct Colonel. We did, as did France. But the United States didn't. Understandable of course given your isolationism at the time. Obviously, a lot has transpired in the ensuing years. Things have changed. There are jet planes now. Rockets. Atom bombs. War crimes trials. There's no going back to the way things were."

"Burtons right." said Tucker, tamping out his cigar. "We've got to be forward facing here on out. There's a lot to sort out." Tucker leaned forward and put his elbows on knees and looked straight at Doug. "How about this Doug. If you happen to come across any information, evidence, about this Katyn, Polish thing, we keep it to ourselves for now. The Germans don't need to know. The Poles don't need to know. And certainly, the Soviets don't need to know. You get my drift?"

"Yes General."

"Good. Keep Timmerman here, and Burton I guess as well, updated on anything you come across. Let's keep things pretty tight. I'll keep working on the Soviets to drop this bullshit so we can get on with these trials." Tucker stood and pulled his jacket down tight.

Doug stood, as it seemed the meeting, or at least his portion of it was over. He saluted the General.

"Keep it tight Doug. The fewer people involved the better."

"Yes Sir General." Doug turned and exited the office.

TUCKER SAT DOWN after Doug left the office. "So, what do you think?" he asked.

"He was honest with us about the Poles. That's a good sign." offered Timmerman.

"And you Burton?"

"Good sign, agreed. But he didn't offer up the info about his brother or the Poles. We had to ask him for it." said Burton. "That gives me pause."

"I'm giving him the benefit of doubt." said Tucker. "For now." He rose again from his chair. Both Timmerman and Burton stood. Tucker looked at Burton "Plus he's got us a possible lead. More than you and your people have Old Boy." He patted Burton on the shoulder. "He came highly recommended. Let's see what he turns up." He patted his front jacket pocket. Inside was another cigar, which he pulled out and took a quick sniff of. "I'm off to Berlin, then London. Got to put out a few fires. I should be back in about a week. Seems like we have to help you Brits out of another jam." Tucker chuckled as he headed for the door. "Word from up top is that this needs to go away. They're counting on me. I am counting on *you*." With that he put the unlit cigar in his mouth and walked out.

DOUG LEFT THE meeting with mixed messages. Was he being told to steer clear of anything related to this Polish thing, or was he being asked to make a concerted effort to investigate it? He had remembered the discussion last night with Timmerman and Burton at the party, and something that Burton had said. Something about some men being sent to investigate something related to this. Were they looking into the same thing, or something else entirely? He hadn't asked about this in the meeting, and they didn't bring it up. That was probably a sign that he shouldn't be in the know about it. But maybe he *should* ask Timmerman about it, or wait and ask later. He decided to hold onto that for now.

If he was being expected to investigate this, he needed a plan. But he had so much other work that needed his attention. He decided he would first follow up with Chet find out more about the meeting he had. From the note he had gotten from him, he had questions. Then it hit him. Why had Timmerman asked him if he had come across any information to share? It seemed odd. Was it because of Jodl's comments? Maybe it was his comments last night with Timmerman and Burton. Or did they already know about his brother and the mystery man? Not sure how they would know about that.

Doug put a couple of files he needed to review tonight in his case and left the Palace. When he arrived back at the hotel, he stopped to check for messages. The Lieutenant handed one message to him and he tucked it into his shirt pocket. He was hungry, so he went to the canteen to see what was being offered for dinner. The dinner plate they were serving was a fried pork and noodle dish. They gave him a good helping, along with two slices of buttered bread. It tasted good. He also decided to have a glass of fresh milk as well, something that was in short supply in the city. Just like the office supplies.

He sunk his fork into a slice of apple pie and took a bite. He pulled out the message from his pocket and opened it. He started reading it and stopped chewing. The first line of the message read FROM GEN. JODL. It was written by a German lawyer that was supposedly assisting Jodl in his defense. It said that he wished to provide Doug with information about Katyn. He could meet Doug at the hotel or at the Palace if he preferred. He planned to be at the hotel tomorrow morning at 8 a.m. if Doug was available.

Doug put his fork down and pushed the pie away, no longer hungry. This was becoming stranger by the hour. For whatever reason, Doug had become the focal point of an investigation on a subject he knew virtually nothing about. And yet he was being asked to meet with a mystery witness, a hush hush meeting with General Tucker, and now he was being given a lead, by an imprisoned potential war criminal no less, to investigate a possible Soviet war crime.

He needed to think this through. He pulled out a legal pad from his case and flipped to a clean sheet. He rubbed his temples, then he picked up a pencil. In the middle of the page, he wrote KATYN (?). Then he listed

SOVIETS (INVESTIGATION, MOTIVATION)
POLES (MYSTERY MAN, MOTIVATION)
AMERICANS (TIMMERMAN, TUCKER)
GERMANS (JODL, LAWYER, INVESTIGATION, MOTIVATION)
BRITISH (BURTON, MOTIVATION)
TWO INVESTIGATORS (?)

He looked at the sheet for several minutes. He needed more information to answer the questions. He needed time to think, but he needed to read through files tonight. He placed the legal pad in his case and went up to his room. He had a meeting at 8 a.m. the next morning, and a long night ahead of him.

CHAPTER SEVENTEEN

August 19, 1945

DOUG HADN'T SLEPT well. Things running through his mind kept from sleeping soundly. He had such a good night of sleep the night before, thanks to Angela. He arrived in the lobby at ten minutes to eight. He wasn't sure how this meeting was supposed to take place, nor who he was meeting. He sat in the lobby and waited.

He checked his watch. It was 8:05. One of the guards from the front entrance walked into the lobby. He asked the Lieutenant at the desk something, and the Lieutenant in turn pointed over to Doug. The guard walked over and told him that a man was out front that wanted to see him. Doug went out of the hotel.

The man stood a few yards away on the sidewalk. A guard standing with him. Doug walked over. The man spoke in English, with a German accent. "Lt. Colonel Walters?"

"Yes, how can I help you?"

The guard said "Are you Okay Sir?"

"Yes Corporal, I should be fine. Thank you."

"We'll be right over here Sir."

The man could be in his late thirties, but it was harder to tell nowadays. Everyone aged more over the past few years. He wore a dark suit with pinstripes over his skinny frame, a black tie, and black shoes. He had blue eyes and light brown hair that was slicked back. His face was nondescript. His right arm was missing. The empty sleeve of his suit was tucked into a pocket. The man bowed his head slightly to Doug.

"You are?"

"Thank you for meeting me, Colonel. I am Anton Bauer. I am here on behest of General Jodl."

"Okay. Who are you?". Doug intended to find out who this man was, and why he had contacted him.

Bauer looked at him, unsure of what he meant.

"Anton Baer, who are you in relation to Jodl.? What do you do? Why are you here?"

"Ah, yes, sorry Colonel. I am assisting General Jodl with his defense in the coming trials. I am a lawyer. And my note yesterday is why I am here."

"What type of law do your practice Bauer?"

"All types, but primarily criminal law Sir."

"Prosecution or defense?"

"Mostly prosecution."

"Did you help prosecute anyone who ended up in a death camp Bauer?"

Bauer took the question in stride "I am not aware of anyone that I prosecuted who went directly to any prison that you refer to."

"But maybe they went there 'indirectly'?

"Again, I am not aware, but it is certainly possible."

Doug looked at where his arm was missing. "The arm?"

"A British bomb."

"Military service?"

"Yes Sir, I served in the Abwehr. Lieutenant in the Navy." The Abwehr was the German military intelligence service. Hitler had long distrusted the service and its leader, Admiral Canaris, believing the service had been infiltrated by anti-Nazis. Hitler fired Canaris in February 1944 and dissolved the entire service, handing over intelligence functions to the SS.

"Interesting. A spy. I assume you've been through a background check?"

"I have Sir."

"And now you, Bauer, an admitted spy and a lawyer, are working for Jodl?". Doug paused "Not sure what I should think of you."

"I am Sir, working for Jodl. And you may think of me as you wish. I have nothing to hide."

"And what do you think of him?"

"My role is to assist Herr Jodl in forming a defense."

"And that includes providing me, and thus the Americans, with information about a potential war crime?"

"The General believes it is important."

"And you Bauer? Do you think it is important?"

"Colonel, I believe in the law. Whatever the laws are. The laws that are being referenced, and developed, for the coming war crimes trials will hopefully lay a foundation that helps to punish those that are guilty. And to deter future wars and crimes against humanity."

"Is Jodl guilty?"

"As you are aware Colonel, I am not the one who will determine that. My personal views are irrelevant."

"What do you think about the process?"

"Those in power determine the process. I have seen this happen first-hand."

"What information do you have for me?"

Bauer reached into his pocket and withdrew an envelope which he held out to Doug. Doug did not take the envelope.

"What is in the envelope?"

"The envelope contains a name, and location, of a man who can provide you with documentary evidence regarding the Katyn incident."

"How did you get my name? Where I am staying? I'm sure your spy background helped."

"General Jodl identified you. He said you met in an interview. Many of those working on your staff are staying here at the hotel. It was an obvious first place to look for you."

"I wouldn't say I met Jodl. I was present in an interview with him. I don't believe we were formally introduced."

"The General assumed you were an investigator. I asked for a list of participants in that interview for our records."

"What does Jodl expect me to do with this information?"

"I believe he expects a war crimes investigator to 'investigate'."

"Is that so? So now I am working for him? As you can imagine Bauer, we have plenty of war crimes to investigate, specifically ones committed by Germans."

"I believe you do as well. But I should remind you that no one has been found guilty yet Sir."

"You are correct Bauer. But give us time. You Nazis left troves of evidence."

"That sounds like the verdicts are already settled. That will make my job that much harder." Bauer chose not to dispute being called a Nazi. This was not the time, nor place, to have a discussion on who was, and wasn't a Nazi. Though he didn't consider himself a Nazi, he certainly could make the argument that, given the circumstances, he was as much a Nazi as any German.

"The verdicts are not settled, but rest assured, you will need to work extremely hard. I hope that you and your client understand that I am not committing to investigating anything, nor helping you in any way."

"Again, we are not expecting anything. But, as a fellow professional, I would assume that you have a curiosity, and possibly a sense of duty."

"Curiosity, yes. Sense of duty, yes. To the United States of America and our allies."

"Understood Colonel" Bauer nodded to him.

"Now, I have a lot of work to do today sifting through volumes of evidence of Nazi war crimes. So, I need to go." Doug took the envelope from Bauer's outstretched hand.

"Thank you, Colonel for your time, and consideration."

Doug turned away from Bauer and walked to the hotel entrance to catch a jeep to the Palace. After a few steps he turned back to Bauer. "And I'll have someone do some follow up on you. You better hope your story checks out."

"I assure you it does Sir." Bauer nodded his head slightly.

"It had better be spotless." Then Doug turned and walked away.

IN THE JEEP on the way to Palace Doug opened the envelope. Sure enough, there was a name and a location. The name listed was

WERNER RUESSEL, MAJ. ARMY
ADJ. TO MAJ. GEN. KARL REINIGER, ARMY
BRITISH MILITARY HOSPITAL, HANNOVER

In his office he found a map of Germany and looked until he found Hannover. The city was located in the British occupation zone. It would be a long drive, or he could try to arrange a flight there. That would be much quicker. He wrote a note out and had an assistant type it out. He sent over to Colonel Burton's office.

CHAPTER EIGHTEEN

August 20, 1945

DOUG HOPPED IN a jeep at the hotel and was driven to the airfield. Colonel Burton assigned an aircraft to fly Doug to Hannover. Doug didn't share why he needed to travel there, but Burton had assumed it was about their discussion from the other day with General Tucker. Doug reached out to Burton because Hannover was in the British zone.

At the airport, Doug found the aircraft that would take him north. At the plane was a Major Harold Bolinger. Burton had agreed to the flight but wanted one of his team members to tag along in case any issues arose in Hannover. A British Major could come in handy thought Doug. The two officers made introductions and then climbed into the aircraft.

During the flight, Doug sat with Bolinger, exchanging backgrounds and what had brought them to Nuremberg. Bolinger was in the Military Deputy's Department and was splitting his time between Berlin and Nuremberg. He was younger than Doug, had studied law, and had spent time with the British Army in North Africa and Egypt before returning to London in 1943. After the

Allied invasion of the Nazi occupied continent, he arrived in France to work on the growing number of German prisoners of war. Later he worked on establishing a prison camp named ASHCAN that held high value Nazis officials, government leaders and General Staff officers. The camp was located at Palace Hotel in Mondorf les Bains, Luxembourg. Interrogation teams collected biographical information as well as information regarding how the Nazi government functioned from the prisoners. All of this information collected during these interviews and meetings would help the Allies prosecute the war criminals.

The flight took about 2 ½ hours. The pilots brought the aircraft down at the airfield outside of Hannover. After deplaning, Bolinger collected a vehicle and a driver for them.

"Where are we heading Colonel?" asked Bolinger.

"We need to get to the Military Hospital." said Doug.

"Right. The hospital Yardley. Thank you."

They pulled out of the airfield and sped off to the hospital. The city reminded me of Nuremberg, and Berlin for that matter. The same sight. Smells. Devastation. Processions of refugees walked the roads like those in Nuremberg. They all looked the same. They driver pulled into a driveway leading to long 3 story stone and brick building. A couple of Army ambulances with large red crosses painted on the side were parked in the drive.

Doug and Bolinger inquired as to where the main desk was located and the guard at the door pointed them in the right direction.

Bolinger introduced them to the Hospital Administrator and explained they were there to see one of the patients. Doug gave them the name of Ruessel.

"Oh yes, he's one of the last Germans here. It was my understanding that he was to be moved in the next few days out of this facility." said the administrator. "I'll take you to him."

They all walked down a long hallway to a staircase that led up to the higher levels. As they walked the administrator proceeded to tell them about this patient "This patient was here before I arrived, but my understanding is that he was transferred here from a field hospital in Halle. If I remember correctly, around June, but I'd have to check his record, what we have of them, to know for sure."

"That would be helpful." said Doug. "I'm sure record keeping is a challenge for these patients."

They were on the second floor heading down another hallway. Nurses were moving from room to room. "Yes, indeed. We prefer proper record keeping, and I can assure you we have been keeping good records since I arrived here."

"No doubt". Said Doug, not sure if he'd touched a nerve of the Administrator.

"This particular patient, a German officer, was brought to us from Halle, where they had performed immediate care for him. He had a gunshot wound to a shoulder, and a fracture to a leg. If I recall he had been fished out of a river, still alive. It's wonder he didn't drown. In any event, he has been with us since June. We've conducted the surgeries to address his wounds. Because of these injuries, his recovery has been somewhat lengthy, he had some infections you see and to be honest, he needs to be moved somewhere else where he can convalesce. As you can see, we are very busy here, being the only major medical facility in the area. "

"Again, thank you for that information." said Doug.

"Ahh, here we are" said the Administrator as he pushed the door open to a room. There were four beds in room, all occupied. He pointed to one of the beds "Ruessel."

"And the others in the room?" asked Doug.

"They are German as well. The last Germans left behind here. We keep them together to make it easier to, well monitor, and care for them."

Doug turned to the Administrator and Bolinger "Would it be too much trouble to ask if you two can find the detailed records on this patient? Any additional detail might be helpful."

"My pleasure Colonel. Glad to be of service." The administrator smiled and nodded then he and Bolinger took off down the hallway.

Doug walked over to Ruessel's bed. The man in the bed had seen the men at the doorway. He was awake and looking at Doug as he approached. Doug smiled at the man "Do you speak English?"

Ruessel shook his head in the affirmative "A little."

Ruessel's skin was a dull grey, and he looked malnourished. His skin clung tightly to his sunken eye sockets and cheek bones.

His teeth were dark and his hair receding and thin. Several lesions that had healed on his neck and small shrapnel scars on his face. He wore a hospital gown and a blanket pulled up to his waist. The room had no window, so the only light came from two overhead hanging bulbs.

Doug grabbed the cloth curtain and pulled it to separate the space between Ruessel's bed and the one next to his. There was a short stool next to one of the other beds and Doug picked up and set it beside Ruessel's bed and sat down. He sat the shoulder bag he had been carrying down next him. "I am Lt. Colonel Walters, and I'd like to ask you some questions. As you might imagine I ask that you provide me with honest, truthful, answers. Making false statements will only cause your problems. Understand?"

Ruessel nodded, presumably understanding Doug.

"Are you Major Werner Ruessel?"

"Yes."

"Were you an adjutant to a General Reiniger?"

"Yes. Is the General alive?" Ruessel had not heard whether the General was alive or dead. The last he could remember was an image of the general disappearing into a dark fog, pistol drawn, yelling at the gathered troops to follow him. He assumed that the General had not survived the encounter. But then again, he had somehow survived that day so maybe the General had as well.

"That I do not know." Doug made a mental note to remember to find out if the general had survived and was being held somewhere.

"I am here to ask you a couple of very specific questions. Are you aware of any documents that General Reiniger had, or was transporting with him, out of Berlin?"

Ruessel nodded yes. He had been questioned three times by British officers. They wanted to know all about him, his service record, whether he was a Nazi party member, his role in the Army, who did he report to. He mentioned in one meeting that he was in Berlin just before the fall of the city, his commanding officer was a General who had been in the Führer bunker. He shared that the General was under orders to bring important documents out of Berlin and get them to the Americans or British. More questions followed. Did he know what the documents were? Where were they now?

There had been an interpreter in the previous interrogations. It was easier to speak German than find the correct English words, especially since he was struggling to recover from his injuries. The interpreter was German. An older man who probably was a university professor or civil servant of some sort. He hesitated at first to share what the documents were and where he had hidden them. He mentioned quietly to the interpreter that the documents were about Soviet war crimes. The interpreter acknowledged what he said but did not translate it to the British interrogators. He had commented to Ruessel quietly, 'later'.

The British interrogators took copious notes, but as they left, the interpreter told Ruessel that he overhead them saying that he was not a priority target. They felt he was probably making up most of it in order to get more attention, better treatment. The interpreter told Ruessel this was a good thing, best to be a nobody, stay under the radar. The last interrogation session was over a month ago. Ruessel was notified he would be moved somewhere more appropriate. Things were not great here in the hospital, but he was certain wherever he moved to next would be worse. Given his injuries, he was not able to work yet. Fend for himself. He would be cast out. It was time to share with this American officer what he knew, as his circumstances might improve.

"Yes. I was with the General. Working on this final mission." He spoke in a low volume as there were three other men lying in beds nearby.

"I see. This was a 'mission'?" asked Doug. He too spoke in a low volume. It would be much better if they were in a more private setting, but given the crowded hospital, this was the best they could do.

"Mission, yes. orrrr... maybe assignment is better."

"Okay. This mission, assignment, who gave it to Reiniger?"

"The General said it was given to us from General Jodl. We had a letter, orders. To help us get to the Allies."

"To get some documents to the Allies?"

Ruessel nodded yes.

"Do you know what these documents where, what was in them?"

Another yes.

"What were they?"

"The General and I retrieved these documents. From Berlin. Reports on Kaytn. The General and I were there."

"Katyn? In Russia?" Doug wasn't sure exactly what Ruessel was saying.

"Yes."

"You said you and the General were 'there'? At Kaytn?"

"Yes. For the investigation."

"Okay. You were not there during the 'killings', but there was an investigation, and you were there for that, correct?" Ruessel shook his head in the affirmative. Doug had thought for a moment that he was saying that he and Reiniger had been at Katyn when the massacre took place.

Things were checking out from the information Bauer had given him. But it seemed there was an added bonus that Ruessel had been at Kaytn as well, at least during the investigation the Germans conducted. He might be able to corroborate what was in the documents. A nurse walked into the room and stopped, surprised to see Doug in the room sitting with one of the patients.

"Can I help you?" she asked.

Doug turned to her "I'm here to speak with this man ma'am. I shouldn't be much longer."

He was clearly an American officer, so the nurse saw no need to stick her nose into things she thought. "I see, very well Sir. I just need to check these men quickly." She walked over to each of the beds in the room and did quick visual checks, then she walked out of the room.

Doug waited until she left, then turned back to Ruessel. "Major. Can you tell me where these documents are now? Clearly they are not with you." Doug looked at the area around Ruessel's bed.

"They are safe."

"Safe? Where?"

Ruessel explained that he had been forced to abandon the documents at the end of his journey as they approached the American lines. He hid them for retrieval at a later date. Ruessel thought for a moment on whether he should divulge the location of the documents to this American officer. He hadn't done so with the British officers that questioned him, as the interpreter has suggested he not do so at that time. Maybe he had made a mistake in not divulging this information earlier.

Ruessel motioned with his hand as if he wanted to write something. Doug reached into his bag and pulled out a pad of paper and a pencil and handed them to Ruessel.

His memory of what happened between when he tried to escape in the river to when he awoke in an American field hospital was not clear. But Ruessel knew he could find the documents if he could return to that village, that church. He scribbled some words, directions. He added a drawing with many details. After he was finished, he handed the pad to back to Doug. Doug looked at what he had written. The words were in German, and it seemed very detailed. The sketch drawing showed a building, a church, and what looked like a graveyard.

"Is this a church? And, this is a graveyard?" as he pointed to the drawing.

Ruessel nodded.

"This is the city, town?"

"Yes."

Doug studied what Ruessel had written. Then he understood. "Name?"

Ruessel motioned for the pad. Doug held it out for him. Ruessel pointed to it a word written at the below the sketch.

"Who else knows of these documents? And the location?" asked Doug. If Ruessel had already given this information to others then they may have been retrieved and long gone by now.

"I had mentioned the documents to some British officers several weeks ago. But I did not say what the documents were, nor where to find them." offered Ruessel.

"I see, and why didn't you may I ask?" If the British had already questioned him before, why didn't they ask more about these documents? He'd ask Bolinger if they could find any records of any interrogations of Ruessel and see what, if anything, was in the notes. Chances were that, if upon first glance, Ruessel wasn't a high value target, he was probably simply ignored. There were hundreds, thousands, of Wehrmacht and SS officers that needed to be screened, and in some cases, apprehended.

Ruessel hesitated before answering. "I have been struggling, as you can see, with my health, my physical wellness. I don't remember exactly what the questions were back then. But I don't remember them asking about the documents." He hoped this answer was acceptable. He wasn't sure if he should mention the German interpreter or not.

Doug stared at Ruessel, wondering if this was the truth or if there was more. Clearly someone else had heard about him, and the documents. Whoever that was had gotten the information to Bauer and Jodl. He needed to press him further. "Well Major, someone else must have known about you, and these documents. Otherwise, I wouldn't be here. I thought you understood what I meant when I asked you to be fully honest."

"Yes Colonel. The only other person that may have overheard this was the interpreter."

"Interpreter? When you spoke to the British officers?"

"Yes. He was German."

Bolinger and the administrator walked down the hallway and came back into the room. Doug turned to them and asked "Any luck?"

"I have located the records Colonel." said the administrator proudly.

"Excellent. I'm finished here." Doug tucked the pad into his bag and stood up. He looked at Ruessel. "Thank you Major for your cooperation. It will be noted in my report." He had gotten what he needed and there wasn't a need to continue the questioning while Bolinger was there.

The men starting to walk out of the room. Doug stopped and looked back at Ruessel who was watching him. "You will most likely be asked to provide additional information Major."

Ruessel nodded at Doug as he and the other men disappeared into the hallway. Now that he had revealed the location of the documents, he wasn't sure what lay ahead for him. It seemed that word had gotten out somehow that he was alive and in the hospital. And that he knew about the Katyn documents. He had now played all his cards. If the American went looking for the documents and couldn't locate them, he would probably find himself in a worse situation. If he was able to locate them, it sounded as though he might still be of use of someone. Being of 'use' in Germany right now could be a matter of life or death.

"Any luck with the German?" Bolinger asked Doug as they walked down back down the hallway.

"I didn't get much, but he may be of use to us later."

"Worth the trip up here then?"

"Too soon to tell."

ON THE FLIGHT back to Nuremberg, Doug pulled out the pad from his bag and looked at what Ruessel had written. He'd need to get this translated. They had a couple of hours until they landed, so he made two handwritten copies of Ruessels notes, even recreating the sketches. He put one copy in his jacket pocket, and the original and copy back in his bag. He dozed off for the last hour of the flight. After they landed, Bolinger arranged a vehicle back into the city center. Doug asked Bolinger if could be dropped at the hotel, and Bolinger arranged it. After he got back to the hotel, Doug asked for a driver to take him to Chet's camp. He needed to catch up with his brother.

CHAPTER NINETEEN

August 21, 1945

THE STAFF MEETING had gone on for two hours before it was Doug's turn to present. He walked through progress reports and his team's upcoming schedule. The first of the International Military Tribunal trials was now scheduled to commence this coming November, barring any delays or disruptions. It was already late August and it seemed they still had mountains of evidence read and process. The team in Berlin was working as fast as they could. Meanwhile, in the bigger picture, Stalin was continuing to push for a propagandistic show trial of the top Nazis, with corresponding pre-determined outcomes. This was fundamentally at odds with the legalistic traditions of the French, British, and Americans. This friction between allies could delay the start of the trials. Or scuttle them altogether. The Soviets could decide to go their own way and conduct their own kangaroo courts, similar to the Nazi People's Court, most famously presided over by its Judge President Roland Freisler. The French, British and Americans wanted nothing to do with these, so keeping the Soviets on board was important.

After the meeting, Burton caught up with Doug in the hall. Doug told him that the man they met yesterday may be of value, at least in regard to the Kaytn issue. Doug suggested that they have the man kept somewhere where he could be called upon to provide more information. Doug suggested the Bolinger could help with the arrangements, and that they should do this quickly as it was understood the man would be put out of the hospital imminently. Burton agreed. He'd put Bolinger on it this day. Was there anything else Doug needed? Doug asked if Burton could provide travel documents for travel to the French and Soviet zones. It would be easier if he had the papers in hand in case he needed to travel at last minute. Doug had been traveling to and from Berlin, in the Soviet zone, but this was accomplished via a flight on a C-47. He didn't need travel papers for that. But if they needed to travel via ground transport, he would need something. Burton agreed, but said the Soviet documents would be trickier, but doable. When did he need them? Doug said by the end of day if possible.

BURTON HAD THE travel papers delivered to Doug a couple of hours later. After wrapping up his work for the day, Doug closed his desk and headed out of the building. Near the exit, he ran into Angela. They agreed to meet again, for 'dinner', at hotel, in a couple days' time. Angela got in a jeep that would take her back to her lodging. Doug took a jeep back out to see Chet again.

Chet had agreed last night to help Doug retrieve the documents. Doug had asked him not to discuss this with the Poles. Chet would take Nichols and a couple other men on this 'adventure'. They would have to travel into the Soviet zone, so special travel papers would be needed, and now Doug had them. Doug had given Chet a copy of the notes and the sketch he had extracted from Ruessel. The found the village location on one of Chet's maps.

American forces had, up until last month, been holding this particular area of Germany which was now officially part of the Soviet zone. The American Army had advanced that far into Germany at the cessation of hostilities, but by agreement, the Americans had withdrawn to the agreed to border and the Soviet forces moved in. It was still early in the hand over process and the Soviets were still organizing themselves and securing the territory. Chet shouldn't encounter any issues, but if he did, the papers, and his smarts, would get him through it. Chet was eager to get out of the camp for a couple of days. Chet had experienced the thrill, the high one felt, from going into battle, facing death during his time in Europe. At the end of the war, there was euphoria that you and most of your men had survived. Then came the dreadful tedium and boredom. The restlessness. This jaunt he'd agreed to pull for Doug potentially had some excitement, even a bit of danger. Something to do other than watch his men watch other men. They'd leave in the morning before sunrise.

CHAPTER TWENTY

August 22, 1945

NICHOLS BROUGHT AROUND the Dodge command car. It was bigger and roomier, especially with a couple of extra guys, and a daylong ride ahead of them. Nichols had picked up some extra fuel. Along with them for the ride was Private Jennings and Corporal Evans. They were happy to get a day out of the camp themselves.

Chet had mapped out the journey. It would take them through Bayreuth, then on to Hof, where they would pass through into the Soviet zone. They encountered some backup as they approached the checkpoint at Hof. The travel papers Doug had secured for them allowed them to pass without undue scrutiny from the Soviets. They were still logged in by the Lieutenant on duty, who thoroughly checked their identifications. He made a special note that the intended destination was Berlin, and that the stated reason for the travel was official business on behalf of the International Military Tribunal. He was personally glad to be able to assist these Americans in their efforts to bring the Nazi war criminals to justice.

More like a bullet in the back of the head. That's how it would be dealt with in the Soviet Union.

A Soviet vehicle arrived at the Hof checkpoint two hours later. In it was a Captain of Military Police, and NKVD officer in his distinctive blue visor cap and matching riding pants and high black boots. The Lieutenant and others in the station office snapped to attention when the men entered. The officers wanted to see the latest reports of traffic. They were on the lookout for Nazi military officers and political figures that were trying to flee the Soviet zone and get into the American zone. The Lieutenant was responsible for ensuring this did not happen. Should any of these prize Nazis escape through this checkpoint, the Lieutenant would be held personally responsible. They provided he lieutenant with an updated list of most wanted, and others to be on the lookout for. They asked him if he had seen anything unusual in the past couple of days. He said he had not, but then thought he should mention the Americans who had passed through earlier on their way to Berlin. It was not especially unusual, but they were traveling on a pass on behalf of the war crimes tribunal. The NKVD officer wanted to know more.

There were still Americans transiting in and out of the Soviet zone, but most of the Americans opted to fly into Berlin rather than drive. The roads were still not good for traveling long distances. Bridges were out, detours around badly damaged areas, and war wreckage still strewn about. And the ever-present refugees. He wasn't sure if it was anything, but they were trained to report everything, no matter how insignificant. After grilling the Lieutenant again about the details, the NVKD officer and the Military Police Captain jumped into their vehicle and sped off.

The Lieutenant was relieved when they departed. There was zero tolerance for mistakes. Minor mistakes found you busted down in rank. Or reassigned to less desirable duty. Bigger mistakes earned you a ticket to a Gulag. Major mistakes could mean a bullet in the back of the head. People just disappeared.

CHET'S GROUP FOUND the way to the area near Lutherstadt Wittenburg where the map Doug had provided lead them. There wasn't much here. The only building that had survived was a pretty beat up, but relatively intact. It was what they were looking for. A church.

Chet followed Doug's notes. The men found what they were looking for. The only thing they encountered was an old German lady who watched them digging in the graveyard. She approached them from across the street, yelling something at them in German, which they didn't understand. It was probably something about them digging in the church graveyard. After several minutes of being yelled at, a man emerged from the church. He was most likely the minister. He went over to the old woman and attempted to calm her down. She turned her attention, and screaming, to him. Taking her by the arm, he led her into the church. He was not interested in disturbing the four American soldiers who were disturbing a gravesite. There was no use asking for trouble.

Chet had the guys load the dirty leather cases in the back of the Dodge. Before departing, Chet walked over to the back door of the church. He knocked and the man answered. The man looked warily at Chet, not knowing what might come next. Chet held out his hand and gave the man four chocolate bars and three packs of cigarettes. Not much of a church offering, but the man could trade them for something he needed. The man thanked him in German.

The journey had taken most of the day. The late August sun was sinking in the sky. Chet decided they should stay there for the night. So, he knocked on the door again. The man opened the door. Chet used his hands to convey to the man that they would be staying inside the church overnight. The man did not seem happy nor was he willing to oppose whatever they were doing. They hauled the dirty leather cases from the Dodge into the church. Chet shared some of their rations with the man, who thanked them and went back into his quarters. The man returned a bit later and handed Chet a bottle of wine. Chet thanked him. The men eventually stretched out on the pews and floor for the night. They'd get an early start tomorrow morning.

CHAPTER TWENTY-ONE

August 23, 1945

THEY SAT IN a queue on the road leading to the Soviet checkpoint at Hof leading back into the American zone. Chet was tempted to open the leather cases and see what was in them. The men hadn't asked him about what might be inside, but he was sure they were curious. He was as well, but he'd leave it to his brother.

The guards asked to see their IDs, which they provided. Chet also handed the man the travel document. He scanned it he was studying it intently. Chet could sense the man was unsure of something. He asked them if they could wait a for a minute while he asked his commander something. Chet said sure, but he knew this wasn't good.

As the guard turned go to the station office, there was some commotion on the road behind him. Some screaming in Russian. Someone blowing a whistle. Chet looked back and could see that one of the guards had pulled a weapon on one of the refugees that was passing in the queue. The guard who had been checking the took off running. The door to the office flung open, and the Lieutenant who had given them the twice over just yesterday came out in a hurry. Other guards followed suit.

The gate was left open on the other side of the road at the checkpoint. The people in the queue entering the Soviet zone were not sure what was happening or what they should do. The all decided it best to stay put. There was enough room for a vehicle to pass through the open gate. Chet nudged Nichols with his elbow and pointed to the gate. Nichols put the Dodge in gear and steered it over and through the opening on the other side.

After the commotion died down, the Lieutenant was certain they had apprehended one of these sneaky Nazi war criminals. The man was taken into custody. One of the guards tapped the Lieutenant on the shoulder. "What was it?" he demanded. The guard asked him to look at this travel document for the vehicle he was checking just ahead. The Lieutenant looked at the document. He had seen this before. This was from the men he had personally checked through this checkpoint yesterday. The ones that may have been of interest to the NKVD officer. He and the guard started walking up the queue to the gate. The guard stopped in his tracks. The Lieutenant stopped and turned around looking. He asked the guard where the vehicle was. The guard was stunned silent. He started turning around, frantically looking for the vehicle. The other guards were returning to their posts and duties. The Lieutenant had a grave look on his face. He told the guard to get back to work. The man saluted and returned to checking identities.

The Lieutenant had a tough decision to make. On one hand, he and his men may have bagged a high-profile Nazi. On the other, they may have let a vehicle through that was under suspicion. The captured Nazi would certainly look good for him. The lost American vehicle would not. How best to deliver this news? If he tried to cover this up, he would be denounced by the guard that was guilty of letting the Americans pass. The guard would be tortured and tell he had reported this to the Lieutenant. Then it would be his turn to be tortured. He made a quick decision to face the problem head on. He summoned his Sergeant. He instructed the Sergeant to arrest the guard in question and take him behind the checkpoint office and hold him there. If the prisoner attempts to make a break for it, shoot him. The Sergeant nodded. The Lieutenant handed the Sergeant the folded travel document of the Americans. He told him to find this on the body.

CHET AND THE others had a good laugh after they'd cleared the Soviet checkpoint. Chet told Evans and Jennings to keep an eye out behind them to make sure no one decided to pursue them. He wasn't too worried, as there we safely in the American zone again. They reached an American checkpoint a mile or so down the road, but they were quickly waived through after ID checks.

Thirty minutes pass the checkpoints, Evans leaned forward and tapped Chet on the shoulder. Chet turned to him.

"Might have someone following us Sir."

[249]

"Are you sure?"

"Think so Sir."

Chet turned further around so he could look. He didn't see anything behind them. "Where?"

"They'll be there a sec... there Sir. That black car."

Now Chet could see a car. Black car. Of the few non-military vehicles on the road these days, most of them seemed to be black. The car was a way behind them.

"You sure they are following us?"

"Think so Sir. They been hanging back just far enough but keeping pace with us."

"Really?" Chet was convinced. He had asked the guys to watch for followers, so maybe Evans is starting to see things. "Let's watch them a bit longer." Chet was thinking that if anyone pursued them it would be some Soviets in a truck trying to catch them. Not someone following them in a car. Not trying to catch them. "What do you think Jennings?" asked Chet.

"I see what Evans is saying Sir."

"Okay. Let me know if they start gaining us."

"Yes Sir."

"You want me to pick up the pace Sir" asked Nichols.

"Nah. Let's give it bit longer." There was intermittent military traffic traveling in both directions. And refugees wandering on the roads. Chet didn't want to risk hitting anyone or causing an accident. A handful of GIs had been killed in accidents since VE day. He wasn't going to be one of them.

Thirty minutes later, Evans could still see the car trailing them. Maybe this was nothing. All this cloak and dagger stuff and they were all on edge. They had faced German artillery, armored vehicles, and tanks. They shouldn't be thinking twice about some fucking car traveling down a main roadway a safe distance behind them. But now it was stuck in his head and bothering him. He waited another mile or so until he saw what he was looking for. He turned to Evans and Jennings and said, get ready. They grabbed their weapons. He told Nichols to slow up. Then he pointed to a group of buildings up ahead. There was a narrow dirt road branching off to the left. He told Nichols to take the left. Nichols braked and slowed down for the turn. After he turned Chet told him to stop. Nichols brought the Dodge to a halt. Chet pointed to Evans and Jennings to get out, one to go left, the other to the right. The men jumped out and ran over to the buildings and took cover. Chet told Nichols to take off and go up a little further, but not too far.

Either they would see the car pass by harmlessly, or... sure enough. A black car turned on the road they took and was rolling toward them. This was going to be interesting. Chet told Nichols to stop, which he did. Chet pulled his .45 out of his holster. Nichols did the same.

The black car had made the turn behind them but then it began to slow, then came to a complete stop in the middle of the road. Chet

[251]

slowly got the Dodge, resting his hand on his .45, and turned toward the car. The midday sun was shining in such a way that he couldn't make out who was in the car, but he could see a driver and a passenger. He just stared at the car for minute. He needed to take action. Don't give them time to consider their options. He slowly walked towards the car, eyeing them carefully as they sat staring back at him through the windshield. Evans and Jennings were off to the sides of the buildings. He nodded to them and they stepped out behind the car with their weapons at the ready. Chet still had twenty yards to cover before reaching the car.

The men in the car watched as the American approached them, slowly closing the distance between them. The driver noticed a soldier approaching the car from behind in the side mirror, his rifle up. The men in the car look back and realize they are surrounded. The driver put the car reverse and hit the accelerator. Dirt flew from the tires as the car raced backwards. Chet stopped and raised his gun and pointed it at the car. Both Evans and Jennings jumped out of the way but kept their guns trained on the car. Chet yelled to them not to shoot. The car flew backwards down the road, the engine revving, until it hit the main road pavement and skidded to a stop. The driver shifted the into drive and swung the car around, heading back down the main road from the direction they had just traveled. Both Evans and Jennings ran up to the intersection and aimed to fire at the fleeing vehicle. Chet yelled at them again not to shoot. Chet walked up to the intersection and watched as the car sped off and disappeared into the distance. The men lowered their weapons.

"Seems you were onto something Evans" said Chet as he patted him on the shoulder.

"Should have let us put a few holes in him Sir."

"I'm hoping that we all get out of Europe without firing another shot."

Nichols meanwhile had backed the Dodge back to where they were standing. "Assuming we won't pursue Sir?"

"Correct. We've got them running as fast as they can in the opposite direction of where we're headed. Good enough for me. And now I think they know better than to mess with us."

The men rolled into Nuremberg after dark. Doug had told Chet that if they found anything, don't bring it to the hotel. Best to keep it with him at the camp and Doug would go see it there.

CHAPTER TWENTY-TWO

August 24, 1945

IT HAD BEEN two days and Doug hadn't heard anything yet from Chet. It was going to take a day there and day back, so maybe he'd hear something today. Sure enough, at noon he was notified that he was wanted at the front gate. He passed the front entrance gate and across the street sat Chet on a low wall. Doug smiled and walked over to him.

"You're back." said Doug.

"Did you doubt me?"

"Of course not." Doug turned and sat next to his brother. "How did it go?"

"The package is here."

"You found it?"

"Just followed the directions."

"No shit." Doug said, amazed that the information and directions were accurate. "Easy in, easy out?"

"For the most part. Had a little run in on the way back."

"How so?"

"We got back in the American zone, and about an hour in one of my guys notices we're being followed. So, I decided we should stop and talk to them."

"Really? You were followed? Are you sure? Who was it? What did they say?"

"We, we got'em to stop, but not to talk. Couple of guys in a black car. We had them cornered, but they high-tailed it outta there when they realized we were onto them, and we weren't gonna take any shit. We had them outgunned."

"Outgunned? You guys had guns out? Jesus Christ Chet. This is getting out of hand. These guys following you pulled guns? Did you get a look at them? Anyone get hurt?"

"Hell no. It would have been them getting hurt anyway. I didn't see that they were armed, but we weren't waiting to find out. Never got a good look at them."

Doug was visibly upset. He had pulled his brother into this mess, and now he was putting him in danger. He felt guilty for asking Chet to get involved in the first place. "Sorry about all this. Who in the hell could it have been?"

"I thought about that too. All I could come up with was the Soviets. We kind of slipped through their checkpoint on the way back. There was a big commotion going on and we tired of sitting there."

"What? The travel docs didn't work?"

"Yeah, they worked fine. It was the Soviets at the checkpoint. They were all edgy, nosing around. You know. They might have wanted to keep us hanging around for no good reason while they filled out some stupid reports. There were people coming and going in both directions, but mostly out."

"Yeah, from my understanding they are really cracking down on the Germans, well valuable or useful Germans, slipping out into the British or American zones." The war was over. Here in Europe, and now in the Pacific. Fortunately, the Americans and Allies came out on top. But at a cost. The Soviets had thrown thousands if not millions of men and vast resources to repel and defeat the Nazis. Britain had survived, but was badly wounded, maybe fatally. France was whole again, but the country had been humiliated and embarrassed. Not sure if the French could regain their standing. The Germans were going to pay. More so than they did with the Versailles Treaty. The country was being carved up into zones of influence. Anything of value, technology, science, weaponry, human capital, was up for grabs. And of course, the victors would exact justice on the defeated, punishing the wrongdoers. Doug was now caught up in this process, this movement, toward finding truth and holding those responsible accountable. That is what he understood it to be.

Chet pulled out his cigarettes and pulled one out. He offered the pack to Doug.

"Since when did you take up smoking?"

"Since I joined the Army." They both laughed.

"You should try giving them up. Not healthy if you ask me."

"Yeah. Yeah, I will when I get back to the States. I'll be damned if I'm going to pay for all these cigarettes."

"The package is safe?"

"Yessir. Two rather large leather cases. Fairly heavy."

"Okay. I'll head out tonight and take a look."

"Oh yeah, the Poles are back at it. They said the brother wants to still meet with someone who can help him, use the information he has, something like that. But I guess he got spooked last time. Seems kinda high strung. Why doesn't he just come forward with what he's got?"

"Good question. I think everyone is so on edge with these trials coming up that maybe he's worried things will get into the wrong hands. Look at this crap we're dealing with chasing this other stuff down."

"Yeah, good point. Way over my head." Chet stood up and put out his cigarette. "Oh yeah, have you had a chance to get 'reacquainted' with your lady friend?"

Doug smiled. "Actually, I have, thanks for asking."

Chet was impressed. "Well, good for you. Anything you can share?"

"With you? No way. Next thing you know you'll be after her."

Chet gave a thoughtful look "Hmm. Now I'm intrigued. Describe her again? Maybe she is my type." He was needling Doug.

He and his brother had never competed for the affections of a woman before, as they were attracted to different things. Doug liked girls on the student council, Chet liked cheerleaders. "Anyway, you seem to be getting more interaction with the opposite sex than me. That has never been the case before."

"Quality over quantity. That's my motto."

"Hey. What are you implying?" They both laughed. Chet had dated several girls in high school, a new one each school year it seemed. He had dated some others after high school, and one girl he become very close to, Deborah. But things didn't work out in the end. Maybe he would 'reacquaint' himself with her when he got back to Michigan. She was a quality person. Someone Doug might like. His brother was a quality guy, always has been. People looked up to him, respected him, went to him for advice. That's probably why they asked him to help out over here. But now it seemed he was getting pulled into some sideshow stuff.

Doug gave Chet a soft punch in the arm "Thanks again. I owe you one."

"Yes, you do."

The two men hugged, then Doug walked back across the street and back into the Palace.

DOUG WENT TO the camp and looked at the documents that evening. Most of 'the documents were in German, with some Polish and some Russian. Lots of photographs. Picture after picture of exhumed and stacked bodies. Pretty gruesome stuff. Whoever was responsible for this, the Germans or the Soviets, it was a war crime. He needed to know more about what the reports and documents were saying. He needed a translator. If the documents weren't real, then he didn't want to bring them out into the open. Introducing faked documents about a war crime wasn't something he wanted to get involved with. But Tucker had put him in this spot. Look into this thing, and if it is something, we'll act on it. If it's not, we'll bury it and move on.

Angela. He could ask Angela to translate a few pages. She's here as a translator, translating hundreds of German documents. She'd be able to give him a good feel for the authenticity of these files, and what some of it meant. He'd ask her tomorrow.

When he returned to the hotel, Doug stopped by the hotel desk. He looked around, but there didn't seem to be anyone there. He decided to grab a sandwich at the canteen, so he headed over there. As we walked away someone called out. "Can I help you Sir?"

Doug stopped and turned back. Alfred was standing there behind the counter. He had appeared out of nowhere. "Yes. Hello, Alfred, isn't it?"

"Yes Sir, Alfred."

"You're just the man I needed." Doug approached the counter and put his hands on it and leaned over to Alfred. "I'm hoping you can help me find something."

"Yes Sir. I can try. What is it you are looking for?"

"Well, things are getting so busy, I don't have time to find one myself, but I am in need of a large case" he held up his hands to show the size he meant. "A leather case, about this size."

Alfred looked at him, trying to imagine a leather case that size. "Okay, are you looking for a new case Sir? I'm not sure I can help you with that."

"No no. A used case would be perfect. Something black preferably. I have a couple of other cases that I'm using for work, but I need another."

"I see Sir. Well then, if it is a used case you need, I am certain something can be located."

"Excellent." Doug smiled at Alfred, who gave him a nod back in return. "Any idea on what that might cost me?"

"It will really depend on a number of..."

"A carton of cigarettes."

"That shouldn't be a problem Sir."

"And a bottle of Whiskey if you have it to me by tomorrow."

"Tomorrow it is Sir."

AUGUST 8, 1945

THE LONDON CHARTER OF THE INTERNATIONAL MILITARY TRIBUNAL DECREE
WAS ISSUED AND SET DOWN THE LAWS AND PROCEDURES BY WHICH THE
NUREMBERG TRIALS WERE TO BE CONDUCTED.

THE CHARTER STIPULATED THAT CRIMES OF THE EUROPEAN AXIS POWERS COULD
BE TRIED AND THREE CATEGORIES OF CRIMES WERE DEFINED: WAR CRIMES, CRIMES
AGAINST PEACE, AND CRIMES AGAINST HUMANITY.

THE CHARTER WAS PRIMARILY DRAFTED BY ROBERT H. JACKSON OF THE UNITED
STATES, ROBERT FALCO OF FRANCE, AND IONA NIKITCHENKO OF THE SOVIET
UNION

"ALAS, THE GERMAN REVELATIONS ARE PROBABLY TRUE. THE BOLSHEVIKS CAN
BE VERY CRUEL."

Winston Churchill to Polish General Sikorski
April 15, 1943

"WE SHALL CERTAINLY OPPOSE VIGOROUSLY ANY 'INVESTIGATION' BY THE
INTERNATIONAL RED CROSS OR ANY OTHER BODY IN ANY TERRITORY UNDER
GERMAN AUTHORITY. SUCH INVESTIGATION WOULD BE A FRAUD AND ITS
CONCLUSIONS REACHED BY TERRORISM."

Winston Churchill
April 24, 1943

CHAPTER TWENTY-THREE

August 25, 1945

BURTON ASKED DOUG to join him in his office. When Doug arrived, Bolinger was there in his office. Doug took a seat.

Burton was looking at Bolinger with a concerned look. "Doug. It seems that we have a bit of a problem."

"How so?"

"Well... Bolinger here went back to Hannover to retrieve the person of interest that we had talked about the other day, per your suggestion." Burton took a long pause. "And you see, the person wasn't there."

Doug looked at Burton, then turned to Bolinger. Bolinger shook his head no.

"Bolinger spoke with the administrator, who said the patient was scheduled to be transferred out of the facility. Two days ago, two men showed up there to retrieve him. Had some paperwork or such, saying they were taking him to the local church medical facility, to assist him in his recovery."

"And let me guess, he's not there. Never arrived probably."

"Actually, when I contacted the church facility, they said they hadn't even known about the patient, nor sent anyone to retrieve him." said Bolinger.

"Interesting turn of events." said Doug. He had made a mistake. He probably should have put Ruessel under guard, some sort of protection. But that would have raised a lot of questions and Doug was trying to do his 'investigation', if he could call it that, out from the open. Bringing Ruessel back with him wasn't feasible either. He presumed it wouldn't look good for the American and British to be holding and protecting someone who potentially had damning evidence of a war crime that an ally committed. It would look like they were siding with the Germans, the Nazis, over the Soviets. As General Tucker suggested, that is not the look they wanted.

"Rather strange, don't you agree?"

"I do."

The three men were silent, trying to process things. Doug thought through various options. The Germans? Why would they get rid of Ruessel, considering that they had led Doug *to him*. They knew where he was so they could have retrieved, or silenced him, earlier. Maybe they used him as bait to get the Americans and British involved. The Soviets. That would be his first choice. After all, Ruessel had information, potentially, to expose them for a war crime. But how did they know about him? Bolinger knew where he was, but not necessarily who he was or what he knew. Burton didn't know the specifics either. Burton may have told Timmerman that

Doug was going to Hannover, but he couldn't have known anything further.

"Where you able to get anything out of him that was useful?" asked Burton, breaking the silence.

"As I mentioned, Bolinger and I found him at the hospital, I spoke with him briefly to confirm his identity, check his basic story, and confirm that he said he was aware of some potential documents. That was as far as we got." Doug we not willing to share any more information with Burton or Bolinger. Something was going on and he needed to try to keep information compartmentalized.

"I see." said Burton. "This is a dead end I suppose."

"Literally" said Doug.

DOUG THOUGHT ABOUT Ruessel's disappearance the rest of the day. Maybe there were some connections. Chet had mentioned that when he went to see this mysterious Pole, they might have been followed. Then Chet is somehow followed during his return from retrieving the documents that Ruessel led them to. Now Ruessel is gone, having disappeared with two mystery men. Timmerman had stressed to the team that even though they were in the American zone, there were plenty of Soviets 'working' here as part of the Soviet delegation to the tribunal. They were allies, so they have permission to be here. Bottom line, it is possible that everyone one of the British, American, and French teams might be 'surveilled' at one time or another, so be aware, stay alert.

All things pointed to the Soviets. They were known to follow people, gather intel, recruit informers. And they had motivation, at least in this case, to find and suppress any information about Katyn, or otherwise, that could embarrass them or, in the off chance, make them stand trial for war crimes. Fat chance of that happening.

Doug arrived at the hotel that evening, and Alfred spotted him when he entered the lobby. Alfred waived and Doug walked over to the hotel desk.

"I have your request Sir."

"Excellent. I appreciate your assistance."

Alfred opened the door behind the counter and reached down and picked up a case. It was black and close to the size that Doug had requested. It was in fairly nice condition, more than what he needed. "It is of very high quality, not easy to find. I hope this is to your liking. If not, another one can be found." He placed the case on the counter for Doug to inspect.

Doug looked the case over, opened it, checked the handle. He noticed some initials embossed under the handle. FWS. "This should do nicely. By the way, who is FWS?"

"FWS?"

"Yeah, FWS. The initials right here" as he pointed to the initials.

Alfred glanced at the initials. "I would assume a prior owner." He looked back at Doug, wondering if this would kill the deal. The man had not been specific on the requirements or lineage of a used leather case.

"Prior owner. I hope the prior owner was not a Nazi bigwig. Nor a Jew. That would be embarrassing for me." Doug wanted to put Alfred on the spot, see how he reacted.

Alfred didn't flinch. His expression stayed the same. "I am not fully versed on the background of this item, so I cannot vouch for it. It is here for you now via a reputable source."

"Reputable." said with a hint of sarcasm. "I'll take it."

Alfred was glad the uncomfortable questioning had concluded, and the deal was going to happen. He had been subjected to numerous screenings with uncomfortable questions already since the end of the war. Germans who had felt oppressed by the Nazis were now turning the tables and incriminating those they had grievances with. To even get this job at the hotel he had to undergo several screenings. The Potsdam Agreement was recently signed by Truman, the new American president, Attlee, the new British Prime Minister, and Stalin. It laid out a denazification program that would eradicate Nazi influence from German society. One of the first steps would be to remove those who had been Nazi Party or members of the SS from positions of power and influence. This is what caused concern for Alfred, and many of this colleagues that were still around. More uncomfortable questions were certain to come.

Doug opened the shoulder bag he had with him and extracted a carton of cigarettes. Lucky Strikes. He placed the carton on the counter and pushed it to Alfred. Then extracted from his bag a bottle of whiskey. He handed this to Alfred. "I hope you enjoy these."

"Thank you again Sir." Alfred picked up the cigarettes and bottle and set them behind the counter, out of sight. "I actually don't drink whiskey, nor do I smoke. But I know others that do. So, these are very valuable. As good or better than currency."

"Good to know."

"Please let me know if you have any further requests Sir."

"I certainly shall." With that, Doug picked up his case and went to his room. These Germans sure knew how to suck up to you. Nice. Friendly. Civilized. Wait until these trials start and all of evidence of the Nazi atrocities is made public, for all the world to see. The 'master race' alright.

CHAPTER TWENTY-FOUR

August 26, 1945

IT WAS SUNDAY, and Doug made arrangements to pick up
Angela. They were going to have lunch at the hotel, and then spend
some quality time together.

They ate some lunch at the canteen. Doug opted for the sausage
plate with sauerkraut, and Angela opted for some roast chicken. But
neither of them was there for the cuisine. Their conversation was
playful, and they struggled to contain the sexual tension between
them. They quickly worked their way through the food and headed
up to Doug's room.

Doug had been over-worked, and over-stressed, the past two
weeks. In his room, he set it all aside and was able to focus all his
attention on Angela. They had all afternoon to spend together, so
they were not rushed like before. He had time to explore her body.
And she explored his. Afterward, as they lay in the bed together
relaxing, they both shared more about their pasts. Both had been
married and lost their spouses. Angela's husband had been a Royal
Air Force pilot assigned to the Desert Air Force based in North
Africa. He was killed while flying Hurricane fighters out of Tobruk.

They had only married just before the war started, so they had never really had a chance to get their life together started. After his death, she wanted, no needed, to focus her attention on something. So, she applied for several opportunities within the government and military, and they were happy to utilize her language skills.

Doug shared a bit about his wife and the illness that took her. He too became heavily involved with the war effort and had done his part on the home front. He had been persuaded to join the legal team working on the tribunal and felt it was his duty to do so. Angela said she was lucky he was doing his duty.

After more lounging, Doug asked Angela if she could help him with something.

"Sure, I can try. What is it?"

Doug got off the bed and put his shorts on. He pulled a leather case from under the bed out, opened it, and pulled out a file folder. He closed the case and pushed it back under the bed. He sat on the bed and she sat up next to him, pulling the bed sheet over her shoulders and covering her breasts.

"What have you got there?"

"I've come into the possession of some documents, and unfortunately there are all in German, maybe some Russian or Polish in them as well. I know you are an expert at translation, so I was hoping you could translate a few pages for me and let me know they say, and if they are authentic."

Angela leaned her shoulder into his and gave him a push. "You want me to work on my day off? Really?"

"I know, I know, I shouldn't ask. I'm sorry."

"Why don't you give them to your team and have them translated? Aren't they getting paid for that?"

"Yes, they could do it, and I will bring them in for them to work on, but before I did, I wanted to make sure they were legit. If you gave them a first pass and said they were, I'll bring them in and I'll put them to work on them. I don't want to waste their time, and I don't want to look stupid for bringing in something that is worthless."

"I see. Where did you get these files?"

"That I cannot say."

"Not even to me?" Angela said in a pouty voice. "Is this some hush hush thing?"

"Well, if it were 'hush hush', I wouldn't be asking you to look at them, would I?" he said with a big grin.

"That's true, I guess. Let's have a look, shall we?"

Doug handed her the folder and she opened it. There were several loose pages inside. She read over the first page, then turned to the second, and read over that page. She studied all of the pages one by one but didn't say anything. Doug was watching her as she read.

She stopped and looked at him "Do you want me to translate this for you?"

"Yes, please."

"Shall I read it for you, or would you prefer I write it down?"

"Oh, yeah, right. I'll grab you some paper." He got the bed and fetched a legal pad and a pencil. She set the folder down and laid out the pages. She took the pad and flipped to a new sheet. She started writing.

"Do you want me to do all these pages? Or shall I just give you a summary of each of these pages?"

"Maybe just the summary of the pages."

There were seven pages in total. She sat on the bed and wrote out titles of the pages and a quick summary of the page contents. When she was done, she put the pages back into the folder and closed it. She looked up at Doug. "Any more for me Sir?"

"No, that's it. This case is full of the rest of the files, but I just needed this sample. So, what is your impression? Do they look legit?"

"My professional opinion?"

"Of course."

"I'd say they are legitimate German documents." She paused for a moment. "They seem to be German documents about and investigation into a massacre, of Poles, committed by the Russians." She had a concerned look on her face.

"Yes, that is what I was led to believe the documents were about."

Angela put the papers with her translation on top of the folder along with the pencil. Doug picked it up and glanced at her translation to English. Then he bent down, pulled the leather case out again, and laid the papers inside. Angela laid back onto the bed. Doug pushed the case under the bed and laid down beside her.

"Thank you for doing this. I owe you a favor now."

"Mmmmhmmm." She rolled over and snuggled next to him, putting her arm on his chest. "When can I collect?"

"Whenever."

"Is now a good time?" She slowly moved her hand and put it inside the front of his shorts.

AFTER DOUG HAD escorted Angela back to her lodging, the driver dropped him back at the hotel. Doug thanked him and the driver replied "Anytime Sir" and gave him a wink. Doug gave him a smile and a wink back. Before he turned to go inside, he saw the man across the street. Standing there in his dark pin-striped suit. It was Bauer.

Bauer was looking right at him and they made eye contact. He had not expected to see he man again. Ever. Except maybe in the courtroom as defense for Jodl. They way Bauer was looking at him, it seemed obvious he wanted to talk. Unless he was here waiting to talk to someone else.

After his conversation with Alfred about the value of cigarettes, he had started carrying them with him. He didn't intend to smoke them, but they could come in handy when interacting with people. He had put a pack in his shirt pocket, so he unbuttoned the pocket and pulled the pack out. He walked across the street, pulled out a cigarette, and put it in his mouth. He leaned on the steel fencing that surrounded the parking area. He looked over at Bauer.

Bauer slowly walked over to Doug. Doug said hello and offered him a cigarette, which he took. Doug lit Baeur's cigarette for him, then lit his own. Bauer thanked him. Doug puffed on the cigarette a little to get it going.

"I was not expecting to have another encounter with you Mr. Bauer."

"I was simply hoping to find out if you had made contact with the lead I provided."

"It checked out. And so did you."

Bauer nodded.

"Was the lead able to assist you with locating any evidence?"

"Not yet, but he said he would be willing to." Doug did not want to share anything with Bauer about what he learned from Ruessel, and that he was in possession of the documents. He'd let him think the documents were still out there. He also didn't mention that Ruessel had gone missing

"I see. I hope that he shares this information with you soon. Time is of the essence."

"Maybe this guy is playing an angle, he might not have anything at all."

"That I cannot guarantee. But we have confidence."

"Okay. I could have been seen talking to you twice now. I'm not comfortable in talking to you again. Not unless you have something you can provide me in return."

"Such as?"

"I'm sure Jodl, with his great memory and attention to detail, can help us with a few of these nasty political characters. Fill in some gaps. Give us some names. Help us find other documents. That sort of thing."

Bauer thought for a moment. "Would this type of cooperation coincide with any dismissal of charges? Leniency?"

"What?! Are you crazy? Any cooperation he wants to do, and should do, is up to him. I'm in no way setting up a horse trade or negotiation here. I'm simply saying that I'm going out on a limb, and I don't like it. Understand? "

Bauer nodded. "I will see if there is anything that the General feels might be... shall we say, useful."

"You do that. And we'll see if we can get Ruessel moved down here."

Bauer looked surprised. "Do you think that is wise?"

"Why wouldn't it be?"

"Well, you see, I'm sure you can understand, that there are a number of..."

"What are you trying to say?"

Bauer looked for the right words. He decided just to be blunt. "I'm not sure it would be safe for him here Colonel."

"Why not?"

"There are many Soviets here, in Nuremberg. Actually, all over your zone. So bringing someone like Ruessel, to Nuremberg, could put him in danger."

"Well, I don't plan on going to Hannover again." Doug was not lying about that, now that Ruessel was gone. And from the way the conversation was going, Bauer was not aware that he was missing. Talk about being in danger here. He was nabbed out of a British hospital.

"Understood Colonel."

Doug had not been smoking the cigarette, just holding it. It had gone out already in fact. Doug tossed the cigarette on the ground and walked across the street and into the hotel.

Bauer watched Doug disappear into the hotel. He bent over and picked up the barely used cigarette and put it in his pocket.

NOVEMBER 28, 1943 | 8:30 PM

TEHRAN CONFERENCE - TRIPARTITE DINNER
ROOSEVELT'S QUARTERS, SOVIET EMBASSY

DURING THE DINNER, STALIN PROPOSES TO ROOSEVELT AND CHURCHILL THAT
THEY SHOULD 'PHYSICALLY LIQUIDATE' 50-100,000 GERMAN COMMANDING
STAFF OFFICERS AS A MEANS TO CONTROL POST-WAR GERMANY.

ROOSEVELT JOKED THAT PERHAPS 49,000 WOULD SUFFICE.

CHURCHILL REACTED NEGATIVELY AND TOOK STRONG EXCEPTION TO WHAT HE
TERMED THE SUGGESTION OF THE "COLD BLOODED EXECUTION OF SOLDIERS WHO
FOUGHT FOR THEIR COUNTRY".

CHAPTER TWENTY-FIVE

August 28, 1945

GENERAL TUCKER'S OFFICE in the Palace of Justice complex was spacious, but very utilitarian in design. A large wood desk that was sourced locally. When Tucker arrived in Nuremberg had asked for a desk that had belonged to one of the local 'Golden Pheasants', a Reichsleiter or Gauleiter, he didn't especially care. As long as he could tell visitors to his office that he was working to bring justice to those bastards using one of their own desks to do his work. The office had a large window with greyish, plain curtains. The window provided warm, outside light, but the view had much to be desired, as there was nothing pleasant to see. Just grey, black, and brown devastation of what had once been a beautiful city and popular tourist destination. Hanging on the wall behind his desk was a large map of Germany. The map showed the Allied occupation zones, with a large zone covering all the eastern part of Germany, including Berlin, designated to, and currently held by, the Soviets. There was large bookshelf along another wall, full of legal texts, including those from the Prussian and Weimar eras, and some from the Third Reich. The Germans had, at one time, a respected judiciary and legal system. After the rise of the Hitler, they found themselves wanting, succumbing to the depravation and moral distortions of the Nazi Party. A large ornate floor globe sat in one corner, another 'acquisition' from another local golden pheasant. The only items on Tucker's desk were a lamp and a carved wooden cigar box. Two upholstered armchairs sat opposite.

Soviet General Belov, a counterpart of Tucker's on the Soviet legal delegation, had requested a meeting today at noon. Meetings with Belov were typically planned well in advance with a specific agenda of things he wanted to cover. Tucker had not received an agenda for today from Belov so he asked Timmerman to put together a few items they could discuss with the Soviets in the meeting. They hadn't had time to put together a spread of refreshments for Belov, which he always seemed to enjoy. Had Belov given them more advanced warning, they could have put something more substantial together. As it was, all they had to offer today was coffee, tea, and some German apple strudel.

Timmerman arrived at Tucker's office with a folder for the General that outlined some potential talking points to cover with Belov. Timmerman had detailed information in folders he would hang onto and provide as needed. Tucker looked it over quickly and was satisfied. "Any inkling as to what Belov is coming over for?"

"No Sir. As you know we weren't scheduled to meet with them for another two weeks."

"Right. This is probably some ploy by our friend Belov to catch us off guard on something. Have I got something here I can come back at him with?" Tucker looked at the notes in the folder again. There was a knock on the door. Belov had arrived. Another ploy. Arrive early so they wouldn't be ready and make them feel bad if they made you wait. No problem, Tucker was ready.

Belov strode into Tucker's office, followed by his aide, and a female translator. Belov spoke English with a thick Russian accent, but some words or phrases he needed assistance with. His translator looked, and acted, like she did more for the General than just translate, but Tucker had no proof of that per se, but he had a gut feel. Belov was about Tucker's age, slightly shorter, rounder in the face, clean shaven, and considerably less hair. His official title was very long and complicated. Tucker could never remember it. His green dress uniform was well tailored and covered in gold insignia, and various medals and ribbons. This guy would give Göring a run for his money with this fancy uniform. Reichmarschall Hermann Göring, the high-ranking Nazi leader and one-time head of the Luftwaffe, was known for his elaborately designed and adorned military uniforms.

"General Belov, so good of you to come over on such short notice." Tucker made it sound like 'he' had summoned Belov, versus Belov demanding the meeting. Keep him off balance.

Belov was caught by Tucker's welcome, but quickly recovered. "General Tucker, it is I that should be thanking you for making yourself available at my request."

Tucker nodded. "You know Timmerman."

"Indeed, Colonel." said Belov, nodding to Timmerman.

"I apologize that I don't have a have a full spread to offer you today, but I promise to make it up to you."

"Understandable" said Belov. He turned and walked over to the side table where the food and drinks were. He frowned. He nodded to his aide who proceeded to get him a plate with strudel and some coffee.

"And what do we owe the pleasure today? Won't you have a seat?" Tucker motioned to a chair facing his desk.

Belov walked over and took a seat. General Tucker walked around his desk and sat down, pulled his chair forward, and crossed his hands on the desk. He didn't have to tell Belov the story about the desk, he'd already told him. Belov had seemed to enjoy the joke. He looked at Belov and waited for him to begin. His aide handed him a plate with strudel, and a cup of coffee, extra sugar. Tucker motioned for the aide to set the coffee on his desk.

"Oh yes, before I forget." Tucker picked up the cigar box on the corner of his desk. "I have a gift for you. I received my shipment of cigars. I think you'll like these. They are Cuban." Tucker opened the box to show the cigars to him. Belov leaned forward and looked at the long dark cigars filling the box. The smell of the tobacco was strong and fragrant. He nodded and smiled at Tucker. "Please take some." Tucker offered.

At that moment, Belov was taking a bite of strudel. He nodded to his aide who stepped forward and took a cigar out of the box.

"Please take a couple more." Tucker added.

Belov nodded and the aid took two additional cigars. He stepped back from the desk and well behind Belov. Tucker set the box down. Belov had not brought any gift. Another point for Tucker.

"General Tucker, I will get right to the point." said Belov, setting down the plate of half-eaten strudel on the desk.

"I appreciate that about you General, you are a man who doesn't mince words."

"Yes. Well, I, representing our delegation, have a concern that has come to our attention."

"What is this concern General?"

"We, I, demand to know what evidence is being uncovered that is not being shared with us. We are aware that some U.S. officers are working with the Polish extremists to introduce lies about the USSR in order to discredit us and to help Nazi war criminals escape justice." Belov picked up the plate and finished the strudel in a large bite. He handed the empty plate to the aide. Belov reached for the coffee then reclined back in the chair.

This was typical Soviet tactics. Come in loud and bold. Demand this. Make accusations. "Okay, there was a lot there General. First and foremost, I know for a fact that Timmerman and his team have been in close, and constant, contact with your team in sharing information as we prepare for these trials. This was all laid out in the policies and procedures we all agreed to. Is that what you are having an issue with?"

"Not exactly General Tucker. The sharing of information between our staffs has been 'proceeding' per our agreements. But, I must demand that all evidence be shared regarding the Nazi defendants, nothing should be left out or omitted."

"Yes General, I understand. Of course, I too would request that the Soviet delegation reciprocate and give us access to all the evidence you have uncovered. You currently occupy half of Berlin, the eastern half of Germany, and all of Poland. There certainly must be a wealth of documents and evidence there" Tucker turned to look at Timmerman "and I don't know if we can say we have seen everything you have uncovered yet. Have we seen it all yet Timmerman?"

"I don't have a basis to make that claim General." said Timmerman.

Belov sipped his coffee, indifferent to what General Tucker was saying.

"So, you see General, I would need you to be more specific about what you mean exactly." said Tucker as he turned back to look at Belov.

Belov looked at Timmerman, then back at Tucker, who had now leaned back in his chair and crossed his legs. "Very well." He hesitated for dramatic effect. "We demand that any documentary evidence, all of it being falsified and manufactured, pertaining to, or about, a massacre in Katyn, Poland, perpetrated by the Nazi invaders. Any and all evidence discovered will be needed. We plan to add these charges to the indictment of the Nazi defendants for these crimes against the Poles."

The Soviets were not going to back down on this Katyn issue. They were just not going to let this go thought Tucker. "So please indulge me here General. Why would you need us to, if we had any, provide you with additional evidence, given that you have already stated, enough evidence against the Germans to include this in the indictment? This 'Katyn' case sounds closed to me, at least from what you have told us." Tucker leaned forward and opened the cigar box and pulled out a cigar. He used a cigar cutter to clip the end, then lit the cigar. He leaned back in his chair and gave out a puff of smoke that rose into the air.

Belov had been selected to work at the tribunal amongst many vying for the posting. He was expected to make things happen on behalf of the USSR. One of the things he was expected to do was get the indictment to include a charge against the Nazis for the Kaytn massacre. How he did it, it didn't matter. But it would be done. Stalin demanded it. If Belov was unsuccessful, he would be removed, and most likely disappeared. This discussion with the Americans was one step in that process. Similar discussions would take place with the British and French. Today's meeting with Tucker would help keep the pressure on the Americans. "We are only attempting to work together as allies, and comrades, to ensure that we have any, and all, evidence for these trials. All we are asking is that any evidence that you turn up, that may help us in prosecuting these war criminals, you share with us." pleaded Belov. "As you mention General Tucker, the Burdenko Commission report is conclusive and definitive. The Nazis committed this atrocity. We provided the undisputed evidence to the world in an open forum. Your American journalists were there, as was Miss Harriman. They all endorsed our findings."

Tucker took his cigar out of his mouth. "Then again, I ask General Belov, what other evidence do you need if the case is conclusive?"

Belov decided he needed to cut to the chase. "We are aware General Tucker, that some of the Nazi sympathizers and Anti-Soviet Poles have been fabricating lies and falsehoods, and planting evidence about this atrocity for years in order to cover their own guilt and ruin the reputation of the great Soviet Union. It is quite probable that they are working together to plant more of this false evidence with our allies, in order to cast doubt on their overwhelming guilt of their crimes and many others. By doing this, they help to cast doubt on the legitimacy of these trials themselves, and ultimately on the punishment that they rightly deserve." Belov had stop and take a breath. He needed to convey to the Americans the concern, certainty, indignation, and righteousness on this issue.

He was reciting the script the NKVD had prepared for him. He was an actor, and Tucker's office was his stage. He added another theatrical flourish. "This is just another Nazi ploy to help cover their tracks and lay the blame of their murderous ways on the feet of others." he spat out in a disgusted tone.

Tucker had heard most of this before, from Belov and other Soviet delegates. He took a long drag from his cigar, then he exhaled slowly and let the smoke linger. "Interesting General. But this part gets me." He paused, leaning his head to one side as if thinking. "Why would the Poles want to work with some Nazis, 'if' the Nazis were guilty of the massacring their countrymen?" He puffed on his cigar again, watching Belov and waiting for his response.

"Because the London Poles are Anti-Communist and they would work with the devil himself to disrupt and discredit the Soviet Union… the country that helped to liberate their territory from the Nazi invaders. The same Soviet Union that spilled the blood of millions of Russian men and women, and tons of war material, setting their country free. What thanks do we get? They have been working against us at every turn. And now joining the Nazis in trying to blame us for killing some of those Polish prisoners. This is clearly a continuation of their deceitful and cunning ways. Falling into their trap can be dangerous." Again, Belov followed the well-honed script.

Timmerman stepped forward beside the General, leaned down, and whispered something to him. Tucker listened and nodded.

"General. We have had, shall we say, rumors really, that some files, documents, that we believe are from the German Wehrmacht pertaining to Katyn, and some possible witnesses, one of whom may be Polish, come to our attention." Tucker was now trying to push Belov, flush him out a bit more.

Belov hadn't gotten to where he was today by accident. He knew when to be loud, bellicose, brash, and when to remain calm, unflinching. He took in Tucker's words without batting an eye. For all he knew, Tucker could be playing with him, trying to distract him. "I see General. I thank you for this information. I should let you know that we have hundreds of Polish witnesses that have testified about the German atrocities at Katyn. And, we have located a cache of falsified Nazi files on Katyn that were bound for Anti-Soviet elements. These fabricated documents were clearly being spirited away from Berlin in order to be used against the Soviet Union." Belov was referring to documents found with a dead Nazi General who was attempting to break out of Berlin just before the city fell. The dead General had been carrying orders from the German High Command to get the records of the German investigation into the Katyn massacre to either the British or Americans zones.

"Very interesting General. This is new information. Maybe we have come across some similar "falsified" documents also. Would it be possible to see the documents that you were able to liberate?" Tucker had no clue as to whether Walters or anyone else had come across any information yet, but he wanted Belov to believe they might have. He wanted to turn the tables again on Belov.

Belov considered whether he should share any further information with Tucker. If the Americans had come across documents from the Germans, it would be best to discredit them now. "As the Red Army valiantly surrounded and reduced the German capital, we intercepted some documents being transported by a detachment under the direction of a General Reiniger as he fled Berlin. He was operating under direct orders of the OKW Army High Command. Some of the documents were destroyed, but some were recovered. We believe that these documents were clearly falsified and were to have been used to discredit the Soviet Union and spread lies and misinformation."

"I assume that means that we can't see these documents?" asked Tucker sarcastically, smiling at Belov.

"It would serve no purpose General. It does mean that clearly falsified, and incomplete, documents being transported out of the Nazi capital on the orders of the General Staff surely cannot be legitimate. The only reasons possible for the General Staff secretly taking documentation would be to sow disinformation and distrust somehow, or as a means to try to save their own necks. Clearly both of these reasons make sense and are plausible. Don't you agree?"

"I think I have my answer." said Tucker, giving up on his request.

"Very good General. I will assign Captain Sergeov on our staff to work with your staff regarding this evidence and any others that may show up in the course of your investigations."

"Thank you General for the offer, but I think we should examine the evidence first in greater detail, just to make certain that it is not legitimate or admissible. As you said, these Poles and Germans are a pretty cunning lot, and I am almost certain now that we have received the same type of falsified documents you have. Thank you for your offer of assistance though." said Tucker. If Belov thought they had some evidence, and the Soviets wanted it, then why not let him think he had it.

"May I remind the General that we are against any evidence being introduced by these war criminals regarding Katyn as part of their defense. This would be a breach of our agreement." Belov rose from his chair and gave Tucker a smile and nod. "Very well General. I believe we are done here today." He turned and headed out of Tuckers office, followed by his aide and translator.

Tucker turned in his chair and looked at Timmerman, rolling his eyes. "What do you think?"

Timmerman walked over and took a seat. "I'd say they seem to know a lot, and, they seem worried about having this stuff come out."

"Agreed. Let's get Walters in here."

BELOV KNEW THE Americans and the British were aware of, or in possession of, some evidence. NKVD men had been watching and following several of the staff and investigators, and they had informants working at the hotels and within the Palace itself. Tucker said he had some evidence already, or that he was going to receive some. He wasn't sure if Tucker really meant it, or not. If they did have it already, Belov would have to arrange for it to shared officially, so he could discredit it. He had just delivered his verbal request, now he would put it in writing. If Tucker was waiting for documents or evidence on Katyn to surface, he would have work hard to make sure it didn't reach his desk, nor any of the Nazi defendants.

The Nazis and Soviets had competing investigations and conclusions as to who was responsible for the Katyn massacre. Belov had briefly worked on the developing the Burdenko report. The conclusion as to who was responsible, the Germans, had been decided before the investigation began, so the job was simply to make the facts fit the conclusion. Belov had no idea if the Germans had committed the crime, or if it had been his own countrymen. And he didn't care. His job now was to follow orders and relentlessly push the narrative that the Germans must pay for this atrocity. The Nazis were clearly war criminals, the evidence abundant and overwhelming. The Soviet Union would not be branded the same.

DOUG JOINED TIMMERMAN and Burton in General Tucker's office later that afternoon. Doug struggled with whether or not to inform them that he was in possession of the Katyn documents. He hadn't actually gone through the contents of the cases, but he felt confident that they were authentic. Whether what they said was true or not, he didn't know. Anyone could manufacture evidence or come to a convenient conclusion about the facts of a crime. Doug decided he would omit the truth about having the documents. For now, at least.

In the meeting, Doug explained how he had met with a German officer in Hannover on the lead he'd received from Bauer. Ruessel said he had been at Katyn during an investigation by the Nazis, and that he could provide documents of some sort. Doug had planned to meet with him again, but then Burton explained that the German had 'disappeared'.

"You mean he just walked out of the hospital? Did you guys have him under guard?" asked an astonished Tucker.

"Not exactly General. You see, he was 'taken' from the hospital. We're not sure by who, or where to." offered Burton. He was embarrassed to have to admit this, but he tried to put a good face on it.

Tucker looked at everyone in the room. "So, this guy was some sort of potential witness, and had documents to share, and he gets nabbed?" Tucker had a disappointed frown on his face.

Timmerman shared with Doug and Burton what Belov had said in the meeting about documents and witnesses. When he mentioned

Reiniger, Doug interrupted him. "Excuse me Sir, did you say Reinger, General Reiniger?"

"Yes, I believe that is what General Belov said. Why, does it mean something?" Timmerman asked Doug.

"Actually yes. That is who Ruessel, this German Major, said he was an adjutant to, and that they had been on an assignment, on orders from Jodl."

Tucker looked at Timmerman.

"Belov said they had intercepted documents sent out by the German High Command." recalled Timmerman.

"Are we talking about the same documents?" asked Tucker.

The men sat thinking for a moment. Then Burton offered "Is it possible there were multiple sets of these documents?"

"If that were the case, then it seems the Soviets have their hands on one set." said Timmerman. "Said they got them off a dead Nazi General trying to escape Berlin."

"It's possible." said Tucker. "And if they do, they know what is in the documents and they don't want anyone seeing it. Belov comes marching in here accusing us of having documents and information, and not sharing it with them. Hell, I just let him think that we might have our hands on a set. I don't mind seeing that blowhard squirm."

Doug was now in a bind. He had the documents. The Soviets are accusing the Americans of having these documents, and the General just made the Soviets think he had them. If he confessed to having the documents, what would happen to them? What would be done with them? Would they be obligated to sharing the contents with Jodl's defense team? We would look like we were siding with the Germans over the Soviets. The Soviets would not be happy about that. Or would we not admit to having them and just hold onto them, which then put us in the position of withholding evidence. Doug knew that evidence got withheld in cases all over the country, all over the world, and big and small crimes alike.

But the whole point behind these trials, at least to his understanding, was a bigger, more profound sense of justice. Not just finding fact, the truth, and making a historical record of the crimes committed during the war. But as importantly, establishing what conduct political and military leaders would be held accountable for in the future. These trials were high stake, for everyone personally involved in conducting them, to countries like Germany and Japan, and to the rest of the world who was watching.

And then there were the Poles. The Poles believed it was the Soviets who committed the massacre, and that it was their right to demand justice. Just as important, they wanted to return to their country and govern it as they saw fit. But the Soviets had invaded Poland, first in 1939, then again in 1944 while pushing the Nazis back into Germany. Now at the conclusion of the war, the Soviets occupied their country. The Soviets sat as members of the tribunal and Stalin seemingly had no intention of handing over Polish territory to those who accused him of war crimes.

"Maybe they learned about Ruessel?" said Doug, coming back to the conversation.

"If so, then they may be responsible for his disappearance." said Burton.

"Any more follow up with this Pole you were talking about before?" Tucker asked Doug.

"No more contact yet Sir, but I was hoping to try to meet with him sometime soon. The Poles are really wanting me to meet with him."

"Well, when you can, do so. But let's be careful about this. We know the Soviets have eyes and ears all over." Tucker knew the Soviets were watching the Americans and British, and in turn, Tucker knew that the Americans were watching the Soviets.

"Maybe take Bolinger along with you, you know, for safety reasons." said Burton.

"Good idea" agreed Timmerman.

"As usual, keep us posted Doug." said Tucker. He tamped out his cigar and rose from his chair "If you gentlemen will excuse me, I have another obligation to attend to his evening." The men rose to leave. "Another meeting, and the Soviets will be there blathering on about how we aren't listening to or respecting them, not sharing information, this or that wasn't what was agreed to, the same bullshit."

DOUG HAD A driver take him out to Chet's camp. Chet hadn't been expecting him, but Chet treated him to dinner at the camp mess. The food inside the American camp was plentiful and nutritious. It didn't taste bad either. Food in the Stalag housing the DEFs was not. Food was scarce as well to civilian population, though there had been a plan to attempt to increase food available through the International Red Cross. Displaced persons, including Holocaust survivors, were allocated more generous rations, where available. General Clay, the Deputy Military Governor of the American zone, was becoming increasingly concerned about the humanitarian and political situation due to food supply and distribution. As Doug ate his plate of pork chops, mashed potatoes, corn, and bread, he realized that food was now a weapon, a punishment, or a reward. All the Nazi prisoners in the camps and the multitude of displaced persons aimlessly wandering the cities and countryside of the devasted country were nominally at the mercy of those with eggs, butter, milk, bread. These things may actually be more powerful than machine guns, artillery, or even atom bombs. Food could motivate, intimidate, and kill, depending how it was used.

Doug had agreed to come to Nuremberg work on the war crimes trials because he felt it was his duty to his country, and because he felt bringing justice to those who had abused power and brought cruelty, oppression, and inhumanity to millions of people. After all that had happened before and during the war, those responsible had to be held accountable. The decision of the victorious Allies to pursue justice through these war crimes trials was a noble one, or at least he had thought it was. Now as he sat here eating unlimited food, he thought about the women, children, and elderly that were starving outside the camp gates. About the city devastated by Allied bombing. The bodies still being dug up from beneath the rubble. The prisoners in the Stalag next door being slowly starved to death. The Poles desperately trying to find someone to help them attempt to regain control of their country from a new world power. And the utter destruction of two cities in Japan, and the inhabitants within them, by his own country.

And then there was this current mess he found himself in with this information about a massacre, and atrocity, in Poland, seemingly by an ally of America, who would shortly be sitting alongside us in judgement of war criminals. His time here in Nuremberg so far had been non-stop. The work preparing for the trials was stressful, almost to the point of being overwhelming. He was mentally tired. And this Katyn investigation, or whatever he could call it, was still puzzling him. He understood why the Soviets would want this whole matter buried. He was still trying to figure out what the Americans, or the British, angle was. Tucker had indicated he was happy playing cat and mouse with the Soviets about the information they may have, but ultimately it seemed that they simply wanted the Soviets to stand down from their demand to blame this atrocity on the Germans. That would mean that Tucker, and presumably others, already knew that the Soviets were responsible. Why else fight them to keep it from becoming part of the indictment against the Nazis? Why would Tucker want him chasing down these documents, the witnesses? Was he after the truth? Wasn't that what he and Tucker, and all the others working on the tribunal, there for? The truth? Maybe, maybe not. Maybe this whole Katyn thing was embarrassing. Troubling. Inconvenient.

Chet watched Doug work his way through his meal. Doug hadn't said much and was clearly in one of his deep thought moments that Chet had witnessed from his brother over the years. Sometimes it happened during a meal, or other times during a car ride, or when they were alone, fishing on the banks of the Shiawassee River on a hot summer afternoon. Chet was fine with those silent times with his brother. After a time, Doug would emerge from these deep thoughts and engage with him again. Until then, Chet would leave him alone.

"The documents" said Doug, speaking his thoughts aloud. "aren't enough."

"Come again?" said Chet while chewing a piece of bread.

Doug was emerging from his thoughts. He sat down his fork and knife and leaned back in his chair. He looked at Chet. "We have documents, but it's always better to have witnesses." Doug proceeded to update Chet on happenings from the past couple of days. The disappearance of the German Major. The Soviets demanding that all evidence of this Katyn incident be turned over. The Soviets presumably watching, spying, on him and others in the

American and British delegations. Tucker's interest in the documents, and witnesses, if any.

"Maybe it's time that I talk to this Polish guy who supposedly has information about Katyn." said Doug, "The guy you met, the mystery man."

"I'm sure Poles would be happy to try to arrange another meeting. Assuming that the guy didn't get too spooked last time." said Chet. "Like I said, he didn't want to seem to want to be found by the Soviets."

"Right." Doug finished off his cup of coffee. "Can you see if we can arrange a meeting in the next few days?"

Chet said he would talk to the Poles again tomorrow. As he and his brother left the mess, he stopped and grabbed three apples from a bowl of fruit and put them in his pocket. On the ride back into the city, Doug asked the driver to pull over at one point next to a woman carrying a young girl on her back and holding the hand of a young boy walking next to her. The woman was startled and scared when the jeep stopped next to them. She was even more startled when the American officer reached out and placed three red apples in her hands.

CHAPTER TWENTY-SIX

August 28, 1945

GENERAL TUCKER WAS going to stay for ten, maybe fifteen, minutes before he bade farewell to the other guests at the gathering. The party was at the large home of a former Nazi party bigshot, located outside the city center. The house hadn't sustained much damage and was being used by members of the French delegation as housing and office space. Tucker was surprised the Soviets hadn't gotten their hands on this real estate before the French had. Given that the Americans had held this part of the country, they had obviously given the French the first shot at claiming it for their needs. Tucker was tired. The conversations he'd had this evening were mundane. The food was good though, as were the French wines served. The women present at the party were a welcome sight, and that is why he had endured up to this point.

Across from where Tucker was sipping his wine and pretending to be interested in a conversation with some members of the French delegation, Colonel Burton entered the room. The party had started well over two hours ago, so he entered unnoticed. He worked his way through the guests to where Timmerman was standing near the bar, sipping a brandy. Burton asked the bartender for a glass of wine, something not too dry. He then leaned over and whispered something into Timmerman's ear. Timmerman turned his head to Burton, who nodded. After Burton received his glass of wine, Timmerman motioned for him to follow him over to General Tucker.

Tucker saw them approaching and he excused himself from the group he was standing with and walked toward Timmerman and Burton. Tucker looked at Burton "Nice of you to join us Colonel. A bit late though. I'm on my way out actually. How about you Timmerman? You staying any longer?" He sat his half empty glass of wine on tray table of a passing waiter. "Find anything, or anyone, interesting tonight?"

"Nothing especially intriguing General." said Timmerman. "But Burton here has some news."

"Spit it out Burton," said Tucker.

"Well Sir, we have located the documents.' said Burton in a hushed voice.

Tucker raised an eyebrow and looked at Burton, then Timmerman. "Where? Doug?"

Burton nodded in the affirmative.

"Have you looked at them yet? Are they what we thought they might be?"

"Not yet Sir. We've yet to evaluate them. We've just recently secured them." said Burton.

"Okay. Well, let's see what you guys make of them."

"We'll go through them tomorrow General." said Timmerman. He finished off the last bit of brandy and set his glass on a side table. "And Walters?"

"Nothing" said Tucker. "Not yet."

DOUG CHECKED FOR messages after Chet dropped him at the hotel, but there were none. He stopped at the hotel desk to pick up his laundry. Alfred was there, as usual, and he handed Doug three shirts and two pair of trousers. Back in his room, Doug placed the clothes in the dresser and pulled out the bottle of whiskey. He poured a glass and took a sip. He kicked off his shoes and pulled off his trousers. He sat on the bed and pulled off his socks, throwing them into the pile of clothes accumulating on the floor near the dresser. He reached down and felt under the bed. It was gone. The case Alfred had gotten for Doug was no longer there. Doug stood up, walked over to the dresser and picked up the glass of whiskey and took another sip. He grabbed his towel, opened the door, and walked down the hallway to the bathroom.

CHAPTER TWENTY-SEVEN

August 29, 1945

DOUG SPENT MOST of the day working with his team sorting through another batch of files that the team in Berlin had sent down to them in Nuremberg. Sometime around midday, he ventured outside to get some fresh air and think. As he sat on a bench eating his cheese sandwich, Angie had appeared and sat down next to him. She too was on a lunch break. She had a tin that contained a beef stew, food she had brought from her lodging. She had remarked that she hoped it would taste better on the second day than it had on the first. Their cook was a British Army Sergeant whose cooking was considered bland, even for British fare. They both laughed. Doug asked if she would have any free time in the next couple of days. He was scheduled to fly up to Berlin to work with the team there for a few days, and he thought it would be nice if they could spend some time together before he left. She said she should be able to find some time for him, maybe on Friday or Saturday. Or both she said with a sly smile. Doug said he could arrange that. They agreed on Friday night. They both finished their breaks and headed back to their respective offices.

Chet was waiting for Doug when he exited the Palace grounds. He said that that the Poles had been able to arrange a meeting for him and the mystery man tomorrow afternoon. Was Doug available? If Doug didn't meet with him the next day, it might have to wait until his return from Berlin. He told Chet could meet tomorrow afternoon, as he had a meeting in the morning he couldn't miss. Chet offered Doug a ride back to the hotel, and Doug took his offer. On the ride to the hotel, they discussed who should go tomorrow to meet the mystery man. Chet said he figured that the fewer, the better. Maybe just Wojcik and Doug. Doug said that he may have to bring along Bolinger, as instructed by Burton and Timmerman. Chet wasn't sure if that would work or not, but if he had to bring him, the three of them should be it. Doug said he wished Chet would be along, but Chet said he'd already met the mystery man and didn't need to meet the guy ever again. They agreed that Chet would bring Wojcik to hotel before noon. He would have the directions to the meeting place.

CHAPTER TWENTY-EIGHT

August 30, 1945

DOUG WALKED TO Timmerman's office and knocked on the door. Timmerman was in and he beckoned him to enter. "Doug. What can I help you with?"

"Nothing Sir, I just wanted to drop off these reports for you. This one here goes over the schedule for the team next week in Berlin." Doug handed him several file folders.

"Okay great. Thanks for working on these. Do you have everything you need for the trip?" said Timmerman as he took the files and placed them on his desk, opening the one file with the schedule in it. "Thanks for taking this trip for me. The General needs me here next week for something."

"No worries Colonel. Glad to help." It was already 11 a.m. and Doug needed to head back to the hotel. "If that'll be all Sir."

"Yes, yes." said Timmerman as he scanned the schedule in front of him.

Doug turned and headed out the door.

"Oh, by the way, any more progress with the investigation?" asked Timmerman, without looking up from the file.

Doug had decided he wouldn't mention the meeting with the Pole unless he was asked about it. If he didn't have to take Bolinger, or anyone except the brother, that would be best. "As a matter of fact, Colonel, I'm supposed to meet with the Pole who says he may have information."

Timmerman lifted his head from the paperwork and looked at Doug. "Really? When is this meeting supposed to take place?"

"Actually, Sir, this afternoon."

"I see. Have you told Burton?"

"I was actually on my way over there to tell him and see if Bolinger was available to join." This was a lie. Doug wasn't sure how convincing it was, or if Timmerman heard it in his voice.

Timmerman looked at Doug. It was odd that Doug hadn't mentioned the meeting without him asking. "Very good. I'll let you handle it. Just give me a report on it after."

"Yes Sir. I hope this guy shows up and this isn't all just a waste of time." Doug tried to sound as if the meeting wasn't a big deal. He wasn't sure if this was convincing either. Doug saluted Timmerman, who saluted back. He turned and left the office.

Doug walked to Burton's office. His aide said he was in and that Doug could enter. Doug explained to Burton what he had told Timmerman. Burton asked the aide to go fetch Bolinger, whose office was just a few doors down. Bolinger appeared and they discussed that he should accompany Doug to this meeting with the Pole. Bolinger said he would go down and get a jeep arranged and meet him at the front entrance. Doug thanked Burton for his assistance, and as he turned to exit his office, Burton called out "Good hunting."

"BUT THE LAWS OF GOD AND OF MAN HAVE BEEN VIOLATED AND THE GUILTY MUST NOT GO UNPUNISHED. NOTHING SHALL SHAKE OUR DETERMINATION TO PUNISH THE WAR CRIMINALS EVEN THOUGH WE MUST PURSUE THEM TO THE ENDS OF THE EARTH".

From President Truman's Address before a Joint Session of the Congress.
April 16, 1945

CHAPTER TWENTY-NINE

August 30, 1945

CHET AND WOJCIK were waiting at the Grand Hotel when Doug and Bolinger pulled up in a jeep. Doug explained that Bolinger would be going along, but Wojcik was not happy about it. He was uncomfortable bringing along someone he didn't know, especially after how his brother acted the last time they met. Chet suggested that he should go along as well, but Doug said that the three of them would be enough. Chet insisted that Doug bring along his sidearm, so Doug went up to his room to get it. When he returned Chet pulled him aside and asked if Doug wanted him to follow the group, at a safe distance, to the meeting. Doug said he thought they'd be fine, but he knew that there was a fifty-fifty chance that Chet would follow anyways.

Wojcik, Bolinger, and Doug got in the jeep and started off with the directions Wojcik had. After about an hour of turn after turn, they reached an area where Wojcik said was familiar. It was the same square where the church was that they had met his brother at last time. The only difference this time is that the directions indicated they would meet in the four-story building just to the north of the church. Building 744. They parked the jeep near the church, and they all climbed out. They all scanned the area looking for anyone that may have followed them. No one seemed to have followed them. The area wasn't totally deserted, as there were a couple of old men digging through the remains of a building just down the street, and a woman carrying a bucket of water across from the church. She looked at the men warily, then scurried into what had been a front entrance to a building and disappeared.

The men looked up at Building 744. It was relatively intact. There was a front staircase that led up to the front entrance. The railings to the stairs were missing. The front door was wooden with the glass knocked out. The building to the right of 744 hadn't fared as well, with the third and fourth floors destroyed, and rubble strewn on the ground below. The building to the left looked to be habitable, except for the ground floor retail space that had been gutted. Doug told Wojcik and Bolinger to stay with the jeep, but Bolinger said he should go inside with Doug. Doug considered it, then agreed. Wojcik would need to stay with the jeep. Wojcik wanted to go inside to see his brother, but he agreed to stay put.

Doug and Bolinger walked across the street and climbed the front stairs to the entrance of 744. Doug pushed the heavy wooden door open, and they walked into the building foyer. A large staircase led up to the floors above. They stood there for a few moments looking around, but they heard nothing. Then they heard a sound above them. They looked up through the open staircase and saw a man leaning just over the edge of the railing on the top floor looking down on them.

"Colonel Walters?" asked the man.

"Yes, I'm Walters" replied Doug, still looking up at the man standing high above them.

"I thought I made it clear that you were to come alone."

"Well. I wanted to bring a colleague along. Mainly for safety reasons. We don't venture out alone much." offered Doug. "Your brother is with us. He's just outside with our jeep."

"Yes, I saw him."

Chet was right, this guy was very cautious. "We're here to listen to what you can tell us. About Katyn." Doug looked over at Bolinger. They weren't sure what to do at this point.

After a few moments, the man told them to come up. They climbed the staircase up to the fourth-floor landing. To the left, there was a dark hallway leading toward the back of the building. To the right, a short landing with doorways opposite each other. The door on the left was open. Doug and Bolinger walked over to the open doorway and looked in the room. Light from the large front window flooded the room. The window overlooked the church and the square. Below as Wojcik leaning against the jeep, smoking a cigarette. There stood the man at the far side of the room opposite the door. He was wearing a grey jacket with the collar pulled up, and a hat pulled down low. Doug slowly walked into the room, followed by Bolinger. As Doug got within about 15 feet from him, he stopped. He could see the man had been injured on his head, and his right ear was missing.

"I am Lt. Colonel Walters. And this is Major Bolinger with the British Army." They all stood there awkwardly, looking at each other. Doug glanced around the space. The room was a living room area with a large sofa placed against the wall under the window. A small table sat next to it. A kitchen area was off to the right, with a table and chair off to one side. A door led off the kitchen somewhere, and another door off the living room led presumably to a bedroom. The room was barren otherwise, all of the belongings had been removed. "I've, we've, been told you have some valuable information to share with us about Katyn?" Doug figured he'd just cut to the chase.

The man looked at Doug and Bolinger warily, studying them, trying to decide if he could trust them. Finally, he spoke. "Were you followed?"

"We didn't notice anyone following us." said Doug.

"You are working on the war crimes tribunal?"

"Yes, I am a lawyer and investigator on the American delegation. Bolinger here is with the British delegation."

"I have information about Katyn."

"Okay. That is what your brother told us. That's why we've come here to meet you." Doug wanted to put the man at ease as he was obviously not comfortable with them yet. "Do you have some documentation for us?"

"No. I have no documentation per se."

"Okay, then what information do you have?" asked Bolinger.

"I was there."

"You have been to Katyn? Did you see the bodies?"

"Yes. But not after they were exhumed." The man paused. "I was one of the bodies."

Both Doug and Bolinger had to let that sink in. They weren't exactly clear on what he meant. Doug looked at Bolinger, and then back to the man. "Do you mean you were there when the massacre occurred?"

"I was there, but not as an observer. I was a victim. I was shot and thrown into the pit, along with thousands of others. All I have are my identity papers, and a couple of spent cartridges that were used. To shoot us." The man had replayed what had happened in his mind many times in the years since the massacre. He had tried to understand what had happened to him. He had recurring nightmares about those moments leading up to him blacking out. "I lost an ear in my 'murder'." the man said, turning his head slightly and lifting his hat to show where his ear had once been. There was extensive scar tissue and missing hair on the side of his head.

"So, how are you here now?" asked Bolinger, with some skepticism, or incredulity, in his voice.

"And you know who did it?" said Doug. "Tell us what happened."

ONCE YOU'VE CLAWED out of your own grave, there is only upside to your life moving forward.

When his mind started to wake up, nothing seemed to connect in an orderly fashion. He was sensing and irritation in his nose. He couldn't see or hear anything, but he actually didn't understand what those things were anyways at that point. Electricity bolted through his body and his limbs reflexively attempted to pull him into a fetal position. Another jolt. He recognized and felt that one. Again. This time his right arm moved a little, but something was holding it down. Again. His legs twitched and pulled upward toward his chest. As he began to understand that he had a body and was trying to gain control of it, he started to tremble as if he was having a seizure of some sort. His hands tingled and his legs felt as if they were cramping, his body writhing frantically to wake up.

He was lying on his side, with his right arm extending behind him. He lay atop what he seemed like a pile of lifeless bodies, some partially covered with dirt. His right arm was pinned by another body and he struggled to pull it free. He attempted to gain some vision with his eyes, but it was nighttime and pitch black out. He kept blinking and trying to focus on something, anything. As his right arm began to pull free, he lifted his head slightly.

Wham.

That is when he first felt the intense pain. His eyes rolled back in their sockets as he tried not to scream. He now remembered where he was, and a deep sense of fear rushed over him. He lay still for quite a while and waited for the pain to dissipate. As a physician, he knew something was wrong, so he lay there for a moment and tried to diagnose his condition. His limbs, though aching a bit, seemed to be in working order. There was the blood on his face and in his nose, and the searing pain in his head. How had he gotten here? In this condition and place?

His eyes flashed open. I've been shot!!!

Am I dead? Is this my passage to heaven? If I've been shot, how can I be thinking, feeling this pain? Clearly, I'm alive. I remember now the events leading up to his arrival here. The ride in the truck. The smell of pines. I've been shot in the head. Does the rest of my body will work?

He took several deep breaths and made a second attempt at sitting upright. Using his arms, legs, and shoulders he gently raised his head and neck. The intense pain was there again, but having anticipated it, he was prepared. He slowly made it into a sitting position and then stopped, as he dealt with the pain. His arms were secured behind his back, which made the process of sitting upright that much harder. He wriggled his hands and wrists back and forth until the cloth tie binding his hands loosened enough for him to untie himself.

His left hand instinctively moved toward his face. Something sticky covered his face and his hand tried to brush off the caked-on substance from his eyes and his nostrils. As he wiped his face it disturbed the flies that had gathered. The flies reluctantly dispersed. He began to open his eyes, using his fingers to wipe away the blood that had congealed in his eye sockets and in his nose. He spat dirt and blood from his mouth. His eyes slowly adjusted to the darkness and he could see he was sitting amongst many bodies in a ditch. In fact, he was sitting atop several lifeless, unmoving, bodies. His instinct was to check them for life, but he knew that there was no life left in them. There was nothing more than the sound of the woods in the evening darkness.

The intense pain receded, and was replaced by a steady, throbbing pain. He had gathered himself enough and made an additional assessment. He reached up with his right arm and touched the right side of his head, where most of the pain was emanating. It felt tacky, spongey. He gingerly felt around and could feel skin, hair, and his cheekbone. But something was missing. He felt again. Where his ear should be, there was only mangled flesh and an open wound.

Okay. That was the extent of the damage.

In the darkness, he felt around with his hands and was able to find a woolen scarf among the bodies. He fashioned it into a head bandage wrap. There was still some blood flow from the wound, but some clotting had taken place and the bandage was helping to stem bleeding. He eventually clawed his way up the side of the earthen ditch and pull himself out. As he lay there catching his breath on the precipice of the grave, he felt with his hand some spent cartridge casings strewn among the dirt. He grabbed a few and pocketed them. Who knew, one of these casings may have been the one that took his ear and nearly killed him.

Unbeknownst to him, a few yards away in the same mass grave was another body that had been deposited there a few hours after his had been dumped. The body was lain out nicely as a normal body may be put in a grave. The legs were drawn together and the arms folded across his chest. An overcoat was draped over the torso and head, covering the handsome face of the soldier. It also covered some missing teeth, and half of the backside of his skull. A small cross had been respectfully placed atop the overcoat of the fallen comrade. This was the body of the man that had saved his life.

He wasn't sure where he was other than the woods. But all woods have a way out, and he picked a direction and started walking through the brush. Later he would come upon a small village, where he was taken in and cared for by a couple of the villagers. He spoke enough Russian to get by.

Over time, he would move around as necessary to avoid detection from the whatever authorities were occupying the area at the time. Because he was a physician, his talents were welcomed almost everywhere he ventured during his travels. Providing medical care and first aid to those that had little to no access made him, at time, invaluable. Sometimes he needed to hide in the shadows, other times he was able to hide in broad daylight. As the war was drawing to a close and the Soviets were retaking huge swaths of Polish territory from the Germans, he retreated alongside Poles and Germans westward into the German Reich. He spoke some German, so he was able to make his way into the country as the war was playing out its final days.

After hostilities ended in May, he was able to receive food from the Allies, and because of his medical background, he volunteered at medical aid stations run by the Americans. His help to the Americans was rewarded with extra rations. More importantly, he learned from the Americans that preparations were underway to prosecute Nazi war criminals and hold them responsible. That is when he decided he needed to share his story with those that could bring justice to perpetrators of the massacre at Katyn. He set off for Nuremberg.

CHAPTER THIRTY

August 30, 1945

WOJCIK FINISHED A cigarette while he waited patiently outside with the jeep. The late August sun was warm as he stared up at the building that Colonel Walters and the British officer had gone into. It had now been over ten minutes, so he assumed that the men were able to find his brother inside. He kept looking up at the fourth-floor window to see if he could see them, or, get a glimpse of his brother. He saw no one. If the Americans could help his brother, it could potentially lead to helping his comrades in the camp, and other Poles scattered throughout Europe. Maybe his brother could come back to the camp and stay with him.

He had received a partial pack of cigarettes, obtained from Major Walters when they were back at the camp. He pulled the pack out of his front shirt pocket and withdrew another stick. The American cigarettes were good. He put the pack back in his shirt and started to reach into his pant pocket for his lighter. A hand knocked the cigarette out of his mouth and clamped over his mouth. He felt an intense pain in his back. He instinctively reached up with his hands to grab the arm and hand on his mouth, frantically trying to pull it off. As he did so, the hand on his mouth pulled his head backwards. The pain in his back was searing, and his legs were giving way. Then he felt something sharp and metallic push into his neck. His eyes began to close, and he was feeling warm all over. He saw a man moving toward him. Then he looked up at the sun, relaxed, and closed his eyes.

DOUG AND BOLINGER listened intently to the man tell his story. The circumstances seemed improbable, but they couldn't help but believe every word he said. The story was brutal and sad. Doug had been around enough witnesses in his career to know when someone was lying, embellishing, or telling the truth.

After the man finished, they all stood in silence for a minute. Doug spoke first. "What do you want to do? How do you want to proceed?"

"I want to testify about what happened. About how the Soviets murdered thousands of my countrymen. I want justice."

"I understand. I would want the same." Doug said in agreement. "And I understand that this will be very, complicated, and dangerous." Doug was trying to process what he had just heard from the man and try to figure out next steps.

"I am a doctor, and I was, I mean, I am, a reservist in the Polish Army. I want the Soviets to know that they did not kill Captain Piotr..." He stopped mid-sentence. All three men heard the sound. It came from below them, from out in hallway from the staircase.

Both Doug and Bolinger turned their heads toward the doorway, but they stood motionless. They wanted to listen for more sounds, if any. The Pole took a couple of steps toward the window, just enough to look out on the square and see the jeep. His brother was no longer standing by the jeep. He didn't see him anywhere. Maybe his brother had come inside the building.

There was another sound, like a foot stepping on broken glass. Bolinger looked at Doug and motioned for him to step back into the room slightly, quietly. At the same time, he slowly put his hand on brown leather holster and slowly withdrew his service revolver, holding it by his side. Doug had forgotten that he too had a sidearm, so he reached down and withdrew his .45 pistol. He hadn't drawn a weapon in the line of service in several years, though he certainly knew how to use one.

Doug was unsure who could be in the building. Was it Wojcik coming up to see his brother? A local German scavenging? Or....

Two men in dark suits burst into the room with guns drawn, pointing them at the American and Brit. Both Doug and Bolinger reacted by retreating back into the room several feet, with their weapons trained on the intruders. Both of the intruders were sweating, and one of them had what looked like blood splattered on his dark suit. One of the men spoke. "We don't want any problems with you." The man had a noticeable Russian accent.

"It looks like we have a problem here none-the-less." said Doug in a calm voice. His pistol was pointed at the man who spoke, and he stared into his eyes. The man stared back with his gun pointed at Doug. "Who are you exactly, and what do you want?"

"We are here for him." said the man, nodding his head very lightly toward where the Pole stood behind him in the room.

Doug glanced over at the other intruder who was in a standoff with Bolinger. Each man was only about ten feet from each other. If anyone decided to shoot, it would be hard to miss the target. "This man is with us."

The Polish doctor, the Army Captain, the victim of the Katyn massacre, was standing behind the American and British officers. His nightmare had come true. The Soviets had found him, though he assumed they only knew of existence only recently. He had survived his murder at their hands. He had eluded them for years after he had extricated himself from a mass grave full of his countrymen. He knew the fact that he had survived, and was a witness to their atrocity at Katyn, they would do their best to silence him. A witness like him would be credible, believable, and be able to give details like no other witness to mass murder. He had been in the grave itself. He would use his voice to bring the murders, and Stalin, to justice. He may be able to help secure the freedom of his country from the Soviets with his testimony. The Americans, British, and French, and the rest of the world for that matter, would certainly hold the Soviets accountable.

"My orders are to bring this man." said the intruder. A bead of sweat rolled down the side of his cheek. It was clear from his voice that there was no room for discussion. "We can do this without anyone getting hurt." The stalemate continued.

"As I said before, he is with us." said Doug. Adrenaline was racing through his body, so he had to focus on staying calm and not getting too excited. The palm of his hand holding the pistol was getting sweaty, and he was trying to keep his grip on the weapon and not twitch.

Bolinger knew enough about Walters from his file to know that he would not willingly give up the Pole to these Soviets. He had hoped that they could have retrieved the Pole without incident and let him disappear into American or British custody. He too was under orders. As much as he didn't want the Soviets to walk away with the Pole, he didn't plan to get killed protecting him. He was sure that the Soviets wanted to avoid any bloodshed, as much he did. Especially blood from an American or British officer in Nuremberg. The diplomatic and political fallout would be dramatic. It could possibly upset the coming war crimes trials. He also knew that these Soviets were most likely under orders to retrieve, or kill, the Pole. Stalin would not allow a witness to the massacre of Katyn to be heard from. Especially this witness who would speak out about what the truth really was. A witness like this would obliterate the propaganda and lies the Soviets had built over the years regarding Katyn and expose them as the same type of war criminals as the Nazis. The Soviets would never budge. Neither would Walters. Only Bolinger could break the stalemate.

"Colonel Walters" said Bolinger "might we consider a compromise?"

"I'm not sure what options are available Captain." Doug sensed that this was not going to end well. He was putting his life, and that of Bolinger's, on the line. If he gave up the Pole, he knew he would never be heard from again. If he took the first shot, he might survive. They probably stood a fifty-fifty chance. This is not what he had signed up for when he agreed to work in Nuremberg. He wanted to help prosecute Nazi war criminals. Not be in the O.K. Corral facing off with some Soviet goons. Nevertheless, here he was. "Unless our friends here want to reconsider."

Bolinger turned to his left and pulled the trigger. The shot broke the silence and startled Doug and the intruders, but no one else pulled their triggers. Bolinger had hit the target. The bullet had penetrated the right front of the skull and exited the back left, spraying blood and brain matter across the room. The Pole never saw it coming. His body fell backward into the wall and then slumped to the floor.

Doug kept his gun pointed at the intruder but turned his head and could see the Pole on the floor, lifeless. He looked at Bolinger, shocked and confused. "What the hell!!! Why?" he yelled.

Bolinger turned back and pointed his gun again at the Soviet in front of him. The Soviets kept their guns pointed at Doug and Bolinger. "Let's just say I wasn't prepared to get into a skirmish with these fellows. I had no intention of dying for that man. I'm assuming that our friends here might have been given orders to take care of us along with our Pole friend here, if they had to. So, let's all just take it easy. You lads can just plan on going back down the stairs and getting out of here. Remember, you are in the American zone. Let's not make this into an episode that will cause us any more trouble."

Seeing that the Pole was eliminated, the Soviets decided they no longer needed to be there. They both slowly began backing up toward the door, arms still raised and pointing at the American and Brit. They walked backwards out of the room and into the hallway. They lowered their weapons and started down the stairs. Once they were out of sight, both Doug and Bolinger holstered their weapons. Doug walked over to the Pole. Blood was flowing out of his head and spread across the wood floor.

"Why did you kill him you bastard?"

"Good god man... the war is over. We Brits aren't looking for any more fights right now. Let's get on with these trials. The bloody Huns are guilty as hell. We all know it. I'd be happy to just throw the lot of them into the gas chambers." Bolinger walked over to the window and looked out. He saw the two Soviets walk down the front entrance steps. They scanned the area, then started walking down the street toward where they had parked their car.

"You can't mean that... you're a lawyer... don't you believe in justice?".

"Oh, there will be justice alright. The Huns will get what's due them. We British don't have the strength to fight these Soviets. Not right now anyways. And we sure as hell don't want you naïve Americans dragging us into anything anytime soon. Let's just leave this little unfortunate episode alone. It shouldn't stop us from punishing these Nazis."

"What will Burton and Timmerman, let alone Turner, say to all this? How will we explain?"

"Colonel, are you that naïve? Why do you think I was asked to come along with you?" Bolinger thought Walters would have caught on already.

"You let them follow us, right? You used me the whole time." said Doug, disappointed.

"I do as I am told. I am a good soldier. The Poles only trusted you, and your brother. We knew you would eventually find him."

"So, you agree with them, with all of this?"

"Who? Burton? Timmerman? It doesn't matter what I think. Let's be real man. The war is over. Let's wrap up the loose ends and prepare for the next one."

"What about Katyn?"

"What about it?"

"You heard it from guy you just murdered. The Soviets are guilty as hell on this massacre, and you're okay with letting them sit in judgement of anyone?"

"I would suggest you forget all about this Colonel. For your own sake. Go back and tell them nothing. We didn't find anything conclusive. Or tell them that we found the Pole dead. End of story."

"Just like that you can walk away from this?"

"Listen, they respect and trust you. That is why you were chosen I suspect. Now go back and tell them what they need to hear. These trials are too important not to move forward. It's not about the truth, or justice. It's about surviving. We Brits once ruled the world. Now we need to dust ourselves off and rebuild. We need time. We don't have your industry, your firepower. For god's sake, your new atomic weapon should keep these Soviets off us for a while."

"Well, I'm not sure I can walk away so easily from the truth."

"Colonel, overall, I like you. I'm sorry it turned out this way. I think under different circumstances we could be great friends. But I would strongly suggest you 'do' forget about all this. Give the right report. For your own sake."

"Are you threatening me?"

"Certainly not. All I am saying is that this is bigger than you or me. I'm not sure if I am safe or not. I might just be expendable myself. In fact, I'd bet on it."

"What about him?" Doug looked back on the Pole on the floor. Doug's emotions were on edge. This man had been alive and talking with them only minutes ago, explaining to them how he had survived a massacre. He had risen from a grave. Now he lay dead on the floor of an empty apartment, in a bombed-out building, in a

German city far from his homeland. He had wanted justice for those who had perished. He had believed that he could get that justice by reaching out to the Americans. This belief had cost him his life.

"I'll make certain he is disposed of." replied Bolinger.

"Clean operation."

"All accept you. And your brother."

"What about my brother?"

"It's my understanding that he knows something about all of this Katyn thing, and his Polish friends and their stories."

"He really doesn't know anything about all of this." Doug was now worried, as he had been the one to involve Chet in this thing. But actually, Chet had involved him with the Poles after he had first arrived.

"That may be, but they may use him to ensure your cooperation."

"Cooperation?"

"Yes. This thing needs to go away."

Doug was trying to process everything that had just happened. How could Bolinger murder someone? Right in front of him no less. He had misread who Bolinger really was, just as he had misread Timmerman, Burton, and Tucker. He had been so stressed and consumed by his work that he hadn't put all the pieces together. "Ruessel?" Doug asked.

"Ruessel?" Bolinger turned to look at Doug.

"That was you as well, right?"

"It was arranged." Bolinger said as he walked over into the bedroom, looking for anything that shouldn't be left behind.

Doug took a last look at the Pole, and then turned and walked of the room, down the stairs, and out of the building. He crossed the street and as he approached the jeep, he saw the blood. Wojcik. Doug had forgotten all about him. He followed the trail of blood around the jeep and through the gate of the church courtyard. There along the side of the wall was the body of Wojcik. Both brothers had died on the same day, not far from each other.

Bolinger walked through the church gate and stopped. He saw Wojcik's body. "Another casualty. Poor fellow." He turned and walked to the jeep, got in, and started the engine. He sat there patiently, idling the engine.

Doug looked down on Wojcik for a few moments more, then walked over to the jeep and got in.

CHAPTER THIRTY-ONE

August 31, 1945

DOUG COULDN'T SLEEP last night. Everything that had happened yesterday kept swirling in his mind. He didn't know what would happen next, but he was sure that he couldn't continue working with Timmerman, or Tucker. His belief in the purpose, the morality, the integrity of this war crimes tribunal was shaken. Yes, he knew the Nazis, thousands of them, were guilty of war crimes of some sort. These trials would ultimately bring most of them to some type of justice. But maybe he was naïve, like Bolinger said. He felt that if he, or anyone, found evidence of a war crime, whether it incriminated the Soviets, the British, the French, or even the Americans, it should be revealed, and should be prosecuted by the laws and rules that were being developed for the tribunal. From what Doug believed now, this is not how things would happen.

He rose early and got a driver to take him out to see Chet at the camp. He could only guess what laid ahead for him, but he wanted to square things up with Chet before things progressed. Most importantly, he didn't want to get Chet involved any further. Chet was glad to see him and asked how the meeting went. From the look on Doug's face, he knew that things had not gone well. Doug would only tell Chet that the brothers would not be returning. He wasn't supposed to tell the Poles what had happened, simply tell them he didn't know anything.

Then he told Chet to secure the documents he had retrieved from the church graveyard. Doug didn't care how he did it, but, whatever he did, keep it quiet. Doug had no idea what to expect when he returned to work that morning, but he promised to get word to Chet whatever the outcome. Doug hugged his brother and then headed to the Palace of Justice.

LT. COLONEL DOUG Walters was escorted to the interrogation room within the Palace that he been in many times before. He walked into the empty room and the door was locked behind him. After ten minutes, the door opened and a man in a dark suit, carrying a briefcase, enters and walked over to the table and sat down. He beckoned Doug to sit. Doug kept standing. The man looked at Doug "Please have a seat Colonel."

Doug pulled a chair out and took a seat "And you are?"

The man smiled at Doug but ignored his question. "Colonel Walters, I understand you have done some great work for us."

"Who is us?

The man chuckles. "Us. As is in the U.S. The United States of America."

"If you say so."

"I do say so Colonel. And so do a lot of people that matter. This tribunal for one, our government for another. In fact, the entire world will eventually say so. Oh, you might not think that way now, but give yourself some time. You are smart man Colonel. Your work in helping us keep this tribunal together will go down in history. You may be an unsung hero, but a hero none the less."

"I'm not feeling much like a hero right now."

"Of course not. That is understandable I suppose. But I guess that heroes never really feel that way." The man pulled out a folder and a small box from his briefcase. He looked over at Doug and smiled. "On behalf of your great work, we want to reward you. I have here your promotion to full Colonel." He pulled out a piece of paper and pushed it across the table toward Doug.

Doug didn't take his eyes off the man, nor look at the paper in front of him on the table.

"And here are your birds." The man opened the box with the Colonel insignia and pushed it towards Doug. "I think you are up for some sort of medal also. Not sure which one you will receive yet." He continued to smile at Doug.

"A reward huh?"

"Yes Colonel, a reward. I am also prepared to send you home, to the States, to Michigan, on the next flight out. How does that sound? Get out of this place and back where you belong. You will receive a war heroes welcome, and we have some opportunities for you within the State's Attorney General's office. Should you so desire to continue your law career." The man paused to see Doug's reaction, but he was expressionless. "Or we could use someone with your talents in Washington. There will be many opportunities to continue to serve your country now that the war is over."

"I think I have done enough to serve my country already."

The man's smile faded. "Indeed, you have." The two men stared at each other. "I do have a couple of loose ends I'd like to clean up though. Tell me about the files, documents, you retrieved from the Soviet zone."

"What documents?"

"You had asked for, and received, travel documents to travel into the British, and Soviet zones. We believe these documents were used to enter the Soviet zone. And it is our understanding you are in possession of some German documents relating to Katyn."

They were aware of the 'documents' he had kept in his room at the hotel. Or at least they had thought they were documents. Doug had put a bunch of folders, full of blank papers, in the case he had under his bed. He had taken the folder with the documents Angela had translated back to his brother at the camp. Whoever had taken the case thought they were stealing a case of Katyn evidence. What they really stole was a case full of blank paper. Now he had a good idea of who had stolen them. "I don't have any documents."

"Well, maybe our information was wrong. Did you travel to the Soviet zone to obtain evidence?"

"Only my travels to Berlin, which I am sure is noted somewhere."

"Yes, yes. We know of those trips. Did anyone else travel to the Soviet zone on your behalf? Someone like, your brother?"

Now Doug had to decide, should he tell this man about Chet's trip? If he did, he'd have to admit more information about the documents. "Not that I am aware of."

"I see. Again, maybe our information was wrong. What does your brother know about Katyn?"

Doug needed to shield his brother. He had involved Chet in his investigation, but Chet did not really know any of the details. He had kept in the dark about specifics. That way Chet could plead ignorance should he be questioned. "My brother had been approached by some Polish officers, and he referred them to me. The rest I assume you know."

He looked at Doug a bit longer, then reached down, closed his briefcase, and then stood up. "Well then, congratulations again Colonel on the promotion, and best wishes in your future endeavors." He held out his hand to shake, but Doug remained seated. The man ignored the slight. "I will have someone escort you to the hotel, then to the airfield tomorrow for your flight home. I look forward to hearing how things are working out for you."

"What about my report?" When Doug arrived at the Palace that morning, he had written up a report about what had happened yesterday with the Pole, Bolinger, and the Soviets. He included what the Pole had told them, and that Bolinger had shot him.

[339]

"Yes. We have that. Very good indeed. It will be very useful. What about all the documents that you indicated to General Tucker you were in possession of? We would like you to turn these over." The man was trying one more time to get Doug to admit to having documents in his possession.

"As I told you already, I don't have any documents. I was told that the General wanted the Soviets to believe we had some evidence.

"Yes, so you did. Is there anything else pertaining to Katyn that we should have?"

"Nothing." was all Doug said.

"Now, I suggest you take our offer."

"And if I don't?"

"Colonel. You are a good man. A better man than me I suppose. Certainly, braver than me. This is your only offer."

"May I go now?"

"Yes, you may go." He knocked on the door and it is unlocked by two MPs outside the door. "Please take the Colonel to the hotel."

Doug stood up and walked to the door to leave the room. The man put his arm to block the door. "You're a smart man indeed Colonel. Don't play this too smart."

Doug stood there until the man moved his arm, then he walked past him into the hallway.

IT DIDN'T TAKE long for Doug to pack his clothes. He didn't have much else. He expected Angela to be at the hotel shortly. He took the bottle of whiskey from the dresser, opened it, and took a swig. He sat on the bed and laid back.

About fifteen minutes later there as a soft knock on the door. Doug got up and opened the door. Angela stood there with a smile. Doug motioned for her to come in. Angela walked in the room, then turned to give Doug a kiss. Doug put out his arms and grabbed her by the shoulders, keeping her at arm's length. Angela was confused.

"I thought you'd be happy to see me. Is something wrong?" she asked.

Doug took his hands off her shoulders and walked over and picked up the bottle again, taking another swig. He turned around and looked at her. "I'll be leaving in the morning." he said. "But I'm sure you already knew that." He took another swig of whiskey and set the bottle down.

Angela looked at him, not sure how to react. The look on Doug's face wasn't anger, but sadness. Disappointment. Doug was a smart man, so it was only a matter of time until he figured things out. "Yes, I know."

Doug had a suspicion a few days back. But after the case under this bed disappeared, he was almost certain it was true. "You were the only one who knew about the documents, in the case under my bed."

Angela let out a sigh. "Yes Doug. But it seems you pulled one over on them instead. A case full of worthless paper. I told them you were very clever. I was hoping it wouldn't end like this."

"End like what?"

"Well. Like this." She paused, trying to think what words she could say to him. "I wish it had turned out differently Doug. I really do." She attempted a smile, then turned and walked out of the room.

Doug took another swig of whiskey, and it burned as it rolled down his throat.

CHAPTER THIRTY-TWO

September 1, 1945

DOUG PLACED HIS bags in the back of the jeep. He sat in the passenger seat and a Sergeant sat in the back behind him and the driver. He was obviously there to make sure Doug made it directly to his destination. On the way to the airfield, he looked at the war-ravaged city slowly being cleaned up. Though he had only been in Nuremberg for a month, he now noticed that streets were cleared more. The summer heat had receded, and Germans, young and old, women and men, were collecting and stacking bricks that could be reused. Furniture, hardware, anything that could be repurposed was pulled out of damaged buildings. Winter would be there in a couple months, and they needed shelter, fuel, and food.

They pulled into the airfield and the driver drove up to the C-47 parked with the rear door open. General Tucker was waiting in a jeep near the aircraft, puffing on his cigar. Doug stepped out of the jeep and went to grab his bags. "Don't bother with those Colonel, the Sergeant can get those in the plane for you." Tucker motioned for the Sergeant to attend to the bags. "Come Doug, walk with me."

Doug walked over to Tucker and they started walking slowly on the grassy field in the morning sun. "We're sad to see you go, but it's for the best. The decision was made higher up."

"I understand Sir."

"I wouldn't have minded putting a little more heat the Soviets. Belov in particular. That prick. But the Brits were afraid we'd go too far and Uncle Joe will walk away from these trials, maybe even turn nasty. They have a point. He is sitting on half of Europe, with a big, battle tested, well-armed army."

As much as Doug understood what Tucker was saying, he somehow couldn't give up on justice. It wasn't in his makeup. It wasn't who he was. In his mind, he had considered going along with what was happening. Looking the other way. But every time he considered it, he knew he wouldn't be able to live with himself. He wouldn't be Doug Walters, the guy everyone trusted. The guy that didn't compromise when it came to doing the right thing.

"And what about the Poles?"

"That's a mess that's going to take a long time to figure out. Much longer than it will take to put all these Nazis on trial." Tucker's cigar was almost gone. He tossed it on the ground and stepped on it. Then he took a new cigar out of this jacket pocket. He offered one to Doug, but Doug declined. He lit his new cigar. "Figuring out the Polish question is not my department, and above my paygrade." They walked a bit further then turned back toward the aircraft. "My understanding is that you have some opportunities back home."

"That's how it was presented to me."

"Good. See what's available. Something's bound to be a good fit."

"Possibly."

"And Doug, whatever you do, let this Katyn thing go. It could cause a lot of problems."

"For me? Or others?"

"Both."

They finished the walk back to the plane. Tucker shook Doug's hand, then got in his jeep and drove off. Doug climbed the steps and boarded the olive drab C-47. The engines slowly roared to life, and the plane taxied down the runway, reached the end, then spun around in the opposite direction. The pilots gunned the engines and the plane picked up speed, then lifted it off the runway. The plane gently banked as it rose into the sky, then faded into the distance.

September 2, 1945
Nuremberg Prison

A GUARD UNLOCKED the door and opened it for Bauer. Bauer walked into the small room and there sat his client at a small table. Bauer walked over and took a seat at the table across from Jodl.

Making the arrangements to meet with his client were arduous. Paperwork had to be submitted. If there were any mistakes on the paperwork, it was automatically rejected. Physically entering the prison at Nuremberg was also painstaking. It required an interview and several inspections at various checkpoints. Everything was searched thoroughly. If anything was off, you weren't allowed to enter. He did not bring a case with him on this visit, but his clothing was searched for prohibited items. In a prison with so many high value internees, nothing was overlooked.

Jodl sat there with an air of indifference, as if waiting to receive a report from some battle taking place along some front. The man never looked happy, but that was to be expected given his current circumstances.

"What news do you have?" asked Jodl in a quiet voice.

"Herr General, I have some unfortunate news." Bauer hesitated for a moment, looking down at his hands. He was hoping he would be delivering better news. "The Major, Ruessel, has gone missing. Most likely he will not be found. Nor the documents. I must also report that Lt. Colonel Walters in no longer in Nuremberg. It is our understanding that he is returning to the United States."

Jodl was used to receiving bad news, especially over the past few years. He sat there expressionless. "That is unfortunate indeed."

The two men sat in silence for a minute or so, then Bauer spoke up. "Of course, we will continue looking for Ruessel and the Katyn documents. As well as the other items we are currently investigating." After learning that Ruessel had been located in a hospital, and the possibility of obtaining the Katyn documents, Bauer had high hopes that this witness and evidence would provide Jodl and the defense team with leverage in dealing with the prosecutors. Leading the American Walters to the witness and evidence had been a calculated risk. It had not paid off. The most impact it had was causing some minor strife between the Americans. British, and Soviets. Nothing that would help his client.

"Thank you for the update Bauer. That will be all." Jodl stood, straightened his tunic, and walked to the door. He knocked lightly on the door and through the small window in the door he said to the guard outside "I'm finished."

September 3, 1945
Palace of Justice

GENERAL BELOV MADE another grand entrance into General Tucker's office. The two men exchanged pleasantries. General Tucker was more prepared this time for Belov's visit and thus had a respectable assortment of meats and cheeses on hand for him to snack on. Belov presented a bottle of Russian vodka to General Tucker, then took his usual seat across from Tucker's desk.

"Thank you General Belov. Much appreciated." said Tucker as he inspected the bottle. "I'm beginning to appreciate Russian vodka more and more."

"I am glad to hear that General Tucker. I bring it here to you as a gift, in celebration."

"Ah, I see. Thank you again. What are we celebrating?"

"Maybe we can open the bottle and try a bit." suggested Belov.

"Good suggestion." Tucker uncorked the bottle and reached into his desk drawer and withdrew two large shot glasses. He placed them on the table then poured the vodka into the glasses, filing them to the top. He offered one of the glasses to Belov, who sat forward and lifted the glass in toast.

"Here is to resolving a mutual problem" said Belov with a devious smile.

"Mutual problem?" asked Tucker.

"Yes, General. Our Polish problem." Belov still held his glass of vodka in the air.

Tucker stared back at Belov "What Polish problem General Belov?"

"A problem that was most certainly going to negatively impact our working relationship and the progress we are making on organizing and formalizing these tribunals. As you can imagine, I was under great pressure to get this resolved."

"I see. Has it been fully resolved General?" asked Tucker.

"It has. At least for the near term. Of course, new problems involving the Poles will certainly arise in the future, but I am hoping nothing that will affect these trials. That should be good for both of us, wouldn't you agree?"

Tucker thought for a moment. He knew that they were simply kicking the Polish problem down the road. He wasn't certain how far down at this point, but his goal was to get these trials underway and get some Nazis convicted. The Americans, British, and Soviets could sort out the Polish problem later. Tucker slowly lifted his glass of vodka. Both men drank the clear liquor from the glasses. The vodka was smooth and had very little taste. It went down easy.

Belov placed his empty glass on Tucker's desk. He leaned back into his chair with a satisfied smile across his face.

CHAPTER THIRTY-THREE

September 1951

Michigan

DOUG SLICED OPEN the envelope with his letter opener.   The letter was from John Mitchell, Chief Counsel for the

SELECT COMMITTEE TO CONDUCT AN INVESTIGATION OF THE FACTS, EVIDENCE, AND CIRCUMSTANCES OF THE KATYN FOREST MASSACRE

Doug closed his eyes as a sinking feeling came over him. He had hoped this day would never come. He tried putting everything that had happened to him in Nuremberg behind him. It hadn't been easy to forget, even a couple of years after his return to Michigan from Germany in September of 1945. He had picked up his law practice, where he had only left it a few months prior, and kept a low-profile while he reconciled with himself on the events that took place in Germany. He had a witness 'disappear'. Another witness murdered before his eyes. And the issue of the documents that had been recovered. He had not discussed Nuremberg with his brother, nor had he asked to know what Chet had done with the documents. He didn't want to know. It was easier to believe they were gone.

Now the arrival of this letter brought back the flood of emotions and regrets he had from his brief time in Nuremberg. The letter was requesting to provide any information he might have regarding the Kaytn Massacre to the Congressional committee being chaired by a Representative Ray Madden of Indiana. There were a couple of Representatives from Michigan on the committee, Machrowicz and Dondero. He had met them both briefly before at fundraisers and political events over the years.

How had the committee gotten his name? He had only been involved in the Nuremberg investigations for a month six years ago. He never officially provided any research, documentation, or evidence regarding Katyn. The only thing in writing he had produced was the letter he had written about the Polish survivor of Katyn who told him about his near-death escape from the massacre. And his subsequent murder by Bolinger. He had forwarded that letter to Timmerman. The man who had arranged his promotion, and departure from Nuremberg, had mentioned that they had received his letter with the notes. He had no idea what happened to that report after that. A couple of months following his return from Germany he decided to type out another set of notes from memory about the events, which he kept in a lockbox in his home office.

Maybe the committee had been on a fishing expedition, casting their net far and wide, trying to gather as much information they could about Katyn. Doug's name presumably appeared on reports and documents from Nuremberg, so they probably reached out on that basis. He refolded the letter, put it back in the envelope, and placed it in his desk drawer.

CHET PULLED INTO the driveway of Doug's house in his 1949 Chevrolet Deluxe sedan. After he returned from duty in Germany in 1946, he had taken a job at General Motors working at a Buick plant in Flint Michigan. Chet was a natural leader, so he rose quickly to become the assistant plant manager. One of the perks of working for GM was that he got a discount and access to nice vehicles.

It was around 4:30 am on Saturday and still dark out. He was tempted to give the horn a honk, but the early hour prohibited it. He sat for only a minute and the front door opened and out came Doug. He had his fishing pole, tackle box, and a small duffle bag in his hands, and he put them in the back seat of the car. He climbed in car and Chet backed out of the driveway. The brothers were heading north for a long weekend to relax and do some fishing. They planned to arrive in Lake City, Michigan in about four hours, where they would stay in the family's small cabin near Lake Missaukee. They didn't talk much during the drive, as it was early and both men were tired. They would grab a good breakfast along the way and rent a fishing boat once they arrived at the lake.

The sky was filled with early Fall clouds. There was little wind that day, so the lake was nice and smooth, perfect for fishing. Doug didn't usually talk much while they fished, but Chet noticed that this time he seemed unusually distracted, distant. "Everything okay with you?" he asked.

"Huh? Yeah. What do you mean?"

"You seem pretty quiet. Was just asking if everything is okay."

"Yeah. I've been asked if I'd be interested in working for the Attorney General's office. Again."

"Ah. They're still trying to get you to join? You considering it this time?"

"Yeah. Thinking about." Doug's voice trailed off.

"Or are you still thinking about running for office?"

"There's still time...." Doug had a big hit on his line. He ended up reeling in a decent sized bass, big enough to keep. They would have it for dinner that night.

"Anything else going on?" asked Chet. "Girl problems you need help with?" he teased Doug.

"No. I wish I did though." Doug hadn't dated anyone since his wife had died. He had several lady friends, but they were just that, friends. His last romantic encounter had been in Nuremberg. Angela.

"I told ya, I have a nice group of friends in Flint. You need to join us sometime for a cookout or cards. I'll make sure they bring around some eligible beauties for you."

"Oh. You'd do that for me?" Doug asked sarcastically.

"Of course. Anything for my big brother."

"Yeah. Maybe you're right. Let me know when your next gathering is."

"Atta boy."

They fished quietly for a couple more hours, then headed back to the cabin with their catch. They got the cabin opened up, cleaned the fish, and prepared dinner. After they ate, they sat around the fire they had built near the cabin, watching the wood pop and the flames rise gently into the air. They wrapped some blankets around their shoulders and sipped on some whiskey. The sun was setting, and the crisp Fall air was refreshing.

"So. I got a letter last week." said Doug. He couldn't stop thinking about the letter from the Madden Committee he had received.

"Letter about what?" asked Chet.

"About a congressional hearing coming up."

"Hearing about what?"

"About Katyn."

Chet hadn't heard his brother mention Katyn since they had spoken about it back in Nuremberg. Never once had he mentioned it. And he had never asked him what he had done with the documents Doug entrusted to him. Chet had been left to try to explain the Mazur that Wojcik and his brother wouldn't be coming back to the camp. He didn't know any more than that. When they asked about his brother and if he could help find them, Chet told them his brother had gone back to the States. The Poles in the camp were never as friendly as they had been before.

"Katyn. Haven't heard that in a long time."

"Yeah. Had thought that was well behind me."

"What do they want from you?"

"They're looking around for information from anyone that might have something." he paused, "And evidence."

Chet glanced over at Doug. Doug looked at him, but then turned back to watch the fire. They both took sips of their whiskey. "So, what are you thinking?"

"I don't know. I'd like to just ignore it. Let the damn thing just fade away for good."

Chet knew the whole Nuremberg experience had not been a good one for Doug. Everything that had happened over there had left him a different person than what he was before. He had only been there a month but came back stateside with a promotion to full Colonel. He had worked a few months more with the Army on repatriating GIs back to the states, and POWs back to Germany. Easy stuff. Non-consequential stuff. Not like what he had wanted to work on in Nuremberg. His demeanor, outlook, and spirit had changed. His brother had always prided himself on doing the right thing, no matter what the consequences where. He knew his brother well, and he knew that Doug felt like he had let himself down, and in turn let others down. "Is that what you really want?"

"Christ. I'm not sure what I really want. Go figure."

"Why are the holding these hearings now anyways?"

"I'm not sure exactly. But my guesses are that some Polish-American constituents pushed for an investigation. And, or, to try to finally - and officially - stick the blame on the Soviets. Given that we aren't the friendly Allies we used to be, I'm sure that has something to do with it."

"You can say that again."

"I'm still trying to figure out how, and why, they are reaching out to me."

"Sounds like someone dropped your name. Maybe it was the Poles from the camp."

"I hadn't thought about that. I wonder what ever happened to them?"

"They were still there when I headed home. Some were working in some guard units."

Doug reached over and grabbed a piece of firewood and laid it on the fire. Sparks rose up into the air.

"What are you going to do?" asked Chet.

"I don't know yet."

Chet wasn't sure if he should bring it up, but thought he should ask. "Do you want the documents?"

Doug didn't answer. If he agreed to participate in the hearings, he would most likely testify that he had met the Pole that Bolinger murdered. He would tell the man's story. He would also be asked about Ruessel, and the documents he had led them to. He would be asked if he found the documents, and what happened to them. He may be asked why he lied about locating the documents, and why he didn't turn them over to his superiors. They would ask why he agreed to return to the States without speaking up about Ruessel's disappearance, the murder, and the documentary evidence he possessed. In the end, he wouldn't look good, and others wouldn't look good. His testimony might contradict the testimony of others. If he lied, he'd be guilty of perjury. "No." he finally answered. "I don't want to know the whereabouts. For now."

THE FOLLOWING WEEK, Doug received a phone call from a man who identified himself as being a staffer working for the Madden Committee. He had been asked to reach out to Doug to see if he had received the letter, and if he would be willing to appear before the committee. Doug said he had indeed received the letter, but that he had not made any decision on whether to appear.

Doug caught an article in the Sunday paper that mentioned the formation of the committee. The article highlighted the two Congressman from Michigan who had been asked to join the select committee, and it outlined the goals of finding the truth about what happened over ten years ago in the Katyn Forest. The article suggested that truth needed to be brought to light, and those responsible for the murders of thousands of Polish citizens must be held accountable. The article went on to imply that the most probable culprit was the Soviet Union.

Maybe this was his chance. His chance to do the right thing. Tell the truth about what happened in Nuremberg. He had wanted to tell the truth back then, but, had chosen to simply go along and stay silent. The next day, he called the committee staffer and notified him that he had decided to participate in the hearings. The staffer rang back a couple days later with dates and times for his appearance. The staffer asked him to provide his travel itinerary and where he could be reached in Washington. He was going to be staying at the home of a law school classmate who lived in Georgetown, and that he would be via train to D.C. He planned to depart on the weekend. He provided the details of his train departure and arrival.

DOUG PLANNED TO drive early Saturday morning to Flint and drop his car there. He would catch the train in Flint to Detroit, and then onward to Washington D.C. He had talked about his decision with brother on the phone, and Chet supported it. He would be in D.C. for a few days. Doug gave him his classmates phone number in case Chet needed to call him for any reason. He rose early Saturday morning before dawn, put his suitcase in his car, and headed to his brother's house. He never arrived.

CHET WAS EXPECTING Doug early that morning. He made a pot of coffee and grabbed the doughnuts he picked up the day before. He wanted to make sure Doug had a little something to eat before he took him to the train station. Doug did not arrive when he had planned. When he hadn't shown up, and the departure time for his train had passed, Chet became concerned. This was not like Doug at all. He called his house, but no answer. Two hours later he received a phone call from the Sheriff's department. There had been an accident. Could he come down to the hospital.

A farmer had been up early that morning as usual. Far across one of his fields, he noticed a car approaching in the distance with its lights on. It was early to see cars on the road. Especially on a Saturday morning. He was walking from his house out to the barn when he noticed a second car speeding up fast behind the first car. He heard some screeching from tires in the distance, then the sound of a collision, or a crash. It was far off, but he could make out that one of the cars had crashed into some trees at the edge of one of his fields. The sun hadn't risen yet, so it was still quite dark. From what he could tell, it looked like a car had pulled up near the one that had crashed. He thought he saw someone get out and look inside the crashed vehicle. Then the person got back in the car an took off. At that point, the farmer went into the house and rang the Sheriff's department. Then he got into his truck and drove over to the crash site to see if he could help. The driver, a man in a suit, was clearly dead. The farmer had felt for a pulse on the man's arm, but he felt nothing. About fifteen minutes later, a deputy showed up and confirmed the death. In the backseat of the vehicle was a suitcase. It looked like it had been opened and rifled through, with the clothes strewn out and some papers scattered across the seat.

The Deputy found the man's identification in his wallet. In the suitcase, he found a phone number to a man named Chet Walters. It was presumed he was a relative. Back at the Sheriff's department office, the Deputy dialed the number.

EPILOGUE

TWO U.S. SERVICEMEN, BROUGHT FROM A POW CAMP IN GERMANY, WERE AT KATYN IN 1943, WHEN BERLIN HELD AN INTERNATIONAL NEWS CONFERENCE THERE TO PUBLICIZE THE ATROCITY. THE RANKING OFFICER WAS COL. JOHN H. VAN VLIET, A FOURTH-GENERATION WEST POINTER.

AFTER RETURNING TO WASHINGTON IN 1945, HE WROTE A REPORT CONCLUDING THAT THE SOVIETS, NOT THE GERMANS, WERE RESPONSIBLE. HE GAVE THE REPORT TO MAJ. GEN. CLAYTON BISSELL, GEN. GEORGE MARSHALL'S ASSISTANT CHIEF OF STAFF FOR INTELLIGENCE, WHO DEEP-SIXED IT.

YEARS LATER, BISSELL DEFENDED HIS ACTION BEFORE CONGRESS, CONTENDING THAT IT WAS NOT IN THE US INTEREST TO EMBARRASS AN ALLY WHOSE FORCES WERE STILL NEEDED TO DEFEAT JAPAN.

From the CIA website, 2007

HISTORICAL QUOTES

Interspersed throughout this novel are historical quotes from a variety of official documents from the period. Each quote notes the source and date if applicable.

ABOUT THE AUTHOR

Brian Walker was born in Michigan in 1964. He has lived in Michigan, Illinois, Texas, and California. He holds bachelors, masters, and doctoral degrees, and has worked in higher education for 20 years. His hobbies include history, art, and aviation.

CPSIA information can be obtained
at www.ICGtesting.com
Printed in the USA
BVHW041913010623
665242BV00003B/32